The Fire Drake

Book One

By Glenn W. Cunningham

Hidalgo Trust AAR-0002-04021943

Futch/Wolf Publishing
2017

This is a work of fiction. Names, characters, places and incidents either are products of the author's imagination or are used fictitiously. Any resemblance to actual events or locales or persons, living or dead, is entirely coincidental.

Printed in the United States of America
ISBN: 9780999148709
www.TheHidalgoTrust.com
Cover Art by Christopher Blum

Dedicated to:
Rhonda Cunningham
Van Wolverton
Bob Christian
And especially William (Bill) McCabe whose young adventures at
the end of WW2 and during the Korean War inspired large parts
of this book.
Thanks for all the support.

For Family and Friends:
Alan Cunningham
(1946-2016)
Loretta Wolf Cunningham
(1914-2016)
Susan Brodeur
(1950-2016)
Maureen Christian
(1953-2017)
Michael Hamm
(1952-2017)
Better men and women won't be found.

It has been two hard years with far too many friends and relatives dying while this book was being written. I have often used the names of relatives and good friends for characters in my stories and Susan, Maureen, and Mike will be sorely missed.
Even more I will be missing my older brother and my mother whose lives informed some of my major characters as well as demonstrating to me how life should be lived.
Glenn Cunningham

The Fire Drake
Book 1

Hidalgo Trust AAR #0002-04021943

THE HIDALGO TRUST
December 23, 1944
Atlanta, Georgia

A Trust to provide for the security and education of our children and their descendants.

Hidalgo Trust AAR #0002-04021943
Board of the Hidalgo Trust

Foreword
Malois' Retreat, Helotes, Texas
10/18/2013

IN RECOGNITION OF THE SUCCESS of the previous After Action Report the Board has determined to continue with a report from the archives. We would like to present these archival reports while Trust members who were involved can still edit Sherlock Mk. III's synthesis and check it for accuracy.

Reports are assembled from Trust Member narratives, deductive supposition and analysis from other Members, plus narratives and data provided by or obtained from non-members (including adversaries), covert recordings, wire and telephone taps, and radio intercepts. In addition we have used research by various Trust organizations, their affiliates, and inferential analysis based on statistical probability combined with exhaustive searches of thousands of databases.

Initial compilation, synthesis, and composition are performed by the Sherlock Mk. III computer program running on a supercomputer of the Trust's Information Technology (IT) section. Final editing and publishing responsibilities are assigned to a Trust Member who when possible was involved in the action, and in the Board's judgment, seems to possess the requisite narrative skills.

Each chapter begins with a citation of the sources used to prepare it. To help newer Trust members, the first chapter that cites contributions from a Trust member includes a brief summary of that members' biographical information. As readers become more familiar with biographical and genealogical information this information will be moved to a secure data site accessible to Trust members.

Due to the length of the report and the extended time frame represented the report will be presented in two books.

Note from Sherlock Mk. III- The recordings and notes from the period around WW2 were replete with slang and nomenclature no longer in common use. While both the slang and scatological references would impart a truly colorful character to this AAR, at least 84% of the current Trust members will have no reference for their meaning. It is only by use of an extensive database, examination of context, and a rare request to the 16% that I was able to understand all the recordings and narratives. E.G: A *flea* can be an insect pest or a small, underpowered English Ford automobile. Therefore trouble with a *flea* or *fleas* could have numerous meanings. I endeavored to only use slang or acronyms that are still in current usage or were so texturally elegant that the literary algorithms in use could not be overridden. Likewise foreign military will be first presented by their rank in their service, however further mention will use the American equivalent ranks for easier understanding.

Note from Marie Donovan and Lysette Malois-Dumars: In fairness to Thomas Larsen, we both must admit how pleasantly surprised we were with the success of the first novelized AAR, The Hidalgo Trust, Report #0001-04082011. One can only imagine the epic battles over punctuation in which Sherlock and Thomas must have engaged. We still have writing examples from Thomas' time at the Ranch School for any interested members. We wish to thank Sherlock for his patience as our narrative often took flight as we reminisced over people, places, and actions. Sherlock will retain those wanderings for our possible future use of the Tell Me a Story program.

Book One

Chapter 1: Count Voronstov

Report by Brigadier Gen. Ernst Johann Dietsch, United States Army (Progenitor)
and Count Alexi Voronstov's Memoirs
April 10, 1919, 16:40: Near the end of the Bolshevik Revolution: Southwestern Russia, the burnt remains of the Voronstov mansion:

"THANK YOU SIR!" the old man said in a voice shaded with death.

"Bless you Mikhail, rest in God's hands." Then Count Alexis Voronstov steadied his revolver below the old man's chin and pulled the trigger. Reverently he lowered Mikhail's body to rest on the ground. The movement was gentle, though made awkward by the count's wounded shoulder.

Brigadier General Ernst Dietsch looked up at the gun's report; he had just finished digging a shallow grave. "Michael, Petro, help the Count. We need to hurry." The general's brusque words and cold tone were belied by the tears tracks marking his dusty face. [1]Corporal Michael Donnel USMC and Petro Romaniuk hurried over from where they were filling in the last of several graves. No markers graced the last resting place of the Counts parents, wife, and child. Their heavily charred remains were consigned to two graves. The count's parents in one and his wife and young son in another. A larger area held the charred remains of some of the Count's retainers, those who had attempted to defend the Count's home from a roving group of Red Cossacks, adherents of the Bolshevik Revolution.

"You disapprove Ernst?" the count asked as Donnel and Petro carried the body to the grave that General Dietsch was stepping from.

"Did he really need to tell you twice which of your men aided the Reds? You should have provided mercy and shot him sooner. The old man was in great pain." Dietsch responded. Mikhail, the old stableman, had been left for dead on the edge of the fire. Twice wounded and badly burned, he had managed to drag himself from the fire, bearing immense pain long enough to provide witness to the Count and his companions, attesting to the Red Cossacks deprivations.

9

"Mikhail also had great pride in serving my family, he wanted to be sure I knew who was involved. I too must be sure. I would not waste my vengeance on the wrong people." The count's voice was as haggard as his bloodstained and wounded body.

As the count and the general looked hard at each other, Donnel and Romaniuk lowered the old man's body into the grave; their actions a mix of reverence and haste. As they gathered the charred planks they had used as shovels the general and the count stepped up to the grave. A short moment of reverent silence was followed by action as the four quickly backfilled the grave.

A low whistle caused them to look toward where a wiry man was trotting toward them on horseback. Drawing to a halt he addressed the general, "Time to go Sir. There is a large dust cloud headed from the west. From the size probably a lot more men than we want to engage." [2] Staff Sergeant Ian Pratchett, the last member of their party, had been on watch for any more Bolshevik reavers.

"Alexis, can I trust you to come with us or should I have you tied to your horse and let Petro lead you?" Dietsch asked.

"I will come with you. A futile gesture that leaves me and a few of the Red Cossacks dead is not retribution, I have larger plans for the revolutionaries." The count limped toward their horses, followed by the others.

"*I'm sure you do Alexis. I'm sure you do.*" Dietsch thought as he mounted his horse along with the others and they headed southeast. "Ian, scout ahead, use the skills you used chasing Pancho Villa and keep us away from the Reds and anyone else. We don't want the damned Bolsheviks chasing us through the countryside. I don't think our so-called diplomatic cover will stop bullets."

Sergeant Pratchett saluted, "You know we never caught Villa. Pershing was some pissed off; he also had a lot of respect for Villa." He turned his horse and trotted away, sitting his horse like the cavalryman he was before the war. The son of a Texas Ranger, Pratchett had begun riding shortly after he was out of diapers and became a Ranger chasing rustlers and border bandits before WW1. Ian served as a scout for the U.S. Army when they chased Villa's Division del Norte after the raid on Columbus, New Mexico.

As they rode from the scene of destruction Ernst considered the Count. They had met at a London Embassy function five months before when the young Count introduced himself and commented on an engineering book Ernst had written five years before. The Revolution was in full swing, yet the Count was not worried, he assured Ernst that his retainers were loyal and that he had divested himself of any land claims as well as starting manufacturing plants that employed hundreds of people at wages far higher than anyone had ever been paid. His plant was also a school that was training machinists and engineers and providing an education for the employees' children. "I saw the writing on the wall years ago. I'm sure that my people are loyal to the new life I have provided."

The two men had a mutual love of engineering, and Count Voronstov had a personal fascination with flight. He was particularly intrigued with what the early aviators called ground or screen effect, the compression of air between an aircraft and the ground which added additional lift and support. He thought that it could be used to carry heavy loads over water as well as the immense grassland prairies of both Russia and the Americas.

When Voronstov invited the brigadier to visit his home and factories, Ernst was happy to agree. Especially when the count offered to meet him at a train station 90 kilometers from his home and provide horses for a two day ride across the steppes. Accompanied by Sergeant Pratchett, United States Army, and Marine Corporal Michael Donnel, the general left London and after several days travel, met the Count and his assistant Petro at a station on the edge of the plain. The first day's ride was idyllic and they spent the night talking around a low fire and enjoying the immense spread of stars, normally not seen except at sea or in the desert.

April 10, 1919, 10:05:

The second day was much the same until they were within thirty kilometers of the count's mansion when they noticed several plumes of smoke on the horizon. They increased their pace to a fast trot and as they neared the closest plume Petro stated that it appeared to be coming from a farm that supplied the factory and the count's home. Cresting a low hill they saw the smoldering ruins and several bodies on the ground.

"Red Cossacks." Petro declared as they approached the farm's remains.

"My home!" Voronstov cried, he turned toward a plume of smoke in the direction of his home and spurred his horse into a gallop.

Dietsch shouted toward the rapidly advancing count, "Alexei, you'll kill your horse. Damn fool. Petro can we catch him?"

"There is no faster route and none of our horses are equal to his. We have twenty five kilometers to reach the Count's home".

"Ian, set the best pace for a fifteen mile ride and still have some reserve to run away." Ernst ordered.

"Yes, Sir. Troop ho." Pratchett set off at a lope and the others followed.

"I thought the Cossacks supported the White Russians." The brigadier said while turning to Petro.

"Most do, some of the poorer groups have gone over to the Bolsheviks. The richer clans have a communal democracy that leaves them independent from both the Russian nobility and now the Soviets."

When the brigadier looked at Petro with raised eyebrows, the man let out a grim laugh. "Don't be surprised General, I am Cossack and the Cossacks have always supported good schools and military service for all males. I have also attended many discussion groups held at the Count's factory schools. I am willing to debate any form of government that you wish."

"Maybe later, I am impressed and I hope I haven't offended you. I'm afraid that I classified you as a man servant at first. I apologize. You haven't even corrected my poor Russian."

Petro answered in English as precise as a don's; "It is easier to appear so to strangers. Your Sergeant Pratchett sets a good pace and rides well. After I show him where some water hides in a small stream, I will ask him to become a Cossack." Grimly chuckling to himself Petro sped up to ride alongside the sergeant while pointing out some features of the land to him.

"Well Donnel, you aren't even snickering. Is it hard to keep from laughing at your commanding officer?"
"No sir. General his English is much better than mine and I'm only catching about two thirds of the Russian. You're correct, he is surprising."

The small group continued in the Count's wake; hoping to catch him up before his enemies did.

[1]*Cpl. Michael Donnel is the paternal grandfather of Ginny Donnel R.N. Both are Ranchistas. See Report #0001-04082011. SMkIII*

[2]*Sgt. Ian Pratchett is the paternal great grandfather of Dr. Ben Pratchett. Both are Ranchistas. See Report #0001-04082011. SMkIII*

Chapter 2:   Red Cossacks Attack

Brigadier General Ernst Dietsch's Memoir and Narrative

April 10, 1919, 12:30
5 kilometers from the Count's home:

NEAR A SMALL STREAM, only a few feet wide, Ian and Petro discovered the Count's horse. Staggering, the hard ridden horse had barely the energy to drink. Petro quickly dismounted and led the horse a few feet away from the stream. "He may founder if he drinks too much."

As the spent horse slowly regained strength, Sergeant Pratchett was looking at tracks in the mud and soft dirt leading from the stream. "He abandoned the horse here and ran on ahead. The Count will kill himself if he keeps up that pace for long. Look at the length of the stride and how his toes are heavily imprinted. The man's sprinting. He won't get far at that rate."

The four men heard shots and yells in the direction of the Count's flight. They raced to the crest of a low hill and saw the Count, lying in a low depression firing his revolver at six men on horseback. Two bodies on the ground showed Voronstov's marksmanship, but a widening stain on his left shoulder showed that the battle had not been one sided.

Brigadier Dietsch issued quick orders; "Donnel use your rifle from here, Ian left flank, Petro right and bring Donnel's horse, I'll go straight. Stay out of saber range Ian or they'll cut you in two." Corporal Michael Donnel pulled his Model 1903 Springfield from his saddle scabbard and his pack with extra ammunition off the horse as Petro grabbed the horse's reins. Donnel went prone at the crest and raised the sights on his rifle, adjusting for the range and glancing at how the tall grass was blowing, giving him an idea of his windage. His first shot kicked up dust a few feet in front of one of the Red Cossacks and a foot to the right. His second shot took the man in the chest flipping him over the back of the saddle. The man's companions sent a useless fusillade at Donnel and then noticed the three riders approaching at a gallop.

Guiding his horse with his knees, Petro tossed the reins of Donnel's horse over its head, knowing that it would follow him; he drew his saber in his left hand as his right brought up a large Webley revolver which he quickly fired, emptying it more in hope of disrupting the Red Cossacks rather than actually hitting someone. A horse reared its head in time to take Donnel's third shot instead of its rider. The horse dropped trapping his rider underneath. The remaining riders decided that closing with the three rescuers was safer than staying exposed to the lethal rifle and spurred towards them. They dropped low on their mounts reducing exposure and began firing their pistols as they neared the three men.

One Cossack targeted Sergeant Pratchett; Ian drew his Model 1911 Colt and standing in his stirrups took a two handed grip and slammed the first heavy slug into the chest of his opponent's horse. The animal staggered and then went down as a second round hit within inches of the first. The Cossack leapt free and continued to run forward firing his pistol only to stop short as a .45 round took him in the chest and a second exploded his head.

Ernst had two of the brigands headed toward him and his horse flinched as a pistol round went between Dietsch's leg and the horses flank, the wound was unimportant, however the saddles girth was partially severed and Ernst could feel it begin to slip. The Brigadier jumped off just before the saddle slipped under the horse's belly. Rolling forward with the momentum Ernst moved to his right placing both riders to his left so only one had a clear shot. The closest Cossack let his empty pistol drop on its lanyard and pulled his saber. Ernst stopped his roll sitting on the ground and facing his closest enemy and opened fire with his .45. The first round caught the front of the saddle and deflected into the Cossack's stomach, it was not fatal and the man leaned down to use his saber. Without time for a second shot, Dietsch quickly lay flat and rolled toward the horse which jumped to avoid the general and spoiled the sabers line, causing a slice of leather to fly into the air from the shoulder of Ernst's jacket and barely nicking the flesh underneath. Ernst arched his back, brought the gun over his head, and fired three rounds into the horse and rider dropping both. The third Cossack was turning to ride at the General when the Count stood up and fired his last shot, staggering the man who continued toward the Brigadier. Both the Brigadier's shot and a long shot from Pratchett hit the man simultaneously, knocking him out of the saddle and sprawling him on the ground.

Petro and his opponent were circling each other in a fast and violent exchange of saber strokes when Petro jumped his horse into his enemy's and managed to slice the man's throat as the horse staggered.

The three rescuers were converging on the Count when they were startled by a shot from Corporal Donnel. The Cossack whose leg had been trapped under his horse had freed himself and brought up his rifle, aiming at the Count. Donnel's shot took him in the head and dropped him instantly.

Count Voronstov looked toward his saviors and then dropped his head as they approached; "I'm sorry. I've been a fool. What could I have been thinking?"

"You were thinking of your family, of your loved ones. Now think with less emotion and take one of the horses. We'll head for your home and then do what we can." Brigadier Dietsch responded. Then the Brigadier went to his friend; "take off your coat, we need to stop the bleeding so that you can continue."

As Sergeant Pratchett bandaged the count, Ernst took off his own coat exposing a small wound. "Not much to that one General, let me bind that." Petro said as he dismounted his horse.

Corporal Donnel walked down from his hill leading the Count's horse which appeared to be reviving after its long run. "Give me a few minutes and I'll bring in the surviving horses." he said as he approached. He led the count's horse in a large circle, seeming indifferent to the excited animals, as one horse began following him the others approached and by the time he returned to the group all the remaining Cossack horses were strung out behind him.

"Not bad for a Yankee farm boy. We might have to have Petro invite you into his clan as well." Sergeant Pratchett joked as the corporal joined them.

"Considering how well Michael shoots, I may ask to join his clan." Petro added.

"Corporal, I believe you are out of uniform, another stripe should be on your sleeve if I have anything to do about it. And I do." Ernst said adding to the corporals growing embarrassment and pride.

Once Dietsch's saddle was repaired and the spare horses collected the men cantered toward the count's home, their thoughts a mixture of hope and fear.

Chapter 3: The Fire Drake

Captured German reports and the personal diaries of Count Voronstov and Generalleutnant der Artillirie Manford Von Erlich

Peenemünde
August 02, 1942

THE BRIGHT ARC of the welder died, Jerzy Mandelbaum raised his hood and inspected the weld. "Will it hold?" asked Milo Balogh.

"I'm afraid so. I can't make a weld that will fail and still pass inspection."

"Pity that." Milo responded while making sure the guard couldn't hear them.

Jerzy was a Polish Jew, a former ship fitter from the Danzig shipyards, forced into labor by the Nazi war machine. Milo was a member of the Rudari Romani, a group historically persecuted by most of Europe. They were inside a large concrete bunker finishing a mockup of a ship's hull. It was an accurate reconstruction that would simulate the hull of a freighter or a thin skinned warship like a destroyer. A mockup of a cruisers hull had been previously built which included a section containing a ship's brig. Each section was about twenty meters wide and each had a white path with black marks every meter extending through the bunker entrance and two kilometers out into a field.

"You still think this is to test a new weapon?"

"Yes Milo, I do. All they do at this site is design and build death in more and more forms."

"Why the brig in the warship? It worries me."

"I'm afraid too; the only prisoners here are our own people."

As the two policed their work site and gathered tools, two guards approached with another guard pulling a cart. While one guard took inventory, the two men placed their tools into the cart and started to follow it out. "Hold there." One of the guards ordered. They waited until the cart had turned into a side tunnel, headed for the tool storage area. Once it was out of sight the guards directed them to the front of the hull. Gathered between the two hulls were all the slaves who had constructed the mockups. They were quickly herded by a large group of guards towards the cruiser hull section. When a couple of the laborers slowed, they were quickly clubbed to the ground and their companions forced to carry them. The prisoners entered the hull section and some were placed in the brig's cells while others were simply left in the brig's office. As the guards left the compartment hatch was closed and dogged tight from the outside.

In the field two covered trucks backed up to the end of the paths. Several staff cars parked to one side and a group of officers and engineers gathered in front of the trucks. A tall man in a brown wool suit led the group to one side. "General von Erlich, I think you will have the best view from here."

"Thank you Graf Voronstov. Shouldn't we be closer to the bunker to see the results?

Alexei Voronstov, still carrying the scars suffered when his family was executed twenty four years earlier, looked at the General and his staff. "Believe me; you do not want to be in proximity to the targets in the bunker. The high speed cameras will show us how well the drachen work. The cameras have been placed in heavily reinforced revetments and will be unmanned, operated remotely. I expect to have to dig them out of the bunker to obtain any film."

The group watched two missiles being prepared. The two missiles had short and unusually deep wings, but otherwise resembled an enlarged Henschel HS 293 antiship missile.

A large open Mercedes pulled up to the group and Reich Marshall Herman Göring descended ponderously from the back seat. "Heil Hitler" exploded from General Von Erlich as the general and his staff raised their arms in salute.

Voronstov ignored the display as he watched the technicians prepare the missiles and set up two tripods with a light projector on top of each. Göring waved a sloppy response as he approached the group. "So these are the *Feuerdrachen* (Fire Drakes). They don't look like they will fly well with that absurd wing design."

"Herr Marshall, let me introduce Graf Alexei Voronstov, the scientist in charge of the project."

"I am not a scientist Herr Marshall. A scientist builds theories; I am an engineer and I build weapons to defeat Stalin and his allies." Voronstov answered. "The wing is not designed to fly high; it is designed for stable high speed in screen effect, what you call ground effect. In this case it will be over water and used to attack Allied ships. The wing and ground effect allow us to carry a far heavier payload than the rocket can normally carry."

"Surely that is mostly a HS 293, its warhead was designed to attack ships; will your new warhead have a greater effect on a ship?" Göring asked.

"Indeed much of the design resembles the 293 though scaled upward; why not use what already works. The warhead has been enlarged and redesigned as a shaped charge. The effect will be to blow a hole in the hull and over-pressurize any ship. The 293 and the larger 294 that is being designed need to hit below the waterline, optimally under the keel. The Fire Drake can hit most anywhere on the ship's hull and destroy it. That is one of the factors we are investigating today. Primarily we are investigating the shaped charge. The simple explanation is for the shock wave to propagate from within the ship and move outward rather than from the outside in. We are doing it in the bunker to prevent any reconnaissance flight from seeing an actual ship attacked."

"And if the penetration does not hit fuel or armaments, what have you gained, just a hole in the side of the ship, probably less than an artillery shell would deliver." Göring replied.

"The wing and the ground effect allow for a warhead weighing over 930 kilos. Larger than the proposed 700 kilo warhead for the 294 and more than twice the warhead of a Heinkel 293. The overpressure force, even without hitting munitions or fuel, should rip the ship apart, quite possibly separating the hull at the waterline. The bunker has numerous large vents to the outside and the test charge is reduced, however I expect the bunker to be destroyed. A ship, especially a warship with all of its watertight hatches dogged down should erupt like a balloon bursting." The Count answered.

"Who else has seen your mockup here?" Göring asked. "If this works we need to keep any information as secret as possible."

General Von Erlich answered. "*Ja*, Herr Marshall, a brig has been constructed in the cruisers hull and filled with *Juden* and *Ziguener*. The Jews and the Gypsies built the mockups; we can't risk them informing anyone. It is a shame to lose their services, but there's always more we can use."

A technician approached the group, saluted and said that all was ready for the test.
"Who will guide your missiles?" Göring asked.

Voronstov pointed to the two light projectors, "The two technicians at the projectors. They need only direct an invisible beam of concentrated ultraviolet light onto the hull and the drachen will guide themselves to the exact spot. This is much easier for a person with minimal training to accomplish than to have a pilot try to control the drachen with radio or wire guidance controls. It is more secure also, as radio transmissions can be jammed and wires can drag in the water or suffer failure.

"Gentlemen, let's move to the bunker upwind. The rocket turbines have been bolstered with solid rocket boosters, this allows them to accelerate faster and extend the range. You will see the missile rise a few meters above the path. Fortunately there is a crosswind which will also test the stability control as well as helping to keep the exhaust away from us and the cameras." Voronstov explained.

When the group of officers and engineers had moved to safe positions inside heavily bermed concrete bunkers and donned safety goggles and ear protection, Voronstov raised his hand then quickly dropped it. Both missiles quickly accelerated in front of a large plume of smoke. They rose about three meters above the ground and in seconds entered the construction bunker. A huge cloud of smoke erupted from the bunker; however the explosive reports were curiously muffled. All of them felt a sharp jolt to their feet as the shock wave hit their site. Tremendous jets of smoke and dust erupted from the vents in the bunkers roof before the entire bunker seemed to expand into a giant cloud of dust.

As the smoke and dust cleared the group resorted to field glasses to see into the bunker. Neither hull could be seen; as the bunker, and all it had contained had become a large crater in the ground.

"I am most impressed." Göring said. "General, come with me." he added as he walked toward his car. He entered his car, and then turned to the general. "General Erlich, you have leave for anything required so that this weapon is operational. Can this Russian count be trusted?"

"Herr Marshall, the results were predicted by the Graf. He said that outward destruction would be immense. This may be the key to decimate an Allied invasion. The technicians will be developing the film immediately and workmen will be digging out any surviving cameras. Let me bring the films to your quarters as soon as they are ready. As for Graf Voronstov, he is both an engineering genius and the most implacable foe of the Communists you will ever meet. I believe that if we had not been destined to attack Stalin, Voronstov would have made a pact with the Devil for his revenge."

"For both your sakes, I hope you're right. Bring the evidence too me as soon as it's ready." Göring replied as his car started forward.

Chapter 4: Approach to Peenemünde

**Narratives of Vincent Fuller, Marie and Lysette Malois,
Logs of UK Bomber Squadron (617) the "Pathfinders"
Marie and Lysette are the twin daughters of
Hiram Marcus Snowden (Progenitor) and Irene Malois-Dumars.
Vincent Fuller (Progenitor) with Frankie Bourland Fuller are the
parents
of Magnus and Morganna Fuller.**

April 1, 1943   02:25
Aboard Flight 1272, 617 Squadron
**A Lancaster Bomber approaching Peenemünde on the island of
Usedom on the German Baltic course.**

THE LANCASTER'S COPILOT shuffled back to the bomb bay and looked down at the man serenely sleeping on top of the Bat. "Mr. Smith, he shouted as he carefully touched the man's shoulder; Mr. Smith, fifteen minutes to the bay."

Mr. Smith opened his eyes and a huge hand came up to wipe his face; "Thank you Sergeant. I'm glad you woke me before you dropped the package."

"The Royal Air Force does have a certain reputation for manners to uphold sir. That and having a Yank of your size upset with us would be strategically unsound."

Smith's chuckle sounded like an empty wooden barrel rolling over cobblestones. "I doubt my ability for revenge would be of much use if I dropped while asleep. Has the navigator been able to find our drift? The wind data will be critical to the launch point."

"Yes sir. Leftenant Higgs has had several sights and says he has it pegged; eight knots from East Southeast."

"If a Pathfinder navigator says it, it must be true. Please thank him and the rest of the crew. I take it there's been no trouble."

"Quiet as church. The raids north and south have drawn the Nazi's attention and we won't pop up to where their radio ranging can see us until right before we drop you. After that well stay on course for another ten minutes, drop some leaflets and head for the treetops and back home."

"Excellent! If you will hand me that lanyard by my feet, I'll zip up my harness and get ready to drop."

The sergeant quickly gathered the lanyard and extended his right hand as his left brought up the lanyard. "Good luck Sir." He was once again astounded as his own sturdy hand was engulfed by the Yank's giant paw.

"If my and Barnes Wallis' numbers are right, let luck look out for itself." The large man struggled a bit to zip the tight canvas harness up to a position under his arms. He then fastened the rotation strap to a hard point on the edge of the bay, pulled heavy goggles down from his parachutist's helmet and placed both hands on the black aluminum tube over his chest.

A few minutes later as the Lancaster climbed and slowed to 120 knots a yellow light, attached to the ceiling above the bomb bay, glowed to life. *"One minute."* thought Smith as he reviewed his actions when the Bat left the aircraft. Below him he heard and then felt the bay doors opening and felt the wind buffet start. A second yellow light came on; *"thirty seconds. I hope Leftenant Higgs is as good as his reputation."* The green light flashed on as Smith felt the package start to drop. The rotation strap rolled him face down as the package nosed down and the shroud that covered the wings was pulled off. Several G's of force pulled on Smith as the lightweight unit decelerated. His right hand pulled on a handlebar control and the two outer arms were unlatched at the rear. Pushing the control bar forward and his body back, he angled the nose up. This was the most critical point of the flight. Too much and the wings might shred as they deployed, or they might stall; too little and they might not get enough air to deploy. With a loud pop the black fabric delta wings deployed and Smith's stomach headed south. *"Too steep, pull in, nose down, a hair more."* And then the delta-winged glider settled into the stable flight Vincent (Mr. Smith) Fuller had designed it for. Hanging prone in his harness beneath the large center strut Vincent glanced at the compass on his wrist, next to a pilot's chronograph; north northeast, head a little more east, a quick glance at the altimeter on his left wrist, 4,800 feet, have to stretch the glide a little. Finally look down, on course for the shallow cove; *"Bless you, Leftenant Higgs."*

A piece of yarn was hanging from the nose where the two outer tubes joined the center spar; the yarn streamed a little to the right and Fuller unconsciously corrected, allowing the yarn to stream straight back. Fuller's mind clicked off the options of lift over speed. You could decrease speed and slightly slow the loss of altitude, however you also had to gain sufficient distance over the ground or all the altitude in the world wouldn't help. Fuller's mind went into auto-pilot mode and the glide was soon at the optimum to allow him to cross the mouth of the cove at the right height and right speed. Fuller's mind then clicked into a picture of the cove gained from multiple aerial photos. He quickly caught the darker thread of the small stream that emptied into the northern quarter of the cove. A small light flashed occasionally from a quarter mile up the stream. Glancing toward Peenemünde, five miles away, he was not surprised to see only darkness. The Germans were very serious about the area black out.

The delta wing's fabric fluttered as Fuller's glide took him over the beach and the air was ruffled a small amount by the dunes. Adjusting course, he followed the stream to the small light and its occasional flicker. Nearing his landing site he raised the nose and as he came up into a near stall his feet came down into the two foot deep stream; two, three steps and he was stopped. His left hand unzipped the heavy canvas harness as his right hand pulled a M2 paratroopers carbine complete with folding stock and a thirty round clip, from an attached scabbard. Vincent hand loaded his ammunition; a 130 grain half jacketed wad-cutter bullet and a few extra grains of powder in the case; the hand load round was faster and far more lethal than the standard 110 grain military ball ammunition. The carbine's pistol grip had been enlarged and Fuller could handle the gun easier than most people could fire a .22 target pistol.

A familiar voice spoke in German; "Uncle Schmitt, what would you like for breakfast?"

"Hola fraulein menudo y nopalitos would be sehr gut..." As the carefully chosen response came in mangled Spanish obscured with a heavy German accent.

A dark lithe figure appeared from low under a bush and splashed into the stream. Vincent braced himself as a tall, strong woman ran into his arms and hugged him fiercely around the neck as her feet dangled a foot in the air. "Uncle Vincent, you idiot, what made you come here in that, that thing."

"Lysette dear, I came because of the reports you and Marie sent in about the aircraft being built here. I hate parachutes and the winged thing you disparage gives me much more control of where I land and who I land near. I can also carry some of the supplies you requested. I'll throw in a couple of extra hugs that your father would have sent if he knew I was coming."

"You big idiot. What will the Germans do if they catch you?"

"Well, if they don't shoot me on sight, I would probably end up with at least one last meal with Willy and Franz and possibly the new wunderkind Von Braun. Let's vamoose out of here and put off my final dinner."

"I hope it is menudo. Serve you right; I never could develop any liking for it."

"You probably weren't sufficiently hung over when you had it. Get plowed on beer and tequila and menudo is a balm old bible characters would have died for."

"Ugh, maybe I should have had it for breakfast at UT instead of aspirin and pancakes."

"Help me fold this up. Here's some piggin strings to lash it with. Your supplies are inside the center tube." After stowing the body harness inside a folded wing the two quickly lashed the delta wing into a long compact bundle. "One second while I install a safety pin." Fuller quickly inserted a quick-pin near the front of the main tube. "That red yarn at the nose is attached to a time pencil and if pulled would have detonated the plastic explosive in the center tube after twenty seconds. Nobody can get the wing or your supplies."

"You should have told me sooner. I was going to pull it out for a hair ribbon... I didn't, but I should have known sooner."

"True; no other surprises on the wing." Fuller slung the M2 muzzle down under his right shoulder, he then loosened a suppressed .22 Colt Woodsman in the shoulder holster on his left.

"Want a howitzer or maybe a German 88?"

"I'd love an 88. Best field gun yet. However as I detect a hint of sarcasm I'll just ask you to pick up the nose. How far will this stream take us?"

Lysette shouldered her end of the delta wing; "We can follow it for a mile to a hard packed road. Tide will be going out shortly which should erase any tracks we leave in the stream."

"Good! Any places to watch out for?"

"No. Marie is up at the road watching for any interference. We liberated a couple of plow horses from the Germans. Once we get to the farm we'll lead them back toward the Germans and let them go. We have a set of wheels from one of the German heavy machine guns. We can lash your wing to it and make better time."

The two were soon moving upstream, nearly inaudible except for an occasional swish in the water. They stopped at random intervals to listen for any sound and to check behind them. Aside from surprising one thin cow, wild enough to evade the German soldiers, the two remained undiscovered until they approached the small bridge. The low sound of a disturbed duck greeted them and Lysette replied softly; "Quack yourself. Come give us a hand."

Marie, Lysette's identical twin, flipped over from a beam underneath the bridge and quietly lowered herself into the stream. "About time you showed. Uncle Vincent, late again? Just like supper at the Ranch; you would start talking to Ernst or Max in the den and the three of you dreaming up new ships and planes and the rest of us sitting hungry at the table until Frankie or Mama Lea would say "screw it" and everyone at the table could finally start to eat."

"Marie get over here, I have something for you from Hiram." Marie received a gentle hug. "This next one's from me."

"Oh damn, stop. I cannn'dt breeeve." Marie hissed.

"I don't think Max was ever late to a meal. And I apologize for all the times I held up supper. Shouldn't we be quietly and stealthily moving back to the farm," Fuller asked?

"Let me catch my breath. A German patrol is due to come down the road in fifteen minutes. There is a lovely ditch fifteen yards upstream that will hide us and that huge bundle. Let's move."

Twenty minutes later a small patrol came down the road, one soldier was in front by twenty yards; 4 more were strung out in an extended line behind. As they approached the bridge a feldwebel took a shrouded flashlight and shined it low and parallel to the road, looking for any fresh signs of passage. Next he went down the bank with a Schmeisser machine pistol in one hand and projected the pencil thin flashlight beam under the bridge. Satisfied the sergeant motioned to his men and they quietly proceeded down the road.

The three allies remained in their ditch. Ten minutes later they were rewarded by two more Germans quietly following their compatriots, hoping to discover anyone who may have hid from the patrol. The two stopped at the bridge and watched their back trail for a few minutes, then continued to follow the rest of the patrol.

After waiting five more minutes the trio cut across the flats until they entered a small thin copse of trees that only hinted of the dense forest inland, to be greeted by two large horses happily munching oats from nose bags.

"You owe us two weeks ration of oatmeal."

"I'm glad to see that [1]Leboo's and [2]Captain Quartermain's lessons were not forgotten." Vincent whispered.

"If the Captain caught you during a lesson, you had to listen to all the different ways he or Leboo could have killed you. They gave me nightmares; and that was just two years ago. Worse was when Max came up behind you and blew in your ear. Those are lessons you never forget." Lysette answered.

"Where is the Captain?" Marie asked.

"Gil always liked the Germans; however he hates the Nazis with a passion. The English still want his hide, but your father and Bill Donovan snuck the little Welshman into Poland a few months ago to investigate the concentration or more correctly now the death camps. Hiram says that they have followed his progress across Poland and into Germany by intercepted reports about the mysterious death and disappearances among some of the more virulent Nazis in the SS."

"How does he report?"

"He doesn't. He has two cameras and multiple rolls of film. When he finishes his trip, he'll exfiltrate himself and find the nearest OSS officer to report to."

As the trio and the two farm horses made their way east, the twins still had some questions.

"Any other news from home, only important stuff please?" Lysette asked.

"Well let's see. Hiram is in London, making nice with the British and more importantly with the SHAEF staff. Everyone hates the OSS as long as they can't run it. They would all be happy to take it on as a favor to Marshall and the President."

"Damn, desk jockeys wouldn't know what to do with it if they did get us," Marie grumbled.

"The only other possibly interesting thing to report is that Frankie is pregnant." Vincent continued.

Both girls stopped; "You're going to have a baby?" Lysette quietly squealed.

"Well Frankie will have the baby, I'd just as soon be handed the final product after she does all the work."

The twins launched themselves on their friend, and after hugs and kisses he was heartily if quietly admonished for calling a baby the final product.

"The farm's about fifteen minutes from here. Time to let Fritz and Brunhilda amble back to the Germans and we'll carry your flying gallows the rest of the way." Lysette said three kilometers later.

They released the two horses and ran the set of wheels into a small pond.

"I don't think flying gallows will be a popular name"; Vincent mused as they skulked toward the farm.

[1]Leboo Larsen, a Maasai tribesman who befriended Max Larsen and became the self-appointed guardian of Max's biological son, young John Wolf. Leboo continues to live at the Ranch and teaches survival and war craft. SMkIII

[2]Captain Quartermain: Gilvaethy Argull ap Cynwris ap Larnuuocan, a Welsh ex-patriot who joined forces with German guerilla forces in East Africa to fight the British during WW1. A close friend of Ernst Dietsch, he taught warfare and survival at the Ranch. SMkIII

Chapter 5: *LaDonna Johnson*

Compiled oral wire recordings of Maxwell Larsen and Brigadier Gen. (Ret.) Ernst Dietsch, (Progenitors) Admiralty logs and the log of the S.S. *LaDonna Johnson* Larsen is the father of John Marcus Wolf, Maria Zaragosa Morales, Thomas Challenger Larsen, Theodore Roxton Larsen, and Katherine Irene Larsen

April 1, 1943, 17:50
Onboard the S.S. *LaDonna* Johnson 300 nautical miles WNW of the Shetland Islands:

THE LONELY LIBERTY SHIP was limping behind the convoy and showing a lot of black smoke from its funnel. The destroyers shepherding the convoy had been forced to leave the ship behind as they protected the bulk of the convoy. The wounded Liberty ship was still trying to zigzag for its own protection, however the speed continued to decrease and the turns became sloppier and wider as if the ship had control problems as well as engine problems. The thump of a triple expansion steam engine continued to slow until the ship barely had steerage way. Two figures could be seen on the port wing of the bridge.

"MmMmMmm. This is another fine mess you've gotten us into." said the short active man in a fair imitation of Oliver Hardy. Heavily bundled he seemed unable to stop bouncing on the balls of his feet, as if his energy could not be contained. "It's damned cold too, you big oaf, and I'm freezing my balls off."

The other figure was a very large and wide person, wearing only an old sweater over his coveralls. "Go inside, I'll be just a minute. Tell Sparks to slow down the sound of the engine and to let it die an agonizing death while the ship slows down."

"Gladly." answered the smaller man as he bounced into the bridge. Shortly the sound of the engine started slowing and decreasing as the ship slowed and wallowed more as the waves rolled the ship. The huge man looked toward the concealed speakers that gave out the sound of a typical Liberty ship, then he looked around at the sea once more and entered the bridge.

The bridge was nearly vacant aside from the helmsman, an officer, and a yeoman-talker entering a note in the ships log. The log was actually kept on a teletype machine similar to those used by news wire services. A coded punch tape came out of the side even as the log was printed on the large roll of paper that fed through the machine. A duplicate tape and scroll were appearing in the heavily armored combat control center two levels below the bridge. "Max, Sparks is reporting that they're starting to hear some activity besides the convoy. Apparently a wolf pack is out and hunting. He says he'll call as soon as he hears anything coming toward us." the talker said.

"Well Max, let's see if your proof of concept works or gets us blown up. You know the Navy will never buy this thing, too expensive, too many toys." Ernst Dietsch stated while standing in front of a warm radiator on the aft bulkhead of the bridge.

"Oh I know, I've already signed off on *LaDonna's* successors. Victory class transports, actually the Haskell attack class variant. Slower, fewer guns and their sound ranging and other detection equipment will be of good, but far lesser capability. They won't have the Big Ears, our parabolic microphones, or the dual sonar domes fore and aft. I structured the contract so I could buy the *LaDonna* back after the war; supposedly to convert her into a fast reefer ship for perishable produce. Actually I will keep her as is and visit a few places in Africa where certain imperial and local dictatorships have enslaved their people far too long."

The helmsman, a medium sized and wiry African black looked over to Max with a hard smile and a nod. "How far upriver can we take her Max?"

"Far enough Mobuto, far enough. What's our speed?"

"Less than two knots and she's a pig when trying to steer with just one screw turning." Mobuto answered after a quick glance at the repeater instruments.

Suddenly a buzzer rattled and a few discrete red lights flashed. "We have a U-boat headed our way." the talker reported.

"Everyone down to the CC. The bridge is usually one of their first targets." Max said as he ushered Ernst and the crew toward a hatch and companionway. Two lookouts who had heard the buzzer joined the bridge crew. As the men descended shutters started closing behind the bridge ports.

Two decks down, they entered the armored command center. Mobuto took over the repeater helm as the talker and officer slipped into padded swivel chairs bolted down in front of a panel that allowed them to communicate with any compartment as well as listen to any radio or sonar traffic from the sensor suite safely hidden below deck. The talker had a small situation board where he could keep a simple representation of the tactical situation. One small and heavily protected port gave the helmsman a restricted view ahead.

"The board is green, all weapons manned and ready, steam pressure is up, turbines ready." The officer reported.

"Thanks Rob," Max replied quietly from his similar station. "What's your best guess, torpedo or deck gun?"

"Deck gun; its dark enough and the sea smooth enough that they'll have a good platform far enough away that our popguns won't bother him." Rob was referring to a 20mm twin Oerlikon forward of the bridge and a couple of .50 caliber Browning M2's conspicuously displayed on the wings of the bridge. The guns were mostly designed to give merchant sailors a false sense of security while allowing them to spit in the face of either long range aircraft or U-boats. "He won't want to waste a torpedo on us; there are too many hard targets in the convoy that he'll want to save his torps for. Probably not the smartest action for the sub, we're nearly dead in the water. He should be helping in the attack on the convoy; they can pick us off at their leisure later. Either that or he wants to encourage the convoy to continue on their current route."

"And that's why all the attack class transports should be crewed by the Navy. Thank you Commander." Ernst said addressing Lieutenant Commander Robert Archer, U.S. Navy Reserve.

Max chimed in, "I agree. Merchant Marine sailors are some of the bravest people I know, their loss ratio is as bad or worse than the daylight bombing crews; however brave crews still need training and there aren't enough experienced combat officers to train the Merchant Marine and fight the Nazi's and Japanese. My group of pirates has more experience than most in mayhem, but you need the institutional knowledge as well as the technical expertise with all our weapons to fight a ship effectively. The naval personnel and my men have meshed better than I would have hoped. A testament to you and your men Commander."

"General, Max, thank you. Max, your men are some of the best blue water sailors I've ever met. Even my chiefs are learning new procedures. We forget how shorthanded most merchant ships are and how they manage to accomplish tasks with far fewer men than we usually have. And the makeup of your crew is definitely an eye-opener for a lot of my men, frankly myself included." Archer answered, referring to the broad racial and ethnic makeup of Larsen's crew.

"Conn, we have a bearing on the U-boat, it's ahead, 70 degrees magnetic and moving south, coming down our starboard side, range 3000 yards. The boat is blowing ballast, preparing to surface."

"Copy that Chief. Five inch mounts track starboard, but keep the screens up." Lt. Cdr. Archer answered. "We'll use just the five inch as they will sound more like the U-boats deck gun in case the rest of the wolf pack is listening. He'll probably attack from just aft of the beam as that takes out the risk from the Oerlikon."

"You fight the ship as you want Lieutenant; most of the action my men and I have seen usually comes at a much more personal range." Max replied.

The two twin five inch gun turrets were each behind a scrim of what appeared to be deck cargo. The heavy armored carapace of the turret was hidden by a simple framework of light weight steel tubing and heavy canvas disguising the turrets situated fore and aft of the bridge.

"Sonar to Conn, target now directly abaft the beam, range 1200 yards. Target is slowing and should be near the surface."

"Conn, Big Eyes, we've spotted her periscope five degrees abaft the beam. Range finder also shows 1200 yards."

"Number 2 five inch, prepare to fire at my command."

"Aye sir, we have her spotted."

"We'll wait until they pop the hatch and the gun crew starts out before we fire, she'll be most vulnerable then. Max have your engineer ready, they still might have a torpedo ready and try to fire even if we hit her." Archer ordered.

"I'm on the phone to him now; he can give us full power on the turbines as soon as I say the word. Should we task the 40s to target any torpedo? If we put a bunch of H-E into the water next to it we can either destroy it or maybe get a sympathetic explosion before it gets close."

"Hadn't thought of trying that before. This ship is the first I've been on where the Oerlikons can depress enough to use them that way. Yeah, tell them to fire if they see any wake and not wait on my command. A quad-40 can put a hell of a lot of metal between us and them."

"Starboard quad-40s, lower armor, retain screens and prepare to engage any torpedo that comes our way. If you see the wake engage."

"Starboard 40 director aye. Engage any torpedo we see."

"Conn, Big Eyes, sub is surfacing now. "

"Sub surfacing"

"Her hatch just popped gun crew coming out."

"Number 2 fire." Archer commanded.

The starboard screen shrouding the turret instantly fell forward and the report of the twin five inch sounded a moment later.

"Conn, two hits at the base of the conning tower."

"Number 2, hit them again."

The two 5 inch sounded together, answering Archer's command. Suddenly a terrific explosion shook the ship.

"Conn, Observation, U-boat destroyed. Looks like one of the 5 inch hit forward in her torpedo room."

"Conn, sonar, U-boat is breaking up and sinking."

"Copy sinking, sonar. Any other activity around us?"

"Nothing at this time. Several explosions from where the convoy is tracking."

"Big Eyes, Conn, can you sight the convoy?"

"Affirmative, looks like one tanker on fire and smoke coming from at least one other ship."

"Helm, course 110, all ahead flank." Archer was determined to avenge the ships lost.

"Commander, if we go busting in there doing fifteen knots more than any Liberty ship can, the Germans will know we have Q ships. It only takes one to see us and transmit to lose our advantage." Ernst pleaded.

Archer rounded on him in anger, hesitated and thought for a moment; "Helm, make turns for ten knots. Brigadier Dietsch, thank you, you're right. We'll hunt at low speed and see if we can pick up a boat making an end around. Have Sparks start the amplifier for the engine sounds and match the wire recorder speed to our actual speed."

"It's a new type of warfare Rob. Rules will have to be made up as we go along and learn. Hard rules that may be hard to stomach. I've a translated copy of the log of the Emden you may want to read," Max added.

"Wasn't that a disguised German raider in the first big war?" Archer asked.

"A damned effective one too." Max answered.

"Sonar, Conn, anything coming up along our track?" Archer queried.

"Sir, I can't say for sure at this time, using just passive measures our ability to hear decreases as speed increases. My last best guess had the U-boats in front and to the north of the convoy and maybe one sub inside the screen."

"Thanks Chief, I'll take your best guess any day. Keep me informed."

"Big Eyes, Conn, keep watch for any survivors from the convoy as well as U-boats."

"Big Eyes aye."

"Now I know how sub officers feel, I hate fighting a ship without being able to see the action. It feels unnatural. It works, but I don't like it. Maybe we should install a periscope." Archer commented.

"It's safer, maybe more efficient, but I agree it stinks. I'm working on possibly adapting the Big Eye to work with a televisior camera and we could pipe the take down here. Maybe several cameras for a more panoramic view." Max said. "With that new gyroscopic mount for the Big Eye that Vince Fuller designed we can hold a steady picture even using a forty power night glass."

"I was amazed the first time I used that new mount. Before it was hard to even hold the horizon steady, now you can focus on something nearby even when the ships going hard into a sea." Ernst agreed.

"That and using the British advances in passive sonar and the twin domes to provide stereoscopic tracking audio may be the most important result of this experiment." Max added.

The *LaDonna* continued its slow and lethal rendezvous with the convoy.

Chapter 6: The Twins' Lair.

Notes and narrative of Vincent Larsen, Marie Donovan and Lysette Malois

April 1, 1942, 05:11

An Abandoned farm 8 Km from Peenemünde

IN AN ABANDONED BARN Vincent and the twins tilted an old hay wagon to one side, sacks full of moldy feed draped over one side of the bed and an arrangement of rusty hooks buried under inches of old straw and holding the heavy-side wheels in place acted as a counter balance to the wagon. Lysette gave a quiet screech like a barn owl and was answered by the rapid knocking of Shave and a Haircut followed by slide bolts moving, then a section of floor complete with a fringe of straw quietly rose up showing a heavy ladder, nearly a staircase, leading down. The Bat was quickly lowered rear first into the gloom and Vincent followed it down holding the front end and protecting the detonator safety pin from being dislodged. The twins grabbed some brooms and working from the field back and into the barn erased their tracks all the way to the hatch. Marie made the last two swipes needed as the hatch closed. In the now silent barn the wagon slowly settled back and the rusty hooks that held it in place were raised, rotated and withdrawn through gaps in the floor boards. A few small flashlight bulbs dangling from wires lit the underground lair. Vincent looked around, a young man; skinny with big ears held a Schmeisser machine pistol in one steady hand and the rear of the Bat with the other. "We can put this over to your left." he said while motioning with the Schmeisser.

The two moved their bundle and set it down carefully. Marie made the introductions, "Mr. Smith meet Corporal Wild Willy McCabe of the Army Air Corp."

"Sir, please just call me Bill. The ladies here hung that name on me and I'd rather it didn't go any further."

"Do I detect the sound of the Bronx Bill?"

"Yes sir."

"I thought so; I'm originally from there many years ago. Catholic school? It's usually only the nuns who can knock the accent down that far."

Bill grinned, "St. Ignatius and they wore out plenty of rulers."

"No offense Bill, but you look like you should still be there."

Marie jumped in; "I'll save Willy from further embarrassment, although it's awfully cute how his ears turn all red. He joined when he was 15 and he's a ripe old 16 hoping to make 17 before we get him killed helping us."

"How did you all meet and how did you find this surprisingly efficient lair; you haven't been here long enough to have done all this work?"

"Actually the Dutch resistance told us about this barn. It seems a family of smugglers, with relatives in both countries, were using this place for years. I don't think smugglers usually think of themselves as criminals, and an awful lot of small time crooks really dislike the bigger crooks like the Nazis and especially the Gestapo and the Sicherheitspolizei that have attracted a lot of really sadistic and mean bastards to them. A surprising number of these small, you might say genteel crooks, are members of the resistance. We've been assured that no one in Germany or in German hands in the Netherlands knows of this place and there are signals that will come in if that situation changes."

"And Wild Bill?'

"Willy, Wild Willy. He just dropped in while we were traveling here. The Pathfinders dumped us out near where we could hop a train coming this way. We jumped off the train on the far side of Züssow to avoid the yard bulls and were walking around the outskirts when we stopped to answer natures call in some trees and brush off the road. At the most embarrassing moment possible, two German soldiers stood up from behind a bush where they were similarly occupied. They had the drop on us even if their pants were around their ankles. Willy dropped out of the tree above them, obviously intending to knock them to the ground. They were big and he's not and probably wasn't all that high to begin with. So there he is swaying back and forth with each foot on one of the German's shoulders, trying to get his balance. The soldiers were dumbfounded, they didn't know whether to laugh or shoot. Willy solved the problem by pushing his .45 into the top of one of their heads and shooting him, then as he and that German fell he pushed his pistol into the other soldier's chest and tapped him. We had our Walthers out, our pants and underwear around our ankles and all of us are pointing guns at one another. Willy's staring at us, but not at our guns and his ears were fire engine red; I started laughing, it was just too bizarre. That broke the dam. We laughed and rearranged our clothes while Willy turned around and swapped magazines in his pistol. Fortunately the contact shots weren't as loud as they could have been. We dragged the Germans farther into the woods, took their weapons and helped Willy adapt a shirt and pants off the smaller German into something that didn't look like a uniform. Next he climbed up a tree and hid his flight gear in the crook of a tree. He climbs like a squirrel."

Vincent turned to Bill and gestured for him to continue. "Well, like Lysette said I'm good in trees. I used to carry rivets on Saturdays and during my last summer at home so I learned to climb high steel. I was a radio operator and gunner on a B-17, the Texas Tease, we got into a furball on the way back from a raid and I had just moved over to a side gun when a rocket exploded on the other side. The other gunner was blown into me and the next thing I know I'm falling through the air. I held off opening my chute, part to get out of their as quickly as possible and part scared shitless at all the tracers and 190s and B-17s flying around. I had to parachute once before when we were nearly over the English coast. I landed just a few yards into the water. Anyway, I landed in some trees which suited me just fine. People just don't seem to look up much. I cut up and hid the chute; I saved the risers for rope and started moving towards the sea. I almost always slept in trees or inside a big bush. I traveled at night and had climbed up just a little while before everyone in the world gathered under my tree; first the Nazis and then the ladies. I was just going to lay low until the bastards aimed their guns at the ladies; and yeah, I thought I would just knock'em flat; didn't turn out at all like I imagined. It always seemed to work for Errol Flynn."

Vincent just looked at Bill and the twins for a moment;" I don't think Errol even on his best day could have pulled off that trick. How did a fifteen year old get into the Air Corp?"

"One thing all those rulers at St. Ignatius did was to give me great penmanship. I stole a birth certificate out of the rector's office and forged a new one that gave me a few more years. Uh, I think one of the corpsman thought I was a fag maybe, but I kept saying how much I liked girls and that I was joining to impress Bernadette O'Malley, so he finally signed off and here I am."

"Willy, you didn't tell us there was a rival for our affections." Marie exclaimed while pouting her lips and batting her eyes.

Bill's ears again signaled his embarrassment while he stammered "'I just used her name, she never said word one to me."

Marie continued, "We thought it was better to bring Willy with us and use his abilities to help."

Vincent read between the lines, they either needed to bring him or kill him; they couldn't afford for him to be captured. "All right, let me ask a few questions. Bill do you speak any language besides Bronx?"

"I speak a little Italian from my mother's side of the family. I understand a fair amount of Yiddish because I help some of our neighbors on their Sabbath when they can't do any work. I don't think Yiddish would be a good language to use in Germany."

"Oy vey! Right about that I think you are. Next question; how close can we get to the field and bunkers at the test site?"

Lysette answered, "Using a ghillie suit like Quartermain showed us how to make I snuck in one night to the edge of the airfield. I backed out about 200 yards and had to stay there all day long. They have an occasional patrol around the perimeter of the field; sometimes they even have dogs. I don't think you can get much closer and stay for any length of time."

"You probably shouldn't have tried to get that close. If you had been captured or killed it would have alerted the Germans and probably screwed any further reconnaissance."

"We needed to get close enough to show the slave labor in our pictures. We think some of the technicians and engineers are from France and Poland and they're basically enslaved as their families are held hostage."

"In the Bat's tube I have a Contaflex camera and Kodak made a special mount that attaches a 10x50 Zeiss monocular to it. I won't have to get anywhere near as close to get some good pictures."

"Vincent, why don't you let me or Marie shoot the pictures. You're needed for the war effort much more than either of us."

"That is debatable. And the person I would have to debate with is Hiram. I'm not going there."

"Just because we're women is not a good reason for you to risk your life."

"I'd agree if you were just women, however you are the two people Hiram loves more than life itself and the apple of my closest friends' eyes. Frankly I'd rather die than explain how I lost one or both of you."

"Excuse me Mr. Fuller," Bill spoke up while getting between the twins and Vincent, "excuse me, but why do any of you need to take pictures?"

"Bill, stay out of this, we have to obtain information on these new designs. The Nazis could really steal a march on us and we can't let that happen." Vincent said harshly.

"I understand that Mr. Fuller; what I'm saying is haven't the Germans taken thousands of pictures and movies and blueprints. Would it be that much more dangerous to find those at night than trying to take your own pictures during daylight?"

"William, may I call you William? That is the most amazingly simple and brilliant thing I've heard in months. We probably need to let you start leading this operation."

"No need to make fun of me Sir."

"Bill, believe me when I say I mean every word. Except I think I'll suggest that Marie and Lysette actually lead the operation as I know that they have infiltrated other offices before and I haven't."

"Bill, how did you know that Vincent is Fuller? We introduced him as Smith." Lysette asked quietly.

"Easy, American airmen go through a lot of schooling about aviation before they turn us loose as crew and you can't study without seeing a picture or two of Vincent Fuller. Also you called him Vincent and that sealed the deal."

"Me and my big mouth. I need to quit getting excited when some man says something demonstrably stupid."

"Girls, it's been a long night. I'm going to sleep for a few hours and when we get up let's sit down and see what we need to do to access those pictures." Fuller suggested.

Chapter 7: "thankfully I don't smell menudo."

Notes and narratives from Vincent Larsen, Marie Donovan, Lysette Malois, and William McCabe

April 1, 1942, 14:00
An Abandoned farm 8 Km from Peenemünde

VINCENT FULLER WOKE and listened without moving. He heard the quiet breathing of the twins as they shared a bedroll, a slight stirring where he thought McCabe was resting. Vince looked around. Only one small light bulb was lit, a hand cranked generator and some old car batteries powered not only the lights, they powered the suitcase sized short wave radio that was sitting on a makeshift desk under the stairs in the most protected part of the hidden basement. When Vincent looked toward Bill's area he saw him sitting up, quietly cleaning his pistol, the Schmeisser resting on a wooden crate next to him. Bill quickly assembled his pistol, his eyes roaming around the room, never glancing at the gun. "Wouldn't it be easier to just close your eyes?" Vincent asked quietly.

McCabe grinned and nodded, "It is easier, I want to be sure I can do it while looking somewhere else. I'm counting rocks in the columns, anything to distract me. Marie mentioned one time that their instructors said that you might want to see what's coming toward you while you're putting it back together."

"Good idea. I have some powdered coffee in the Bat, let me get it out. Do you have a way to heat it?"

Bill grinned and pointed to one of the support columns, "That connects to the old chimney, we'll have to wait until its dark. We only use it after checking the area and then we use charcoal we got from some old burned down buildings. Let me show you something." Bill inserted the .45's magazine, cycled the slide, locked the safety and placed it into a belt holster that had been fastened inside the waist of his pants, pulled a flashlight from a pocket, then rose and moved to the west corner of the basement. Vincent followed him to the corner. "Those Dutchmen were either unusually careful or they had too much time on their hands in the winter." Bill pulled a rag off what appeared to be the marriage of an old stereo-opticon and a flue pipe that ascended up through the floor above their heads.

"You have to be joking," Vincent muttered before bending down to look thru the viewer. "My god a periscope!"

"It comes out inside an old cupola type ventilator on top of the roof, there's one at each corner, you can rotate about three quarters of a circle and the lever on the wall changes the angle up or down. We've risked going out in the daytime to look and you can't see anything in the cupolas. Maybe if you backed off and looked with a good set of field glasses you might see something. The periscopes are fairly useless at night. If someone is showing a light you could see them. Let me show you the back door." Bill said as he led Vincent deeper into the structure.

McCabe walked to a section of wall opposite the stairway from the barn. He walked to a column and disappeared behind it. Vincent walked closer and saw a cavity behind the column. A low tunnel continued away from the barn and McCabe's feet proceeded into the tunnel. A moment later his head appeared and he came out. "It comes out about a hundred yards away in a small cemetery. If you trip a latch at the end a trap door opens and I guess about a foot of dirt or more comes down and you climb up. The tunnels low, you have to crawl, but it's wide enough to turn around in."

"Easier for you than me, I'm sure. I think you're right, the winters are too long. This is all pretty obsessive even for smugglers." Vincent replied.

"I guess anything worth doing is worth overdoing if you're German;" Bill said while brushing off his knees.

"We need to get the girls up and start figuring a way into the archives." Vincent said while walking toward the twins. "Wake up kids, breakfast is ready."

Lysette gently un-spooned from Marie and sat up; "I don't smell pancakes and bacon, and thankfully I don't smell menudo. I hope you can back up your breakfast claim because Marie is a real bitch when you don't feed her on time."

Marie rolled upright, glaring at both Vincent and Bill; "I don't see my breakfast tray. I'll have coffee, orange juice, three eggs over easy and a small steak medium rare. Don't forget a rose in a cut glass vase."

"Girls, you've become awfully crabby in your old age. I'm the guest, you have to feed me."

Vincent and the twins all turned to look at McCabe. "Breakfast in just a few minutes. We have a fine selection of German iron rations. I would suggest the older ones as I believe they were still using real meat in them. I'm afraid that the rose will be a weed in an old can."

"Ugh. Willy dear, whatever you do after the war, don't start a restaurant," Marie replied while climbing out of the bedroll. She continued to the latrine which had an old sheet shielding it. "Vincent, has Willy showed you our luxurious facilities. Please pee in the hole closest to the stairway and poop in the other. There's a sack of leaves and a stack of German propaganda leaflets next to the poop hole."

"I was pretty sure of the location, however I was a little surprised it didn't stink worse. I see you continue to use lessons from the ranch by segregating your waste."

Lysette dropped her voice down and layered on a thick West Texas accent; "Senoritas, crap breaks down faster and with less stink if you don't pee on it. Just throw in some leaves or grass and pee on a rock somewhars else. By damn I can still hear Jack Borden giving us a tour of a cattle camp when we first came to the ranch."

"Bill, did you ever have a conversation with Bernadette on the proper way to make your toilet in the country?" Vincent asked.

"No sir, I don't believe it ever came up." Bill said as his ears turned scarlet.

Vincent grabbed a wooden crate and sat down, "Draw up your chairs and let's see how we get the information we need." The other three pulled stools and a chair up joining Fuller. "Do we go big or small, where do we go, how do we get it out, how do we keep the Nazis from knowing that we got it or does that matter if they know? That should keep us busy for a bit."

Lysette was the first to answer, "I saw some of their routine while lying in the field, at the end of the day men come around with carts and gather all the tools, they also gather blueprints and notebooks. One guard with each cart keeps an inventory, I suppose so the prisoners can't hide a shovel or even a file and they also log in the blueprints. The prisoners or workmen have to strip naked and shake out their clothes before being herded back to their barrack. Even if we could contact them they probably can't get anything out."

"Could they get something in?" Marie asked.

"I didn't see any sign of a search as they entered, however they might check them at the barracks before marching them to work. What would you have them carry?"

"You can secrete one of those little [1]Riga cameras anywhere. Put a condom over it, tie it off, grease it, and no one would find it without a lot closer look and a long finger. We have the one that the OSS supplied us when we went to Paris last year. Vince did you bring another?"

40

"There's one in the main tube of the Bat. I brought you a bunch of extra film as well. However with just two cameras, depending on the prisoners to gain enough access to the photos and prints to copy them, the number of projects we need to cover and the probability that there are some snitches among the workmen; I think this is a blind alley. We don't have the time to set up a ring of prisoners and frankly they're being killed off too quick to rely on them. It might work if I could get into the archive. I could probably determine which projects and what parts of the plans needed to be shot. If I had two helpers I could hand the plans to, I could let them take the pictures while I searched."

"And if we could get a truck backed up to the archive we could load it all up, take the information and deprive the Germans of their working plans at the same time;" Marie chimed in, "and if wishes were fishes we'd be dining on filet of sole right now."

"Bill, do you want to say something or are you still thinking about where the camera would hide?"

"Mr. Fuller, uhh, some of both actually."

"Why Willy what could you have been thinking?" Lysette asked while poking McCabe in the ribs.

"I'm actually wondering why they haven't bombed this place into dust by now," Bill answered while his ears signaled his discomfort.

"Priorities!" Fuller answered; 'there's no need to worry about invention if they don't have any factories to build them. At least that's probably the thinking at SHAEF. I don't necessarily agree. What if you invent something lethal and easy to build, you may not need a huge factory. If they can join parts from existing systems and you can build parts in a number of smaller shops you might be able to marry them together into a lethal combination. Also they know of the large number of prisoners here and are probably reluctant to bomb them."

"If we find enough manufacturing going on here we may change their mind. I think some of the rockets we've seen might be reason alone. I've no idea of their range or payload, but damn they're scary." Lysette said.

"Sir, what did you mean when you asked if we should go big or small?"

"Bill, please call me Vincent. I went from sergeant to major in World War One. I didn't ask to have my commission reinstated and the War Department didn't offer. When I said go big or go small I was referring to different methods of acquiring information. A big elaborate scam where you hide in plain sight, in fact you make sure the light is shining on you so brightly that no one can get a good look. A small scam is all under the table, devise a way to sneak in and sneak out. They both have some problems here."

"According to our teachers in the art of the scam, the big scam usually takes a lot of people, a whole lot of preparation and a fair amount of time; probably more than we have. The small scam is more of an in an out under the table sort of deal. They never see you coming and they never realize you were there. It takes far fewer people, however it usually requires a lot of detailed knowledge of your target. Again that's something we're lacking." Marie added.

"You had a teacher in stealing from people?" Bill asked.

Fuller answered, "You can't protect yourself if you don't know how crooks work. Alas these two fair maidens have put those skills to more nefarious purposes. Their teachers were my wife and father-in-law. Frankie and Merlin were on the verge of skinning me for a small fortune when luck and two good friends stepped in. By that time I was sufficiently smitten of Frankie that I didn't care and fortunately she had similar feelings for me. We managed to coerce her and her father, Merlin, into a semblance of the straight and narrow. They help us avoid being scammed and they have a side business keeping the Las Vegas gaming clubs staffed with security personnel who know every scam, dirty dealing card shuffling type of cheat there is. They keep an eye on both the customers and the staff."

"No offense sir, but you have a strange family."

"Bill, you have no idea."

"Uncle Vincent, the talk about going small and our lack of knowledge has given me an idea. We need two people we met in Paris. They were very effective members of the Resistance. *La Petit Souris* and Robin Jarvis." Lysette announced

"And what can a little mouse and this Robin Jarvis do for us."

"*La Petit Souris*, her name is Susan Brodeur, is the best cat burglar in France. She can hide and go in places no one else could even think about. In an urban setting I would put her up against Captain Quartermain, Leboo, and Max. She'd have their wallets in her bag and their shoelaces tied together before they knew what hit them. Her father was a mountain guide in the Alps and she has been hanging from ropes and cliffs since she was a little girl. Leftenant Robin Jarvis is Susan's partner and lover, an expat British beauty who works for the Resistance and Brit intelligence. Robin is a very expensive hooker who has wedeled out more information from Nazi officers and officials than any ten other spies. Between Robin's skills and Susan's abilities I think we can get both the information and access that we need. We would never have penetrated that provost's office in Paris without their help." Marie added.

"Wonderful, except they are in Paris and we are not." Fuller reminded.

"No, they are in London. Robin's identity was burned by a captured Resistance member. With OSS and British help they managed to escape to Spain. We heard they were coming into England as we were leaving. We need to find a way to get them here."

"No we don't need to find a way. We just need to contact the right people and let them find a way." Vincent stated.

---

[1] *Riga Cameras: Marie is referring to a small camera originally built in Latvia and today known as a Minox. The Minox name was not used until 1948. To avoid confusion the Minox name will be used hereafter. SMkIII*

Chapter 8: Hiram Snowden and the OSS

Compiled OSS records and the narrative of Brigadier General Hiram Marcus Snowden (Progenitor). Snowden is the father of Marie Malois and Lysette Malois

OSS Headquarters in London, England: 70 Grosvenor Street
April 4, 1943, 16:00
Office of Colonel Albert Osgood, London OSS Headquarters XO

COLONEL ALBERT OSGOOD ROSE to his feet from behind his desk and stood at attention as Brigadier General Hiram Snowden strode in. The Brigadier nodded in acknowledgement; "Sorry to barge in on you Colonel, but I understand you have a message for me."

"Yes Sir, please come in. Signals should have the decoded message here in a few minutes. Can I get the General anything while you wait?"

"Al, if you keep acting all proper I'll have to wonder how the Germans snuck in your double. You still keep some bourbon in your desk? You always did back home."

"Hiram, if I don't practice my military Ps and Qs occasionally I'll forget myself when someone really important comes in. Drag up a chair and I'll see if I've got a medicinal dram or two."

"Ouch, someone really important. I'll remember that when we get back in practice." Snowden replied. The two men had worked together for many years. Hiram Snowden had one of the largest and more lucrative patent law firms in the U.S. Osgood was a junior partner, a mechanical engineer whose interest in patent law had led him into a law degree. Hiram was always on the lookout for lawyers with expertise outside of the law. The firm also had a chemist and a physician turned lawyers and one lawyer whose ham radio hobby had turned into a masters in electrical engineering. Hiram's military prowess during WW1 ended with the rank of brevet Major General then reinstated as a colonel in the reserves. His rank had been reset as a brigadier for the duration of the current war. "I'm just passing through here Al, but if you can, will you tell me how the girls are getting information out without getting caught."

"Shoot even if you told the Germans I don't think they could stop it. One of the English boffins came up with a directional antennae and a method to shield any backscatter that the Germans might intercept. They dig a large bowl shape in a dune pointing in the direction they want to send, they line the bowl with a thin copper screen and put the antennae in front. The signal goes out in a very specific direction at a very specific time at night. Both direction, frequency, and time vary by a schedule that we both have. The receiver is in an F4 tasked to be in a certain area and a certain height at the specified time. The only way a Nazi could intercept would be to fly into the cone at the same time. Of course the message is both a combination of coded phrases and one time pads for any info that isn't covered by the phrase book."

"What's an F4?"

"Oh, you haven't heard. It's a P-38 Lightning reconnaissance plane. They take out the armor and the guns, extend the nose and fill it with an operator and a bunch of cameras. We're using a variant with a radio receiver and an operator. The signal is both written down and recorded on a wire recorder. The plane flies off the coast and is too high and fast for the Germans to bother with. Even if they paint it with radar it's gone before they can do anything. If they use a night fighter with radar the Lightning has a receiver that lets them know if radar is being used in the area and can leave before the Germans get in range. The F4 only transmits recognition signals when it approaches its field near Bletchley. That prevents the Germans from using RDF on it or knowing if it answers any signal that they may hear."

"Brilliant. Do you think you can contact this boffin? I have an interest in a few companies that could use someone like that after the war. Would you be interested in setting up a patent office in London and starting a European branch?"

"I'll think about it. Let's end the Nazis and then see if Uncle Joe decides to start number Three."

They were interrupted by a lieutenant who knocked and entered with a folder wrapped in red tape and SECRET stamped in several places. The Lieutenant came to attention and saluted. Snowden returned the salute. "Lieutenant, I know you're just coming over from communications downstairs, but isn't it protocol to put that folder inside of an unmarked folder? There's no good reason to travel up the stairs and down the hall with secret stamped on everything but your forehead."

The lieutenant stiffened to ramrod stiffness; "Sir, yes Sir it is protocol. My mistake Sir."

"Relax Lieutenant. You get any stiffer you'll pass out. I'm sure you were in a hurry. Make sure it doesn't happen again. I'll call you back if there's an answer to this."

"Yes Sir." the lieutenant answered while beating the hastiest retreat he could while maintaining a smidgen of military decorum.

Osgood chuckled and shook his head, "That poor kid is scared to death right now. "He doesn't know whether he's in a lot of trouble or skated. Someone biting his head off he can understand, a general being nice is scary."

"Uh-huh," Snowden mumbled while going through the message, as soon as he finished with the first sheet he passed it on to the colonel. They both read the message, four pages altogether. "This seems like an awful lot to be transmitting even with their un-catchable radio."

"Code phrases, there are a hundred plus phrases, and they only need to send three numbers for each phrase. The numbers are also rotated regularly so the numbers in one message won't match the numbers in a previous dispatch. The longer time is spent with the onetime pad. Their operator has a damn fast hand."

"What operator? Who all is with the twins?"

"You mean besides Vincent Fuller?"

"What the hell is Vincent doing over there? No one tells me anything."

'Need to know Hiram. As long as you promise not to go over to the front I can tell you."

"Donovan doesn't even want me leaving the States. If we hadn't needed to make nice with SHAEF's staff I'd never have made it this far."

"We need to know more about the work being done at Peenemünde. We're getting a little from a couple of Polish workers, but it's slow and all just verbal descriptions. We can't just ask for everything, there's no time and there's no telling whether we'd get wheat or chaff. Vince can tell what is important. We thought he would just be observing, but their idea about copying or stealing the German's own plans is better and probably does not increase the risk that much more."

"How did you convince Fuller to go along with this scheme?"

"One thing that really piqued our and his interest is a report from the Poles of a new missile the Germans are developing. The Poles said it's called a *Feuerdrachen* or Fire Dragon or Drake. They report that a heavily reinforced bunker, where many of the prisoners worked is now a large hole in the ground and none of the prisoners have been seen since. It sounds like a White Russian count by the name of Voronstov is heading the program. You know Vince, he doesn't work full time for any of the aircraft manufacturers, and he only consults; so if he disappears for a while nobody notices. Also we threatened to reinstate his commission, promote him and have him count bolts as a supply officer at Randolph. Actually he probably would have gone just to see what the Nazi's are building even if we hadn't asked," Osgood said.

"Yeah, he doesn't suffer fools very well and he hates company politics. He actually does have a small full time company. He gets a problem from one of the major companies; solves the problem and then has his own guys see if it can be built. They'll build, find flaws and rebuild and they can do it quicker than anyone else. When Vince brings the solution back, he not only has the design and specs, he has the best way to manufacture or make his fix. He also patents and sells them any machine tools that he and his crew design that are necessary to the solution. Most of his mechanics have been with him since the first big war and most of them could be teaching at any technical or engineering school in the country. Quite a few have got their engineering degrees and their professional licenses."

"Yeah, I heard he has a place. Out in West Texas isn't it?"

"Near Midland, lots of room, and all the oil field service companies give him access to a lot of machinists and welders if he needs them. Occasionally Vince or one of his men will get a wild hair and build some specialized plane just to be doing something. They have done a lot of work on crop dusters. The Army Signal Corp and the Department of Agriculture started experimenting back in the 1920's. Vince and his crew think with the end of the war there will be a surplus of engines and airframes that can be converted to crop dusting as well as all the pilots who will want to keep flying; we'll have a new renaissance in both agriculture and civilian flying. Now, who's the radio operator?"

"Corporal William McCabe, he apparently fell into Marie and Lysette's lap. He was a radioman and gunner on a B-17. He was blown out of his plane, parachuted into Germany and managed to evade capture until he ran into the twins. We've confirmed that it's him, both from questions and more importantly the radio guys say that it is definitely his hand. The girls also used a code word to confirm that they we're still free and they believed him to be the real deal. Also their choices were pretty limited, use him or kill him. They can't afford for him to be captured. Oh yes, we went to contact his family and found out that he was only fifteen when he enlisted. They knew he forged his birth certificate, but they have a bunch of kids and were sure he would have joined somehow eventually."

"So my daughters are trying to infiltrate Peenemünde with a giant red headed aeronautical engineer and a fifteen year old radioman."

"Sixteen now."

"Oh, well that's different. My Jewish friends are right; God will get you if your life is too good. And apparently they have seen additional coast watchers and parabolic microphone listening stations since Vincent's arrival."

"Hiram it only gets better. The two agents they asked for; they are an infamous miniature female cat burglar and a British agent who is an extremely popular prostitute. On top of that the two are lesbian lovers."

Snowden collapsed back into his chair, "Oh my God! Hitler will be quaking in his boots. Fill that glass all the way up this time."

Chapter 9: A NAZI jack-in-the-box

General Ehrlich's journal, German records, and supposition by Sherlock Mk3

April 4, 1943, 11:29
Generalleutnant der Artillirie Manford von Ehrlich's quarters in Peenemünde

"GRAF VORONSTOV, PLEASE SIT DOWN. Schnapps?" Lt. General Ehrlich gestured toward the sideboard.

"I'd ask for coffee, but I can no longer stand that ersatz brew. Tea if you have it please."

Ehrlich gestured to his assistant who quickly left for the small pantry adjoining the general's suite of offices. "How is the production coming along? Will the [1]Drachenspringteufel, the self-contained launchers be ready in time?"

"We now have some 1100 Feuerdrachen missiles built. The last hundred or so warheads are being filled even as we speak. They will be ready by the end of the month. We won't be operational until we can finish the [1]Drachenspringteufel. More important is where will we site them? Has the general staff or probably more importantly your fuhrer decided where the invasion is expected?"

"They've spent more time deciding where and when it won't come. They don't expect it before next spring. The Americans and the British are still advancing in Africa. Arnim's Afrika Korps is still holding the Brits and Americans in play, but eventually the enemies' numerical advantage will be too great. Too bad Rommel took ill, but Arnim has done well. We are concentrating on building up our forces in Italy. Also we have the Russian's running from us."

"You must pass the damn Bolsheviks before winter comes. Russia's greatest ally has always been cold and distance. Ask Bonaparte's shade if you need a reminder," Voronstov rejoined.

"Napoleon didn't have our tanks or our commanders."

"Logistics and weather will always be the great equalizer. You have better transport now, but so do your enemies. On the Russian steppes those Studebaker trucks Russia receives from the Americans can go nearly anywhere your Panzers can and faster with less upkeep and the Russian T-34 tanks are fast, rugged and nearly a match for a Panzer. Tiger tanks are too heavy, slow and breakdown too often. The Russian numbers will overmatch your technical superiority. Stalin is as much a megalomaniac as Hitler, and he has killed far more of his own people than your soldiers have, however that won't stop his organizational skills and fear can be as much of a goad as patriotism."

"Graf, don't forget where you are. If the wrong people hear you talking about the Fuhrer like that, even Göring's support won't keep you alive."

"Forgive me General. If being circumspect helps bring down the Communists, then I will better censor myself."

After a knock on the door, a sturdy, athletic major walked in and came to attention. Voronstov noted that the major omitted the heel clicking so many German officers emulated. "Graf Voronstov, allow me to introduce your new adjutant, Major Klaus von Stulpnagel. He has been at the Eastern front acting as liaison to the Waffen SS."

"Major, I am honored to meet any soldier who has been on the front lines. How goes the war against the damned communists?" Voronstov said while rising to shake the major's hand.

"Thank you Herr Graf. The battles go well so far as our supply lines keep up. Unfortunately as we conquer territory our lines get longer and take more personnel and the Russians lines get shorter. I've been in Russia before during the last winter as well as many years ago while accompanying my uncle on a visit. I don't look forward to having to fight the cold and the Russians."

"I agree Major. The general and I were just discussing Russian winters."

"The major's uncle is General Otto von Stulpnagel who was most recently in command of our military in France." von Ehrlich added.

"Your uncle is a soldier of principle and I hope my next observation is not ill taken. I believe Gen. von Stulpnagel's efforts to work with the current French government and his attempts to lessen some of the harsh efforts against the French civilians would have been more productive in the long run than the wholescale looting and mass executions sponsored by the SS and others."

"Herr Graf, thank you for your kind words. My uncle is indeed a man of principle although obviously his superiors disagreed with his actions. Since his resignation he now resides in Berlin with my aunt and is no longer involved in the war. As to the possible efficacy of his efforts I am too involved with our eastern front and too junior to have a legitimate opinion."

"I had the major come in so that you can brief him on the Feuerdrachen. I will be going to Berlin for a few weeks and I want to leave the major behind so he can keep me informed of progress and assist you in overcoming any obstacles that may arise." Gen. von Ehrlich said, both in an effort to move the meeting along and avoid any further discussion on a subject uncomfortable to the High Command. "I will leave the two of you together while I finish some orders before my departure. I'm afraid that the true leaders of our military are the secretaries, who warn of looming disaster if I don't sign all the requisitions they place on my desk."

Count Voronstov remained standing until General Erlich left the room, he then motioned to two chairs in a corner. "What do you know of my work Major?"

"My posting only came in last fortnight and I've been traveling ever since. I'm afraid I have only heard some small talk about your weapon in the last day. It would be best to consider me completely ignorant of the weapons capabilities."

"At least you are willing to acknowledge what you don't know. A sure sign of wisdom and also a sign that you will never advance to the general staff. If, however, you are as open to divulging your ignorance to your underofficers as you are to your superiors, your men will respect and value what you do know even more."

"Herr Graf, I have found that there are very few soldiers who don't realize when their officer makes a mistake. Often long before the officer comes to the same conclusion. Since my mistakes are no secret I find it disingenuous to pretend otherwise. Better to be the first to admit your mistakes, the quicker to rectify them. Also I have found that being the first to disparage myself reduces the need for others to do it more colorfully."

"Well said Major! I realize that you must be faithful to the party line, however can you be candid about the war in Russia now that General Erlich has left?"

"Herr Graf the war in the East is lost. The Russians can lose ten men to our one and still swamp us with numbers. Expecting the Luftflotte to provide sufficient provisions to defeat Stalingrad was a fantasy. The Bolsheviks have adapted to our tactics and our superior training is dying away as their soldiers gain hard won experience. Unless you can come up with advanced weapons in sufficient numbers the war is lost."

"Klaus, I must reluctantly agree with you. Let me introduce you to the Feuerdrachen and the Drachenspringteufel. Come with me to the workshop where we have a unit disassembled the better to visualize its parts."

When they came to the workshop, both men were required to show identification to the guards. The guards acted as if they had never seen either man before and checked the ID pictures against their subjects as well as checking a roster to be sure that the men were allowed.

"The security is impressive Herr Graf. These men must know you well and still they check."

"These men don't know me as well as the previous guards. General Erlich and I walked in last week and the guards simply saluted and opened the doors. The general thanked them, called their officer and sergeant to his office and threw all four into the brig for a week before he demoted them and sent them to the Eastern Front. Since then the new guards have been most careful. Let me show you a Fire Drake."

The two men entered into a cavernous work area inside an earth-covered bunker. Six meters of dirt and rock covered a ceiling of over two meters of highly reinforced concrete. A missile was on a stand, missing its wings and rocket turbine which were displayed on a wall behind it. Much of the covering had been removed from the missile and wings wherever an attachment point or movable surface was present.

"This is our working model. If we need to make an alteration in the design, we can test it out here first just to make sure it will mesh with all the other parts." Voronstov explained.

"Herr Graf, I'm familiar with ground effect, I have flown in Fiesler Storchs and the pilots have mentioned it and how it can cause a landing to overshoot. As I understand it the air is compressed between the wing and the ground adding lift," said the major.

"Yes Major, a light airplane with a large wing and low wing loading easily demonstrates ground effect to the occasional embarrassment of inexperienced pilots. This design uses that effect to carry a load. The effect is maximized as speed and close proximity to the ground coincide. This has allowed us to put the heaviest warhead yet on an anti-ship missile."

"I have heard that the radio controlled glider bombs and other missiles have a weakness as the guiding pilots aircraft must stay in straight ahead flight toward the target so the operator can view and control the missile. This makes the controlling aircraft an easy target for antiaircraft guns or enemy fighters. Would that also cause difficulty in the operator having proper depth perception as the rocket approaches its target? How have you overcome this flaw?"

"Bugs, Major, bugs."

"Bugs sir?"

"Klaus, forgive me, but your expression is priceless. I had a mentor, an American engineer by the name of Ernst Dietsch. He often lectured that there was no mechanism that nature hadn't come up with first and that ideas can come from all the sciences. Biology, chemistry, physics, often reading in other fields enlightens us in our own. I read an article on insect eyes that made me think. Spiders, flies, many insects have compound eyes, nowhere near the resolution or complexity of our eyes, yet by using multiple sensors in each eye the fly or spider is given great acuity and perception within certain ranges and they have depth perception and kinesthetic awareness. In other words they can determine where they are, their relation to prey or enemies and how they and others are moving. How often have flies avoided our best efforts to swat them; it certainly isn't strategy or tactics, it is stimulus and response. I needed to make the operator's job as safe and easy as possible. A shore or ship based operator need only keep an invisible beam of ultraviolet light on the target and the Dragon directs itself. I have used three sensors looking forward from the wing tips and the top of the tail. If one sensor receives a brighter image it causes the controls to act so that all three sensors have an equal brightness of the target. The sensor on the tail is aligned with the initial compass bearing to the target allowing a ninety degree field of acquisition. Once the missile assumes its initial course all three sensors work together to refine the target. Two lights shining under the missile are adjusted so that at the proper height their image overlaps and is read by three sensors along the ventral axis thus controlling altitude. A gyro is fed the initial bearing used to fire the Fire Drake and additional gyros assist in keeping the craft stable and coordinating control movement. There are also airspeed and pressure sensors that aid in attitude control. These also rotate a cam that decreases control travel as speed increases and the control surfaces become more effective. I see by the glazed look in your eyes that I may have waxed too enthusiastically."

"No Herr Graf, It is fascinating although the breadth of your accomplishment is overwhelming."

"Many people have come together to build the Fire Drakes. I've had entomologists, opticians, even an astronomer who is an expert on light waves. One engineer came up with a radical idea to use compressed air to operate the controls and a pipe organ mechanic helped design the quick acting variable response valves. It was lighter than additional batteries and servomotors and need have only enough air for a short flight, most of which can be stored in the tube framework."

"Most impressive Herr Graf!"

"*Sagst du Klaus, sagst du.* Call me Alexei please. We have far too much to do to stand on formality. Come, I'll see if you can help hasten the completion of the Drachenspringteufel, the launchers must be ready to deploy as soon as possible.

[1]Drachenspringteufel, a metal container designed to carry a Fire Drake and act as the launcher. Literally a Dragon Jack-in-the-box. SMkIII

Chapter 10: Just a small invasion

Notes taken by Col. Osgood and reports from Ernst Dietsch, Hiram Snowden and Maxwell Larsen.

April 6, 1943, 15:26
Col. Osgood's Office:

"HIRAM, WHAT'S THE BIG HURRY?" Ernst said as he entered the office and gave Snowden an abrazo that would have done a Mexican bandit proud.

"Unhand me for God's sake. How do you expect me to maintain my military mien when you're pounding on my back and swinging me around like a rag doll?" Hiram exploded even as his smile belied his words.

Max Larsen followed the feisty little engineer into the office and his handshake was much more decorous if just as warm as Dietsch's. "Good to see you Hiram. Hello Albert, it's good to see you." and he advanced across the room to shake the colonel's hand.

"See, you little runt of a square-head mechanic, Max knows how to act like a gentleman, take some lessons."

"I love you too Hiram. Max has gone all soft, I guess it's all those other people's hands and ribs he broke in his exuberant youth. Or maybe it's just respect for the elderly." Said Dietsch, who was only four years younger than the sixty three year old Snowden.

"Careful, I'll have Marshall restore your commission from WW1; and I have seniority by about a month as a Brigadier."

"Hiram, I've wondered, you made Major General back then, why did you come back as a Brigadier?" Larsen asked.

"Brevet Major General. A couple of reasons: first, I reverted to colonel in the peace time reserve. Second, I was out of touch with the new maneuver style of warfare, the lightning war of the Germans. While I recognize it as an extension of their Storm Troop tactics of the first war; I didn't want to be put in charge of someone who knew more than I did about my job. Last, neither I nor Donovan wanted to get in a pissing match with headquarters; I'm senior enough to get into anyone's office without being a threat and the older commanders know I was a major general way back when and treat me accordingly. I donate all my pay to a veteran's relief fund anyway so the extra bump wouldn't make any financial difference to me."

"Did you ever tell Vincent your reasons?" Dietsch asked.

"Oh, God!" Snowden said while shaking his head; "he asked and like a fool I explained and then I had to listen to a five minute diatribe on why internecine politics in the war department is the scourge of success. The sad part is too often he's right. Thank the stars that there are men like Omar Bradley and even Patton when he's actually in the thick of it who are more interested in results than the pecking order."

Col. Osgood broke in; "Gentlemen, I'd be happy to let you reminisce all night long, however time and tide are not waiting and you need to get to work. Max, would you like some coffee?"

"Coffee would be welcome. Thank you Al."

Osgood had brought out the bourbon and three glasses. Max never drank alcohol. Ernst, his closest friend, believed that it had to do with Max being raised by a drunken and abusive grandfather. Max had never told Dietsch the whole story; only Verna Deveraux, Max's fiancée had heard the entire story and the reason for Max Larsen's life long fight against tyranny. He had told her before proposing marriage to give her a chance to refuse after knowing his life's truth.

Once Staff Sergeant Sibyl Futch, Colonel Osgood's secretary, delivered the coffee, the office door was closed and the meeting began. "Screw the Nazis!" Ernst offered while raising his glass. The other three raised their drinks in accord. "Now, Hiram answer my question; what's the big rush?"

"The twins and Vincent are up to here in trouble!" Snowden said while grabbing his throat.

"And this is somehow different from any other time?" Larsen asked.

Snowden looked up at Larsen and sighed, "Damn it this is a little more serious than, than usual. All right, I know Vince and Marie parachuting a barbecued steer onto the University of Texas mall while Lysette tried to drive under it with a flatbed truck set a bit of a precedent, but the current situation is an order of magnitude worse." The other three's laughter quickly died as Hiram gave a quick explanation of the situation at Peenemünde. As the story went on he noticed both Max and Ernst begin taking notes in small notebooks. "So in summary we not only have to get two agents into the area that now has increased surveillance, we also have to figure out how to get everybody and the information out."

"Max, Ernst, those notebooks can't leave this room when you get through. I haven't even tried to get you clearance as so far only the four of us know about this part of the operation." Osgood added when Snowden stopped.

"How do you keep it that close?" Larsen asked while finishing a diagram and setting his notebook on the desk.

"Only two people handle the decryption and encryption, either myself or Lt. Colonel Brewster. We drop the agents far enough away from their target that even if an aircrew says something that gets back to the Germans the best they have is the general area and there are always some plausible targets nearer the drop zone. The F4 pilots only know where to be to get a signal, the possible transmission points could be anywhere within a hundred miles radius of the actual point. And last I coordinate with Dulles and a few others just enough to keep from stepping on each other's toes. We know roughly where all the ops are taking place, none of the operational details or who is partaking in them. If I die Dulles has access to my safe and the info to carry through with an operation. "

"That's a lot of balls to be juggling Al." Snowden remarked.

"Not really, I only have two ops requiring this much security at this time, more routine and lower level ops are handled by compartmented teams. It's a function of span of control. The more intensive the op, the fewer people you can supervise. As I'm not in direct control of how a team accomplishes their task and in more of a support position, I don't have to sweat the minute operational details. You pick good people, train them well, support them as best you can, and then stand back hopefully reaping the rewards. Hiram, your daughters came with more native skills, natural intelligence, and one of the broadest set of tools I've ever seen. They scared the crap out of some of their instructors. A few of the instructors thought they were ringers sent in to test the instruction. It was a shame to move them from France, but we needed our best for this assignment. I'm awfully proud of them as well as being scared spit-less whenever I think what could happen if they're caught."

Dietsch spoke up, "You want us to find a way in for these two agents and then exfiltrate everyone when the time comes."

"You Ernst, and especially Max know more about smuggling people and equipment in and out of coastal areas than anyone else I know. I don't want to get any more people involved than necessary to infiltrate the agents. The twins have also mentioned attempting to bring out some of the non-German scientists when we do bring everyone home," Osgood said.

Max picked up his notebook, did a few quick calculations and then had some suggestions of his own. "If we have a Sutherland amphibian flying with say a bunch of Lancasters on a bombing raid, we could possibly drop the Sutherland out of the formation so that it looks to the German radio ranging like an aircraft with engine problems forced to ditch. We might be able to get close enough to the coast that I could get a small boat in. The Sutherland will have to fly near its max speed and the Lancasters cruise a little slower than normal, but it should look legitimate to the Germans. We'd want to land far enough out to be below the German radar and as close as possible to minimize boat travel. We'll have to check with the Pathfinders as they probably have the best estimates on Nazi radar coverage. The Baltic fishermen use a lot of eighteen to twenty foot lapstrake double-enders. I can rig a small launch to look like one of them and with a high output engine I can sail in late while looking innocent. I imagine that with the manpower shortage quite a few women are working in the fishing fleet."

"How would you get the launch there?" Snowden asked.

"Have you ever seen a Folboat or better yet the British Cockle? The biggest one is seventeen feet long and can carry four men. It collapses to probably less than a foot in width. I think Ernst and I can come up with a large folding boat using rubberized canvas and balsa glued to thin wood veneers. If we add them as a veneer to the Cockle I can put one together in a few days. It should fit through an access door on the Sutherland. The British sent a Sutherland when you needed us to be picked up and the cargo bay was large enough if we keep manning to a minimum."

Ernst nodded in agreement, "piece of cake. I can take an engine from a British Ford and give you thirty percent more power in the engine, lighten it, and add a water cooled exhaust that will make it quieter than one of the one-lungers the fishermen use."

Col. Osgood waved his newly relit pipe for attention; "It doesn't sound like your boat would pass a close inspection. Why not have Vince come out to meet you in a local boat?"

"Time, there wouldn't be enough time for them to steal a boat, get to the pickup point, and return. Unless you have a very secure contact among the German fishermen you can forget a local boat. Besides, we wouldn't survive a close inspection. The German patrols know the locals too well. I'm planning on darkness and similarity to several boats to act as our cover." Max tossed his notebook open to a rough but legible sketch of his proposed boat to Ernst. "What do you think?"

"This will work. We can add sections to bring the bow and stern up a little higher, make the gunwale look like the boat has more rocker, and still get you up on plane. Three days top if we get to work."

"Al, see if you can get us some pictures of the coast in the area. We need both a landing site and some idea of where the fishing and patrol boats are. Also see if the Brits can put a sub in the area; they can pick Max up and drop him off at the *LaDonna* on their way home."

"Yes, General. Hiram you think this will work?"

"I'm willing to bet that Max can get anyone onto any shore he wants to." Snowden turned to Max and Ernst; "What I really want to know is how you two will get everyone off?"

"Give me a couple of days, I need to see how well a new project is coming." Max replied.

Chapter 11:   A reward for duty

Notes provided by Leftenant Robin Jarvis and supposition by Sherlock Mk 3.

April 7, 1943, 01:20
An apartment at Bletchley Park, England:

"OH MOUSE, I NEEDED THAT! I've looked forward to that all day. Aside from say being shot as a spy, the interminable debriefings are the worst part of being in the service."

La Petit Souris, Susan Brodeur, moved forward from between Robin's thighs, pillowing her chin on small strong hands over the taut low mound of her lover's stomach. "My love, my pleasure. Perhaps if your interrogator offered the same reward as I for your patience you might look forward to being debriefed."

Robin burst into a short laugh, "I'm sure that whore dog Commander Ian Fleming would love to give it a try. I think it would be uncomfortable though, as he would need to prop up a mirror so he could admire himself in action. I'd probably have to hold it."

"As bad as that."

"Probably worse mon petit. Now his brother Peter would be worth the effort for a woman so inclined, however he's been happily married for years and apparently wants to keep it that way."

"What do you think of this new assignment?" Susan asked. She raised up and crawled up the bed to lie with her partner. Robin was, as always, admiring of the lean corded muscles displayed in Susan's arms and shoulders.

"I don't think there is much I can do. The Nazis have turned prostitution into a machine, another cog in their war. The soldier takes a number and then has fifteen to twenty minutes to do his business. When the Germans first moved into Paris, a girl could take her time and choice. The higher officers still pretended that we were attracted to them for their own sake. Now it has all the romance of a cattle feed lot. Registration numbers and probably efficiency reports. Once a girl is worn out she is discarded or sent to the camps. You can't have pillow talk when a man is simply masturbating while using your body instead of his hand."

"Sad that the world has come to this and so many of the men on either side who are in charge of the war will never even consider this sanctioned rape as a crime. Someday a dry little professor will find the records and place a side note in some history book that no one will read." Susan shivered as she clung to Robin.

"Pull up the covers. We'll both go to Germany. You, you little thief will be of much more use than me. I still have some skills beyond the horizontal that may be of use." Susan laid her head on Robin's shoulder and snuggled for warmth as they pulled up the sheet and thin wool blankets.

"So we meet our ride tomorrow; who do we meet in Germany?"

"All they say for now is that we'll recognize them." Robin murmured as she turned out the bedside lamp.

Chapter 12: Flying the less friendly skies

**Aircraft logs, and mission reports of
Maxwell Larsen and Lt. Robin Jarvis**

April 11, 1943, 23:10
In the Baltic Sea 40 miles from Peenemünde

THE SUTHERLAND AMPHIBIAN came slowly to rest on the sea's surface, the engines idling just enough to keep the aircraft headed into the wind. "Thank God it's fairly calm tonight. You can't be sure if your altimeter is set correctly until you actually start feeling the water hitting the hull. I would have preferred a bit more moon than we have." Lt. Commander James Wortham said from the command pilots' seat in the Sutherlands cockpit. "One of these days we're going to slam into the face of a rogue wave and disappear in a cloud of spray and rivets."

"How many of these landings have you done Commander? I had the option of closing my eyes and holding my breath, I don't imagine you can do that though." Max said from the back of the cockpit.

"I wish I could. I've landed this way a number of times and each one is one more than I should or want."

The co-pilot, Lt. Bruce Drummond, a large bull chested man, was unbuckling his harness; "Right enough, let's get the pod unfastened and send you on your way Mr. Larsen."

"I'm glad you had a better method of delivery than trying to unfold the shell in the water and then lowering the engine into it." Max said as they went through the amphibians cabin.

"We've been experimenting with delivering Mk 2 Chariots by placing them in a pod next to the hull and under the wing. Your cockle doesn't begin to weigh as much and we could fit it in by partially collapsing it and sliding it into the pod. The crew will get it out and have it ready while you collect your people and gear."

"Thank you Leftenant, we'll be ready." As the lieutenant proceeded to the rear Max stopped and turned to two figures huddled together in a jump seat hanging from the side of the fuselage; "Ladies, time to go."

"I've been going near constantly since we took off; I'd spit in your eye if I had a drop of liquid left in me." Lt. Jarvis declared while glaring at Larsen with eyes showing equal amounts of mal-de-mar and murderous intent. The sturdy waxed paper bag between her knees sloshed with proof.

"Let me have the bag." Susan said while adroitly rolling up the opening. "Should I add this to the evidence cache?" Susan was referring to a collection of used kapok floatation vests, seat cushions, oil and other floating parts from a Lancaster bomber.

"Good idea, lend some veracity to the collection. See Robin, you've already made a significant contribution to our success." Robin's glare deepened as she looked in response to the smiling giant.

"Your boat is nearly ready. Do you want the mast for the steadying sail up or down now?" Lt. Drummond asked, interrupting Larsen's possible demise at Jarvis' hand.

"Leave it down for now, we'll make better time with it down. I won't need it until after the ladies are delivered." Larsen answered.

The trio were soon embarked. Several old sacks containing waterproof duffels were passed over. Arms were limited to a trio of Walther P-38 pistols. As Max had said earlier, they weren't about to outfight a German patrol boat with anything they could carry. Without Brodeur's or Jarvis' knowledge a 10 pound block of plastique and a detonator had been secreted under the engine in the small crafts keel. Max had no intention of any of them being taken alive and jeopardizing his friends on shore. The engine was purring away, barely audible through its underwater exhaust. Lines were let go and the small craft sped away, the occupants' wave to the aircrew was quickly lost in the gloom.

"Godspeed." Drummond whispered as the small craft went out of sight. Drummond then helped the crew throw the evidence over the side. They would wait until they could rejoin the Lancasters on their return. Flying low until past the range where the German radar could get an accurate count. On its return to England the squadron would report one of their aircraft ditching in the area from engine trouble.

Aboard the cockle:

The only light came from the luminous dial on the compass, an occasional star penetrating the light overcast, and a sliver of moon that served more as a reference point than a light source. Max Larsen held the tiller in one hand and followed a preplanned course. There was a certain amount of offset for current, and a little more added for the light wind which was blowing. The light boat was up on plane and making between eighteen and twenty knots Max estimated. A lifetime at sea and a hand dipped over the side gave him a surprisingly accurate approximation of their speed. The wan moonlight and the feel of the sea let him meet the waves, occasionally surfing on the side of a bigger one. "How are you feeling Ria?" Max asked in German. He had an accent that pegged him as an inhabitant of Alsace. As soon as they were on the water the trio had switched to German. Jarvis and Brodeur both sounded Austrian and knew the region well enough to be natives.

Jarvis, or Maria Kessel as her identity papers stated replied; "I'm fine now. I've never been seasick, aircraft though are my nemesis. I hate the lack of control and not being able to see where I'm going."

"Just being able to see the horizon gives your brain a reference to quiet what your inner ear and stomach or reporting. I've never understood people who go below when they start getting nauseous. And throwing up over the side is a lot easier to clean up than puking in the bilges. There are some bottles of water under your seat; you must be thirsty." Larsen said.

"Herr Mueller, you're such a comforting soul. I don't imagine you've ever had a woman friend last a week." Jarvis replied.

"You're not far wrong. A few brief affairs I'm afraid and I'm unfortunately attracted to women smart enough to know better. Actually I recently convinced one to marry. I'm worried because I think she's too smart to have said yes. I think we're both in love." Max said while shaking his head in wonderment.

"Congratulations my large friend, when we return we must drink to your success." Brodeur called from her space wedged in the bow. She was surrounded by their gear, placed there to counter Larsen's weight in the stern.

"It will be my pleasure Fraulein Helga."

"Dieter, you sound like an ancient farmer from Alsace Lorraine. Where did you get that accent?" Brodeur asked.

"From an ancient Alsatian. I knew some old farmers whose families moved from Alsace-Lorraine to Texas before the Civil War and also I've shipped with a few sailors from there. Hopefully we won't have to talk to any locals who will wonder what I'm doing here." Max replied.

The small craft continued to quietly speed toward the bay where Vincent Fuller had landed ten days before.

April 12, 1943, 03:20
A burrow dug into the side of a low dune:

"Time to start your light Marie. Is the hood tight?" Vincent Fuller and Marie Malois were huddled under a tan tarp on the side of the dune facing the small bay. Marie double checked the 18 inch long black round tube that protruded from the front of her flashlight. It would keep any backscatter from the light showing and only allow someone in a very small area of the bay to see the light.

"It's good, Vince. No sign of any German boats out there?"

Fuller lowered his night glass, "No, there's enough light in the sky that I should at least see a silhouette. Go ahead. Two short, one long, and one short every 8 minutes." The two had dug themselves into the side of the dune and Lysette had covered the tarp with sand before erasing their tracks as she backed toward the creek where they had greeted Fuller a week and a half previously.

Bill McCabe was back at the ditch where Fuller and the twins had hidden from the German patrol. Loaded down with extra magazines for both the Schmeisser MP40 and his .45 as well as several German grenades, he was the rearguard and devoutly hoping action would not be needed. While the team might survive a battle with a patrol, if one ensued their only recourse would be to try to escape; their mission compromised beyond hope. Back at the old barn their cache of weapons and explosives were surrounding the radio and their code books. A simple alarm clock was rigged to detonate the explosives and destroy the codes and radio if they didn't return in time. Two pressure switches attached to the ladder's steps would also accomplish the same destruction if anyone discovered their lair before they returned.

"You think Max can find this little cove? It's awfully dark out there and no navigation or city lights to get a bearing," Marie whispered.

Fuller was concentrating on his watch, ensuring that the signals would be sent at exact 8 minute intervals. "Really? You think Max might miss this cove?" sarcasm was ladled generously over his statement.

"Sorry. Dumb thing to ask. Nerves I guess." Marie responded. "I should be worrying about German patrols, coast watchers, MTBs (*Motor Torpedo Boats, SMkIII*) instead."

"That I agree on. One minute to signal," Vincent took a thorough scan of the bay. There was a bit of white foam showing against a darker mass on the bearing of Max's approach. *"Too small to be anyone but Max and his little boat'.* "Time." He said and Marie triggered off her signal. A small light, as deeply shrouded as their own replied. "Two long, one short, one long. That's them. Right on time."

"How does he do it Uncle Vincent? He'll make it in within a few minutes of his estimate."

"Genius and skill. Max might look like a troglodyte, but where boats, tides, current, and wind come together I know no one better at finding his way to an unfamiliar spot on a coast without a single nav-aid than Max."

As the boat continued its approach Fuller and Malois carefully crawled from their burrow. They crawled in opposite directions, parallel to the water, carefully scanning the beach before moving to the water's edge. Fuller waded out as the boat approached. *"Damn that waters cold."*

The low noise of engine and the burble of the underwater exhaust died as Larsen killed the engine then carefully jumped over the side into a couple of feet of water. He and Fuller guided the boat to a quiet grounding on the sand. Larsen stopped the two women from dropping into the shallow water. "Hold on frauliens, no reason to get cold and wet before you need to." He offered a hand to Brodeur who quickly vaulted up to sit on his shoulder. He then scooped up Jarvis in his arms and deposited them on dry sand.

"Hello Mouse, Leftenant." Marie said quietly as she approached the two.

"One of the twins! Lysette or Marie?" asked Jarvis while she and Brodeur hugged Marie.

"Marie. We need to get going. How much more Max?" as she turned to the two large men emptying the boat.

"Last bag." Max stated as he hefted one from the small boat. He crossed to Marie, lifted her up in a gentle bear hug and kissed her on the cheek. "Hiram sends his love. Tell your sister that and you two please be careful."

"I will and we will," Marie quickly promised then turned and hoisted a large duffel onto her back.

"Vince, take care. Bring them all back," Max said as he gave Fuller a quick handshake and a hug.

"Wilco that Max. You be careful." The two men quickly turned the small craft around and as soon as the water was deep enough to turn the prop, the little English Ford four banger started and Max was quickly and quietly on his way.

Chapter 13:   Less friendly waters

Maxwell Larsen and the log of HMS *Satyr*

April 12, 1943, 04:46 Local Time
15 Nautical Miles N.E. of Peenemünde

MAX LARSEN LOOKED forward along his course, 50 degrees magnetic. Sunrise would be soon and the sky was noticeably lighter to the East. HMS *Satyr* (P214) a British S class submarine was due to find him in this area before sunrise. Larsen disengaged the prop from his engine and revved it several times in a row. Hopefully the sub would hear his underwater engine exhaust and investigate. Lowering the dagger-board he and Ernst had designed to replace the centerboard displaced by the Ford engine, he then raised the light telescoping mast, extended it, and hoisted a small gaff rigged main sail. The sail would make his small boat easier to spot, but it would also make him look more like a fisherman. It was an unhappy tradeoff whose calculation could go either way. Max fastened a laughably small jib, back-winded it and eased out the little main, heaving the boat to and holding him steady in the area. A close examination would show his mast and spars to be dull painted aluminum rather than wood.

"Where was Leftenant Oakley and his damned sub?" Max scanned the horizon, hearing the low growl of engines to his west. Probably a German [1]schnellboote; you didn't want one of those anywhere near a surfaced sub. The sound receded from him, *"hopefully they're on their way in and won't bother a tired old fisherman."* He debated whether to send the pickup signal; three shots from his pistol, place the gun in the water and fire away. The muzzle blasts would be picked up by the sub and the bit of exhaust and sound of the action cycling would hardly be heard fifty feet away above water. Before he could put this into action he heard the increased sound of the German MTB. Three powerful diesel engines ratcheting up their rpm and headed his way. Max carefully stood up and looked west. He could see the powerful craft headed toward him by the white foam of its bow wave. *"I should have left the mast down. There's just enough light to show a silhouette. Damn that sharp-eyed lookout. A little too strange to see a fisherman this far out this early."*

Max made his preparations, he had mentally rehearsed several contingencies on the trip out. He made sure that the Walther was firmly fastened in the shoulder holster under his shirt. Next he eased off his rubber boots and as he took his tiller he hauled in his main and let the jib out, the minuscule sails slowly brought his boat to the wind, heeling the little craft over and setting course toward the German Schnellboot. Next he pulled the pin that safetied the detonators for the ten pound block of plastique under his engine and wrapped the pull-cord for the detonators around his ankle. The detonators were the same as used in a British Mills Grenade and with three of them inserted into the plastique, at least one was bound to work.

The German craft slowed, and a loud young officer with a megaphone ordered Max to drop his sails. Max rounded up into the wind and scandalized the main, dropping the gaff and the boom from his position at the tiller. He loosed the jib sheet and left the jib fluttering back and forth across the bow. The little boat bumped up against the starboard side of the German hull as a sailor with a rifle kept his eye, but not his weapon on Larsen. Larsen missed the line thrown to him by a second sailor, one of several eyeing the inept fisherman, allowing his little boat to bump along aft toward the engine room. Max wanted to avoid setting his explosives off right next to the integral torpedo tube built into the side of the S-boat. An angry command from the officer sent a second line toward him and he fumbled with the line until he was leaning backwards off the stern. Max continued his extravagant flailing until he flipped over the stern and into the water. A hard pull on the detonator cord and Max swam as fast as possible under the German hull. He had four to five seconds before the block of plastique went off and he wanted to be on the surface and on the other side of hull before then. Straining every muscle and kicking his legs Max shot to the surface, one long arm grasping the port guard rail stanchion base just as his bomb exploded. The little boats engine disintegrated into a lethal spray of shrapnel shredding the sailors looking over the side for the clumsy fisherman. A large hole was ripped into the thin side of the S boat opening up several rib bays of the engine room to the ocean. Fire erupted through the engine room as pressurized fuel lines were ruptured. The starboard diesel was ripped from its mount and crashed into the center engine crushing two of the crew between the engines.

Max, his feet and lower legs painfully numb from the shock wave in the water, pulled himself up onto the deck as the MTB rocked and started listing to the right. His pistol drawn he fired, taking out the officer who was sitting dazed on the deck of the bridge. He ignored the sailor in the tub mount with the twin machine guns, trusting the Germans to design a gun mount that would prevent the guns from shooting into their own hull. A sailor crawled up the companion way out onto the deck, met by a second round from the Walther, he collapsed instantly with a round to his forehead.

Max sent another sailor, scrambling towards the ruptured engine room, over the side with his third shot. After the massive explosion the shots barely registered on Max's hearing. *"I hope the Germans can't hear any better. There should be about twenty people on board. No, twenty targets and I have five rounds left."* Max mentally made the change from people to targets; remembering one of the hard lessons of his youth.

Larsen hauled himself to his feet, stumbling awkwardly while his feet recovered from the explosion. The sailor in the gun tub was trying to get the attention of his mates while throwing ammo cans at Larsen. Max batted two aside until he reached him, grabbed his shoulders in both hands and heaved the sailor out of the tub, then smashed his neck across the edge of the gun mount. A second officer appeared out of the smoke, leaping from the bridge toward Larsen, an extended arm with a large knife preceding his flight. Max avoided the blade while catching the arm and swinging the man over his head. The officers back snapped as he hit the guard rails cable and Larsen felt the man's arm pull from the socket in a massive dislocation. Dropping the officer over the side Max retrieved his pistol from the trouser pocket where he had placed it during the barrage of ammo cans.

Larsen looked around. A dazed and bloodied helmsman was attempting to pick up his intestines from where a shard of deck had eviscerated him. Larsen used his knife and cut the helmsman's throat as he prepared to go below and see who in the crew was left. As he passed the captain's body, he paused to check for weapons. He found a Naval Luger with the long barrel. He grabbed the weapon and pulled two spare magazines from the holster. Larsen topped off his Walther's magazine from one of the spares. Lugers were normally accurate and reliable if the owner was scrupulous in his maintenance. Between the blast and not knowing the officers habits, he would hold the Luger in reserve.

Lying down on the deck he took a quick glance down the companionway. Smoke and dust filled the air and shafts of light coming from shrapnel holes and ports illuminated the area. Unable to see anything, Max slid down the steps head first. As he hoped there was clear air a foot or so above the deck. He saw two pairs of legs advancing toward him about the same time he heard one of the men coughing. Firing four shots upward through the smoke toward where torsos should be, he was rewarded as both men fell, the first with at least three shots in his chest and abdomen the second man looking around wildly after tripping on the first sailor. His last sight was the muzzle blast as Larsen disposed of the confused sailor.

Knowing that his own hearing was returning after the initial blast Larsen surmised that the S-boat's crew would have also heard the shots; he pulled the Luger and fired one time towards the hatch at the end of the passageway. The bullet struck the edge of the hatch right where Max had aimed. The bullet careened below hopefully slowing anyone advancing from that quarter while reassuring Max of the weapons accuracy and function.

Hearing noise behind him Larsen rolled onto his back and looked up toward the companionway. A shadow through the smoke erupted in flame and noise as a machine pistol opened fire. If he had been standing he would have been riddled. Firing both his pistols into his opponent he was doubly relieved when the sailor fell backwards and a Schmeisser MP38 fell down the companionway ladder.

Scrambling around in an almost futile attempt to turn his bulk in the confined space, he grabbed the machine pistol and continued crawling around the ladder toward the aft spaces. Finding another hatch he banged the Schmeisser's butt on it while calling "*Obermatt, Obermatt, wo bis du?*" He was calling for a petty officer and hoping that if anyone was on the other side of the hatch, someone would answer. Not hearing a response Larsen grabbed a handle to start un-dogging the hatch. The handle nearly burned his hand so he felt the bulkhead with the back of his hand. Too hot, no one alive was inside the compartment and opening it could cause an explosion as oxygen rich air sucked into the compartment to mix with an atmosphere too oxygen depleted to burn, yet hot enough for auto-ignition of fuel and gasses with the right mix.

Abandoning the attempt to head aft Larsen returned to the companionway. Smoke was thinning in the area and no one alive was in the compartment. A notice board with a cracked glass cover showed no ones' reflection outside so Max took a quick look over the companionway sill. The corpse of the sailor who had dropped the MP38 lay next to the companion way. On deck a few sailors under the command of an older Obermaschinist, a chief petty officer machinist mate, were attempting to get the 20mm anti-aircraft gun to fire. Another sailor had jumped into the gun tub and was manning the 7.92mm machine gun and firing to starboard. Aft a fuel fire was raging where diesel was pouring into the engine room through a shattered valve. A shock to the forward hull coincided with the sound of high explosive and the sailors trying to man the anti-aircraft gun were knocked to their knees by the blast. *"Damn, that has to be the Satyr out their firing her three inch. I need to stop this before they kill me."*

With his Walther he put two slugs into the sailor in the gun tub. Running up to the bridge he fired the Schmeisser down onto the crew at the larger gun. The machine pistol had only seven rounds left in it, yet that took out the operator and the loader. The chief turned around and got two shots off toward Larsen with his machine pistol, both caromed off the coaming, one taking a small chunk of Larsen's left forearm with it. Larsen dropped the empty Schmeisser and squatted down. Max emptied the last three shells from his Walther in the general direction of the chief while duck-walking to the other side of the bridge. Pocketing the Walther he transferred the Luger from left to right hand and popped up on the other side of the small bridge. The chief had moved behind the shield for the anti-aircraft gun, however both legs showed under the shield and Max calmly shot both of them, when the chief fell down and into sight Larsen sent a third round into his face.

Seeing a gun battle taking place on the ship they were shelling, the *Satyr*'s captain had halted firing of the 3" gun and was staring hard at a huge man calmly surveying the floundering S-boat. The man waved briefly toward Lt. Oakley, replaced a mag in the Luger and walked forward, checking to make sure the two lying next to the antiaircraft gun were truly dead.

As he continued forward a thin small sailor leapt from behind a ventilator, his only weapon a small pocketknife. The big man moved quickly, turning his body like a matador avoiding a charging bull. As the youth rushed by he used the long barrel of the Luger to knock the knife from the boy's hand. Max's left hand almost casually cuffed the boy on the side of his head, staggering and spinning him around, last a large foot lashed out and took the feet out from under the sailor crashing him to the deck. The big man started to shoot the dazed young sailor, thought better of it and pulled a length of power cord from a spotlight, flipped the kid on his stomach and quickly had him hog tied with both arms and one foot tied together behind him.

The man then turned and walked the length of the foredeck, checked the forward hatch area, made a quick estimate of the sailors mangled by the initial explosion, and then waved for the British sub to approach.

Lt. Oakley looked over to his bosun, who with the other men at the 3" cannon, were still agog at the recent display. "I believe that is our passenger we were tasked to save. Higgins, small arms for your men and prepare to go alongside."

"Aye Captain. Will we be taking the lad trussed up like a pig for market?"

"We'll see. Smartly now, a few Stens for your men and a trench gun for you."

Once again Larsen went below, this time to the radio room where he made note of the settings on the radio, picked up the log and then found a small safe bolted to the wooden bulkhead. It was locked so Max sat down in front of it, put a foot against the bulkhead on either side of it and with one hand on each of the safes short legs he took a strain. Slowly Max straightened his legs and body and the British officer and his bosun arrived at the radio room door in time to hear a groan and crack from the wood bulkhead; they watched as Larsen pulled the safe away. Two large carriage bolts protruded from the rear of the safe and two corresponding holes showed in the bulkhead. "Captain Oakley, this safe should contain their radio codes. Other than the log book I didn't find anything else of value in here. I suggest we pull any charts and listings at the navigation station and leave as quickly as possible."

A dull crump reverberated through the hull. "Captain, we need to leave this bloody ^{2}E boat now," a British sailor called from the deck. "A bulkhead just let loose near the fuel tanks, we need to leave now."

"Go, go! We've been on top too damn long. Grab the charts on your way Higgins." Oakley commanded while pushing Higgins with one hand and offering the other to Larsen to help him up. Larsen grabbed the proffered hand and pushed off the deck to stand beside the captain. Taking the safe in one hand and tucking his pistols into a canvas bag he had liberated in his search the two quickly regained the deck.

"We took the German lad over to our boat Sir. Wallace is sitting on him in the wardroom for now. No one else found alive Sir." Higgins reported as he tried to bundle the last of the charts.

"Thank you Higgins. Don't dawdle now."

Within a minute, a satchel charge was placed in the S-boats port torpedo tube next to the warhead, its time pencil set for a few minutes, and all were back on the submarine and down below, the vessel submerging even as Oakley, the last onboard, spun the wheel to fasten the hatch.

"Let's get deeper and some distance fast. I can't believe all that smoke hasn't roused up another ship or aircraft yet. Send the pharmacist mate to the wardroom," Oakley ordered. After a moment of checking to make sure *Satyr* was safely underway he turned toward Max who seemed to fill most of the forward half of the control room. "I can't have you bleeding on my decks Mr. Larsen. Please go to the ward room and we can patch that arm up."

"Thank you Captain." Larsen's words were cut short by the sound and thump of the *Schnellboote* disintegrating behind them. "Do you do this sort of operation often?"

"Actually Mister Larsen, this is the first time a British submersible has penetrated the Baltic during the current war. This was a playground for my predecessors in the first war, but new detection measures have kept us out for now. This was an experiment for the Admiralty, your recovery was a bit serendipitous. We managed to come in on the lower northern current while barely making steerage way. We were lucky not to get caught in any fishing nets."

Max looked at the young lieutenant for a long moment, "I'm glad your experiment was successful. Remind me to have a discussion with some intel officers on my return. I'd appreciate knowing when I'm a guinea pig." Somber and quiet, Max followed the corpsman towards the wardroom.

"Doesn't appear too happy after surviving being attacked by an effing E-boat." the helmsman said.

Oakley responded, "Just how joyful should you be after killing all but one of the crew of a Schnellboote? Think on that while you mind your course."

[1]*Schnellboote, a German Motor Torpedo Boat. Up to 115' long. Two sizes 104' and 115'. The schnellboote encountered by Max Larsen was a 104' S-7 model. SMkIII*
[2]*British sailors referred to all the German variants of S Boots as E Boats, for Enemy War Boat. SMkIII*

Chapter 14:   Reconnaissance

Marie and Lysette Malois, and Vincent Fuller

April 13, 1943, 16:50 Local Time

An Abandoned Farm 8 Kilometers from Peenemünde

"ALL CLEAR AT ALL STATIONS." Corporal William McCabe called to the conspirators after checking the periscopes at all four corners of the barn. He joined the crew who were going over sketches of the building housing the German archives.

"No windows, the walls are heavy masonry and the door is welded steel. Regular patrols through the site and around the perimeter. At least one person inside the vault during the day and possibly at night." Fuller commented.

"How sure are you of the night staff?" Brodeur asked.

"We can't be sure. We know that some of the German engineers work late hours. We assume that they don't leave plans in their offices when they are through for the night. We have seen a soldier exchange places with another when the guards go to supper. We can't be sure if they stay past the last engineer or if they stay in their all night." Marie advised.

"No windows and the door is shut all the time; how do they breathe?"

"Susan we have seen some large mushroom ventilators on the roof. They stick up just above the parapet. If there is a skylight we can't tell from any angle we can access." Fuller answered.

"They would need two ventilation shafts, inlet and outlet. Would they power both?" McCabe asked.

"Usually only the exhaust is powered." Susan said. "Any idea how large the shafts are? From what I have seen of industrial plants in France and Belgium they would have an air shaft at least a half meter in diameter for a building that size." Susan turned to Larsen; "and before you ask, that is more than I need. How rough is the masonry on the walls and how far apart is the rear wall from the building behind it?"

Lysette answered, "The rear wall is about one meter from the generator building. There are a lot of pipes or conduits running between the two at ground level and the archive wall is almost 8 meters high and a meter and a half above the generator building. I haven't got close enough to determine how rough the masonry is."

"Are there any shadows near noon on the wall? A lot of mottling along the wall from a vertical light would indicate possible finger holds."

"Marie, I remember it as pretty rough when I consider shadows. What do you remember?" Lysette asked.

"I wish we could develop our film here. I agree Lysette, the wall is rough, fairly deep indentations between the brick courses."

"Good, they didn't use poured concrete; it will be easier to access the roof. Now how do I get there and when do we go?"

"The main problems are the guards outside and anyone who might be inside. Easter isn't until April 25th. A holiday like that would find most of the Germans in church or feasting as much as it's possible to feast here." Lysette proposed.

"You're sure that's the date? I never remember the formula for Easter. So many Sundays past Pentecost or some odd time that is reckoned off the lunar calendar." Fuller admitted.

"Heathen, of course I'm sure." Lysette waved a small book, "Never travel without one."

"Really, you always carry an almanac?" Jarvis queried.

McCabe laughed, "You have no shame ma'am. I found that on one of the soldiers I killed. I thought it might be useful for the moons phases and tides maybe. I think Lysette was more interested in it for toilet paper."

"All right, so what. There aren't any more convenient holidays. We'll have to wait until Easter. The best we can hope for is Sunday; the Germans and most of the foreign engineers seem to at least start late on Sundays. Whether for Church or to nurse hangovers from Saturday I don't know." Lysette answered.

Lt. Jarvis joined in, "I see one problem with our date."

"It's a holiday, their routine may be off." Fuller answered quickly, just beating the others who nodded their heads in agreement.

"I once stayed on a roof for four days. I think two should suffice this time. A second skin of water and a bit more food. Not a problem." Brodeur assured the group.

"All right then, two days. How do we avoid the patrols, get Mademoiselle Mouse to the building, and take care of the person inside if he is there, gain access from the outside? Is the door locked by key or combination?" Fuller counted off.

"If Susan can use a vent to get inside I'm sure she can open the door. Germans are fanatical about building codes. A building without windows must have doors that will always open out without needing a key. And once she's inside I don't think any lock would slow Mouse from opening the door if they ignored the building code." Jarvis said. "How to incapacitate the guard inside, I can think of two ways. Knock on the door and when he opens the slide shoot him with a silenced weapon. Or if we were carrying a large armload of fake plans and Vince's German is good enough to convince the guard to open the door and then shoot him."

"I'm dubious of the armload of plans. They will have a log of everything that is out and if there aren't any plans logged out that night he may ask questions we can't answer. Do we know if the attendant has a phone? Is there a regular phone contact? Can we be sure he'll be alone? Susan could you take out the guard if you can gain entry through the vent shaft?" Fuller said while counting off the questions on his fingers.

Susan looked toward Robin and then the twins with a pained expression on her face, "I don't know. I have never had to physically harm anyone in my career. I know that a thief with certain morals seems strange, but I have always taken pride in never physically harming a soul. And when the Germans came and we saw the retribution for Germans killed by the Resistance or even by a jealous husband, I was appalled at the innocents, men women and children killed, ten or even a hundred killed for each German soldier's life. I know that there are hundreds, even thousands of slaves here. What would be their cost for a German life?"

The basement became very quiet, even the light seemed to dim as the group contemplated Brodeur's question. With a start Fuller realized that the battery running the lights was losing power. "Bill, charge the battery please. I'll spell you when you need a break."

"Yes sir." Bill said quietly as he moved to the hand cranked generator. The low whine of the generator replaced the silence as McCabe turned the crank.

"If we take out a guard we could only do it once. Getting all the information we need has to be done either surreptitiously over several nights are one big haul and then destroy what we can't take. Too many questions and not enough answers. I think we may have to reconnoiter and get some answers before we try to actually gain entry." Fuller said. "Let's think about how to infiltrate the weapons area and then go from there."

Chapter 15: Microphones and polecats

Marie and Lysette Malois and Vincent Fuller

April 14, 1943, 02:30 Local Time
An Abandoned Farm 8 Kilometers from Peenemünde

"ALL RIGHT, LET'S REVIEW OUR CONCLUSIONS." Vincent Fuller called the weary plotters together.
"First, Susan reconnoiters for two days. Second, killing any guard inside the vault is our last resort and only if we are willing to destroy any materials we can't carry off. So, we infiltrate Susan to the repository where she will gain the roof and reconnoiter. As there is no external ladder and there are vents on the roof she will see if they have a scuttle for access and try to determine if it is wired against entry. If all goes right Miss Mouse will lower a microphone down whichever vent shaft does not have a fan in it. She will stay for forty eight hours and come back to us the next night with a better idea of the vault routine."
        "You are sure no other building can see the vaults roof?" Jarvis asked.
"Not even the control tower can see the roof. As long as Susan stays below the parapet no one on the ground or in any of the buildings can see her. Our only worry is someone in an aircraft possibly spotting her." Lysette answered.
        "I can carry a piece of tarp with me. Paint it gray on one side and black on the other, I'll use whichever side looks most like the roofing material. I can hide under it during the day. A small amount of water and a few crackers will be all that I need for two days. I have done this before to check on a job. The microphone and headset that Willy and Vincent have put together will be a nice addition. I wish I had this tool years ago; much easier than listening at vents and scuttles." Brodeur replied.
        "The mic and headset aren't much louder than an old crystal radio receiver, but they should let you hear any sound that reaches a ventilator shaft. Just make sure you don't lower it through a vent where someone can see it." McCabe said.
        "Don't worry Willy, I'll be careful."
        "I'll meet you at the same spot in the field where you started from. Are you sure you don't want me to go with you to the building?" Lysette asked.

"*Non*, once I am at the edge of the airfield you would only double the chance of discovery. I know you are very good in the wild, but once it comes to buildings no one will see me. I have been a professional thief since I was eleven years old and I haven't been caught yet."

"What about the guard dogs?" McCabe asked.

Susan smiled and said, "Willy dear, have you ever caught a polecat?"

"What is a polecat?"

Larsen answered as a surprised Susan groped for an answer. "Bill, a polecat is the European equivalent of a skunk. About the same size, but without quite the range a skunk can squirt."

"How do you catch one," McCabe asked.

"Actually, we don't", Susan answered. "I have several vials of smell in the gear we brought. I have used it before to confuse dogs. Lysette will pull a well doused drag behind her as she exits the field. This will keep the dogs much more interested than any smell they get from me."

"Won't the dogs just follow Lysette back to the barn?"

"She'll be provided a rubberized canvas bag to put the drag in. With her surgical gloves also in the bag and a tight seal she should be safe to return. Lysette don't start the drag if you can see a dog and its' handler. The dogs will come quickly as soon as they smell the drag. I would suggest on your way back sinking the bag in a stream and putting a rock over it to keep it in place. Be sure you can find it again when you come to escort me back."

McCabe had one more question, "Where do you get the vials, I can't imagine they sell it in a shop?"

"But of course they sell it in shops. Perfumeries sometimes use it in their products. Stay with us Corporal and stay alive and we will turn you into a true bon vivant."

Chapter 16:   The nefarious scheme

Logs of *HMS Satyr* and *SS LaDonna Johnson*, and narrative of Maxwell Larsen

April 19, 1943, 15:40 GMT
50 Nautical miles NW of the Shetlands

"IS THAT YOUR SHIP MAX?" asked Lt. Oakley. He waved Larsen over to the periscope and maneuvered around Larsen's bulk as he approached the scope.

Larsen saw the *LaDonna*, barely making slow way as it loitered in the area. "Yes Captain, that's her. Right where she's supposed to be."

"Well let's pop up and surprise the old girl. I hope we don't frighten them into doing something rash." Oakley answered and then started tasking his crew.

"Would you care to make a small wager on who discovered whom first?" Max asked.

"What do you mean Max?"

"I'll wager that the *LaDonna's* log has a range and bearing on the *Satyr* two thousand yards before your ASDIC operator discovered my ship. Say five gallons of ice cream against your best bottle of scotch."

"Ice cream, it's been two years since I've had any. I hate to do this to you, but I accept your generous offer. Why on earth would you believe your crew could discover my boat before we show ourselves?"

"When you come aboard to confer with Admiral Sir Austin Miles I'll show you. Did I say that properly; military rank then honors?"

"Admiral Miles onboard your ship! I haven't received any orders for that."

"Officially I don't believe Sir Miles is aboard. Unofficially I believe we will soon be working together and the Admiral was gracious enough to coordinate our activities. Captain you will know more soon; I assure you."

As soon as the sub surfaced Oakley and a signalman gained the conning tower. The signalman quickly used the Aldis lamp to send a recognition code toward the freighter. The proper response was immediately relayed back to the submarine. "Proper reply Captain and johnnie-on quick I must say."

"Very prompt return indeed. Thank you Gannet." Lt. Oakley turned to the intercom; "lookouts to the bridge. Send Mr. Larsen up after them. Ahead one third, course 280 magnetic."

"Max, I take it your vessel is not what it appears," Oakley said as Max worked his way through the hatch.

"*LaDonna's* not what she seems. She's the precursor to a new class of ships. While she looks like a Liberty ship she's a variant of the new Victory class transports. Much faster than the ten to eleven knots of the Liberties. The Victories will do fifteen to seventeen knots. *LaDonna* will do twenty seven knots with her steam turbines wound all the way up. Her hull form underwater is closer to a destroyer than a transport. Of course she wasn't ever designed as a transport unlike the Victory class boats. She was built as a Q-ship from the keel up."

"Armament?" asked Oakley.

"Near to a destroyer again. Four 5" in two turrets, six quad forties, six dual twenties and more .50 caliber and .30 cal Brownings than we can man at one time. We carry a dozen torpedoes with two launch tubes forward and two aft, all below the waterline. A rack of depth charges at the stern. We have one of the new RADAR units, however we're still working on the antennae. I have a few engineers working on one that unfolds like a flashbulb reflector on a pocket camera. Radar is wonderful, but no transports have it yet and the antennae are too obvious. She also carries receivers that alert us if a RADAR unit is transmitting towards us. We've found that we can detect them well before they can register us."

Oakley was most impressed; "My God, I don't see any sign of the additional arms. Where are they? The deck cargo?"

"The fives as well as some of the forties, the canvas is a screen for armor. Deck hatches can pop open, *LaDonna* even has some mounts that extend out from her sides giving her an unmatched ability to depress her weapons for close aboard action," Larsen answered.

"You may win that bottle of scotch after all. Do you have sonar?"

"A bit beyond state-of-the-art. We have a large sonar dome forward and a blister aft and both specialized for passive use as well as active. Anything coming at us from the side lets us use the two domes like the lenses on a rangefinder. Aural Stereo Ranging one of your scientists calls it. England is far ahead of everyone else in the passive use of sound. We have conventional sound ranging that we can use, however we rarely use it unless we're sure of a kill. Can't have the Germans wondering what a liberty ship is doing with sonar. Coming toward her from the side I was sure she'd detect your boat long before you would hear her."

Larsen continued as Oakley gave orders to stop *Satyr* fifty yards and upwind of the Q-ship; "We can top off your fuel oil bunkers and replenish your freshwater if you need it. Our condensers make more fresh water than we can ever use." A fast and rugged looking launch came from around the transports bow. "Here's our taxi. Let's see what Admiral Miles has to say."

"Wonderful, I'll have my Number One arrange for the fuel and water, we can certainly use both." Oakley said.

"Once *Satyr's* hard alongside I'll have my purser see what stores you need. We have fresh frozen meat and some fresh vegetables; you need to figure out where you will put all the ice cream."

"We don't even know yet who won the bet."

Max chuckled and said, "I don't drink anyway and I'm sure your men could use some ice cream in return for their hospitality on the trip."

The Wardroom of the *S.S. LaDonna Johnson*
04/19/1943, 17:12 GMT

ADMIRAL MILES WAS A SHORT thin man well into his fifties. Ungraced by a warm manner or obvious air of command he made up for it with a keen intelligence and an infamous situational grasp of all aspects of marine warfare. As Larsen and Lt. Oakley entered the wardroom, the admiral turned from a conversation with Lt. Cmdr. Archer to greet them. Promptly returning Lt. Oakley's salute the famously stoic admiral broke into a broad smile, "Maxwell, so good to see you again! What nefarious scheme have you been perpetrating upon the Hun?" Then as the two met and shook hands warmly the Admiral turned to Oakley; "Oakley, I've heard your squadron commander speak well of you, I'm especially glad you were able to snatch Max from the sea. I must warn you that Mr. Larsen can get in more scrapes than a platoon of drunken Royal Marines so I'm sure you will have additional chances in the future. Be warned, never bet against this Yank troll; he'll have all of your whiskey and never drink a drop himself."

Taken aback by the notoriously reserved admirals warm welcome Lt. Oakley somewhat sheepishly replied; "Too late for that Sir Miles; I'm afraid a wager has already been set and I'm still waiting to hear the result."

Larsen responded, "Leftenant Oakley let me introduce *LaDonna's* captain, Lt. Commander Robert Archer, United States Navy. Rob, if you'll have a yeoman bring in a copy of today's log we can settle the bet and I'll give the wardroom a fine bottle of scotch to enjoy when no one from the US Naval Command is looking."

The admiral sadly shook his head, "Send for the bottle Mr. Oakley, I'm willing to bet two more that you've lost. Shall we get to work gentlemen while we wait for the log? In theory I'm at a meeting with the general staff, discussing invasion logistics and I'll need to leave in the morning as soon as a Sutherland has light to land by."

As the men assembled around the wardroom table Max deftly took a seat on the side forcing Admiral Miles to the head. A surprisingly large oriental man came in with two trays, the first holding several bottles, a siphon and ice bucket. The second held a large vacuum bottle and a few large mugs. Both trays were swiftly placed on the table, the coffee in front of Max and the tray with liquor before the admiral. "Thanks, George," Max addressed the waiter; "Sir Miles let me introduce George Lee, Larsen Shipping's chief accountant and also my intelligence procurer. You might remember his father Lee Kwan from when I first met you. Pull up a chair George and tell us what's going on in the world."

"Indeed I remember your father, I hope he is well. May I ask what an intelligence procurer is?" the admiral replied.

The large man sat down across from Max and pulled a notepad from his back pocket; "Admiral, my father is alive and well and still working for Max. As to my title, when I first took on the job of intelligence officer for Max, he placed a name placard on my desk with "Intel Pimp" in fancy gold leaf. I asked for something a little classier and Max had it redone as "Intelligence Procurer" in even fancier gold leaf and rhinestones. I decided to quit while I was ahead. Sir Miles, gentlemen, Max; I'll bring you up to speed by area. On the Eastern Front the Germans were knocked out of the Crimea on April 12th and are now holed up in Sevastopol. Stalin has held up further attacks at the moment, however I expect the Reds to renew the attack in maybe two more weeks. In the Med, the Eighth Army broke though Wadi Akarit on April 6th. I expect we'll have Bizerte and Tunis by mid-May at the latest. In the Pacific the Japanese launched heavy air attacks two weeks ago against the Solomons. Their air assets, just don't have the numbers or skill left to sustain that for long. Jap's will lose a lot more than they can ever gain. And too many Japanese troops, transports, and landing craft were lost in the Bismarck Sea in March. Also yesterday from the high amount of radio chatter in between the Jap Navy and Tokyo the Mother Hens believe a high ranking Japanese naval officer, possibly Yamamoto himself, was lost at sea, Whether through Allied action or misadventure we're not sure yet. Max I left you a breakdown on the freight tonnage sunk, new ships launched and my projections on German U-Boat availability with a similar report for the Pacific freight situation. Max I doubt we'll build anymore freight subs, Allied gains and Axis losses will probably negate any need for another *Manta*"

"Where is the *Manta* at the moment?" Max asked.

"North Atlantic, she'll be here in a day and a half at last word."

"Where do you get your information Sir?" Sir Miles icy stare was evidence of his displeasure. "You are privy to material not yet released. In fact I haven't received the information yet about Stalin's success or failure. Much less any rash rumor from the Pacific."

"My job, Sir Miles, is to make sure that Max and Larsen Shipping have the latest intelligence possible. Larsen Shipping had one of the more extensive private radio systems in the world before this war started and it has been expanded whenever possible. Anyone can listen to radio broadcasts and not all the intelligence analysts or code breakers are in the military. Larsen won't send ships into danger without providing the best information and the very best conjecture of enemy intentions given to his captains." Lee said with some heat of his own.

Max decided that some oil needed to be poured on the water; "Sir Miles, George Lee has worked extremely diligently and intelligently to provide the best information he can to the company. He utilizes some of the same mathematical formulas and theories that we have used to predict commodity prices, agricultural yields, oil and coal production, and shipping needs to make sure we have the right ships at the right place at the right time. The Mother Hens are twenty of the sharpest women mathematicians, stock researchers, and analysts you have ever seen; tasked with gathering and analyzing data, using methods that many intelligence professionals have scoffed at until they see that the ladies projections are statistically much more accurate than their own. They have access to two International Business Machines 405 tabulators that they share with my engineers. When possible we share our projections with both the OSS and British Intelligence and they are starting to come to us with requests for analysis. I won't send my ships and their crews out without as much information as possible.

I belong to a group of industrialists that have turned some of our older and wiser heads, especially those with foreign contacts into our own intelligence group. I believe we have a better picture of the industrial, food, and power reserves of all the countries in the world than any of our intelligence services. I certainly have a better picture of Japan, Germany's and Russia's capabilities than Tojo, Hitler, or Stalin, as my people don't risk death by reporting the truth instead of chimeras of wishes."

Admiral Miles accepted Larsen's overture, "Maxwell, Mr. Lee, I did not mean to disparage either your knowledge or methods. George, forgive me, I was taken aback by your knowledge, I truly did not expect to hear some of the information you so matter-of-factly reported. Too often I've seen the consequences of secret intelligence bandied about by politicians and soldiers more interested in preening their importance while safely sitting at home."

Lee responded, "Forgive me Admiral, I shouldn't have responded that way. Long hours are no excuse for being uncivil."

Max replied, "My apologies also Sir Miles, I should have informed you that Lt. Cmdr. Archer and George are both read into all aspects of this action. It was presumptuous of me to have opened this discussion in front of Lt. Oakley without first asking your permission. After he rescued me and the following days of watching the Leftenant commanding the *Satyr* have given me complete confidence in him; that does not excuse my not asking your permission. May we start over with these caveats in place?"

"Certainly no apologies are needed. We are all working toward the same goal and I'm sure we are all tired and on edge. May I suggest we take a moment and sit back have a drink and then resume this discussion? I certainly have no objection to Oakley's taking part in any or all matters that we discuss." The admiral turned to his subordinate, "Leftenant I would appreciate that what we discuss go no further until *Satyr* is back underway."

"Aye sir. Not a word." was Oakley's quick reply.

"Please allow me," the admiral said as he stood to make the drinks, "there is both scotch and bourbon, your orders gentlemen."

Chapter 17: *Manta*

Log of the *LaDonna Johnson* and Maxwell Larsen's narrative

The Wardroom of the S.S. *LaDonna* Johnson
03/19/1943, 18:00 GMT

SQUINTING THROUGH THE STEAM rising from a large mug of coffee, Maxwell Larsen looked at the men who would hold his life and more importantly his friends' lives in their hands. Some he had known for years, Sir Godswain Miles an admiral in the British Royal Navy who had first met Max while a young captain of a British gunboat off of Hong Kong. George Lee, Max's "intel pimp" and one of the sharpest analytical minds Max had ever known. George was the son of Lee Kwan who many years before had joined Larsen in freeing a group of [1]Thai women enslaved by a Chinese warlord. Larsen had sponsored the Lees and helped them gain a home and U.S. citizenship in California. Years later he had also arranged a scholarship to Stanford for George when he graduated from prep school. Max considered it one of the best investments he had ever made. Lt. Cmdr. Robert Archer and Lt. Alan Oakley were both recent additions to the group, but the rigors and intimacy of wartime ships had already convinced Max of their ability and trustworthiness. *"I hope their imagination and mental flexibility match their competence. They have no idea what they're in for."*

      Sir Miles set down his drink, "Gentlemen, let us proceed. I am informed that Mr. Larsen has a mission for us to consider. Other than the rescue of a substantial number of people and possibly a trove of German X-weapons I don't know much more. If he can convince me of its plausibility I will make Lt. Oakley and the *Satyr* available along with any other aid that I can produce. Max, the floor is yours."

      "Thank you Sir Miles. I hope I can convince you to help. At this time a team of British MI6 and American OSS agents are planning to steal the plans and drawings of Hitler's secret weapons from their storage site in Peenemünde. If you are not aware, that is where they are designing and building most of their X-weapons. They range from faster aircraft with a new type of propulsion called a jet engine to self-guided rockets with the range to hit England and possibly eventually America. While the factories arming the Nazis are being bombed whenever possible, we still need to discover what is new in the pipeline. You never know what may become a threat.

There is also a large number of French, Polish, and Dutch scientists being forced to aid the Germans. Their families are held by the Gestapo as collateral for the scientists' best effort. We hope to remove as many of these people as possible, freeing them from the Nazis and gaining their knowledge as well."

"How many people are you talking about and how much material?" Admiral Miles asked.

"Possibly eighty to one hundred people and several tons of plans and pictures," Larsen replied. "Go ahead Alan, I see you're appalled at the numbers."

"Max, I first thought we would be taking off a few agents and a bag or two of plans. Where on earth would you put so many people? You can't imagine putting them in *Satyr*. "

Max shook his head, "No Alan, *Satyr* couldn't handle a tenth of what we need. You will be there to provide security and run interference if necessary. And the *LaDonna* won't be going any closer than somewhere in the North Sea. I have a submersible that will hold everyone and everything we need to pick up."

Admiral Miles broke in, "Maxwell, I have never heard of a submersible with that much capacity. Even the Japanese and German resupply submarine freighters don't have the capacity."

"Admiral, I must digress for a bit and introduce you to the *Manta.* I believe you heard George mention that she'll be here in another day and a half. George if you would pass the files around I'll explain how the *Manta* came to be. Even before the United States joined the war, my company was approached by the U.S. government to see what could be done about the appalling losses of freighters taking Lend Lease materials to Britain. We knew that we would eventually join the war and the Merchant Marine would feel the brunt of the German U-Boat campaign. The tasking was to use a minimum of strategic construction materials while getting large amounts of fuel, munitions, any, and all supplies safely to England. We brainstormed and looked at everything from motorized icebergs to armored and armed freighters." Max paused for a sip of coffee.

"Motorized icebergs?" Rob Archer queried.

"Actually not a bad idea," Larsen answered. "You tunnel into a stabilized iceberg, Load trucks, munitions, whatever. A great way to ship perishable foods and medicines. Plug the hole with more ice, run a couple of ocean tugs out front and proceed at a slow rate while staying in cold water. Ice floats, they're basically unsinkable and inflammable.

You also deliver a small mountain of fresh water. I had looked into it once before with thoughts of delivering water to the Arabian Peninsula, they have more oil than fresh water. Anyway Churchill is building a giant aircraft carrier out of ice mixed with sawdust and with refrigeration pipes running through it to keep it cold. It will be sufficiently large that some aircraft can land on it without using arresting gear. Necessary to be large because it will probably have a hard time getting out of its own way.

 Regardless we gave up thinking about ice, and armored and armed ships capable of surviving on their own would be ridiculously expensive and inefficient. You end up with a warship and hardly any stores. We thought a submersible freighter would have the best chance of survival if we could come up with a sufficiently cheap construction method using less skilled labor. The answer was the *Manta* She is a submersible tug that can pull a string of streamlined submersible barges."

Lt. Oakley interrupted, "Max, a string of submarine pressure hulls, even without engines would still be expensive and use nearly as much steel as an actual submarine."

"Only if they had to resist water pressure. Most are simply a streamlined shell of ferro-cement and are free flooding. They have a buoyancy chamber using a bladder, compressed air tanks and a hydraulically operated compressor and regulator that holds them to a remotely assigned depth. Fuel oil, gasoline, lubricating oil are simply put into a rubberized bladder and exposed to pressure. Tires, rubber goods, who cares if they get wet. Rifles, machine guns, you just cover them with Cosmoline and let them ride. Munitions are trickier, for those we have pressure hulls, although we are exploring smaller canisters that we can pack into a flooded freight shell. We also designed a small all electric tug that can be used to maneuver the barges into a dock or even onto a shore much like a landing craft. The tug is a small submersible that is only used if conventional tugs are unavailable. It stows under the *Manta* and can be boarded through a connecting trunk. I call it a remora."

Admiral Miles broke in, "What is ferro-cement? You're not talking about more of those damned concrete hulls that were built during the Great War?"

Larsen answered, "No Admiral, it's not concrete. Those old ships worked for a while, but between corrosion and weight they were only good for a few years and now they're only good if you want to build a breakwater. Ferro-cement was developed by Professor Nervi in

Italy in the mid-thirty's. It uses a pipe frame and several layers of mild steel fine mesh and quarter inch rebar to build a hull. The keel, ribs, and hull are all made using thin sections and a mortar mix of sand and cement. The hull is only anywhere from two to four inches thick and surprisingly strong. Impact damage is confined to only the actual area of contact, like a dent in an eggshell, easy to repair and easily fothered or stopped up with a simple collision mat. The Italians have made some very nice boats in the one hundred and fifty ton range. My yard has played with smaller designs and I have a pretty little thirty five foot ketch with a hull no greater than three quarter inch thick that sails beautifully. A fifty foot wood motor cruiser ran into it while it was moored and my boat came out much better than the cruiser which nearly sank before they ran it aground. Anyone who has ever tied reinforcing steel or plastered a wall can build a hull meaning that hulls can be built by regular carpenters and the more expensive and skilled welders, riveters, heavy steel workers are not needed. Usually a hull is only about a third or less of the cost of building a ship, with rigging and engines and fittings being the really expensive part. However significant savings in materials of less strategic importance and labor savings can easily cut the cost for a hull to maybe a third of a wood or steel hull."

"Will this ferro-cement hull hold up to pressure underwater?" Oakley asked.

"We're not using it for a pressure hull at this time, although I have some engineers looking into it and I certainly believe it could be used as a pressure hull." Max answered. "For the *Manta* the ferro-cement acts primarily as the fairing and structural bridge while the actual pressure hull is made of steel. We reduced the required size of the pressure hull by moving as many of the components outside the hull and into the fairing which remains wet. If you've ever seen a picture of some of the flying wing aircraft designs you can envision our tug as a stout flying wing. It actually looks more like a manta ray or devilfish. Nature doesn't make an animal look strange just to amuse us. Many of the rays are extremely powerful and efficient swimmers. The *Manta* is also. The screws are placed in ducted fairings at the end of the wings and operated by hydraulic motors. The ducts concentrate the flow and increase power. The props are adjustable in pitch, which is easy to do using hydraulics so we can go for either high speed without a tow to a fine pitch for less speed and more pull when towing a string of shells. The props can even be reversed in pitch which makes the motor easier to build and we use a new bronze alloy with traces of nickel and manganese so that the hydraulic motors can be exposed to the water. The wide separation allows the *Manta* to turn in its own length and the use of elevons and twin rudders near the wing tips give us unprecedented maneuvering control. If you have opened your file you'll see a photo of her."

Admiral Miles flipped open his folder, "My word, she's huge. Is that you standing out on the bow?"

"*Manta* is the largest submersible built yet. I'm out on the nose along with Ernst Dietsch and Vincent Fuller, we collaborated on a lot of the design. Her pressure hull is actually not much bigger than the *Satyr* volume wise. By moving batteries, fuel, propulsion units, and air tanks out into the wet wing areas we have room for some powerful engines and generators while actually having more room for crew. Automation makes our crew smaller than for a normal submarine. We are using a snorkel copied from the same Dutch design that the Germans are using on their subs. It wasn't easy, but we got it to work."

A clamor of questions started up, with Lt. Oakley quickly deferring to Admiral Miles. "How can you put your batteries out in the water, and your fuel tanks as well?"

Max pointed to an area on the sub's schematic. "The batteries are encased in flexible rubber tanks filled with mineral oil, they have a vent that has a check valve allowing hydrogen gas to be released. The fuel tanks are open shells with the fuel itself in bladders. After all a normal submarines fuel tanks are on the exterior of the hull. Since the diesel is only used on the surface or near it while snorkeling we only need to valve off the fuel lines coming into the engine room when submerged. They have a pressure regulator that will accomplish this also if for some reason the valves aren't shut. Buoyancy control is again handled by free flooding compartments encasing air bladders and compressors are used to move air back and forth from bladder to high pressure tank. Our battery reserve gives us more than three times the battery capacity of a normal submarine of equivalent size."

"Armament?" Oakley asked before the Admiral could ask another question.

Again Max pointed to the schematic. "Defensive only. That streamlined blister on the dorsal line behind the nose has a Bofors quad-40 that can pop up. The gunner can remotely switch between three magazines choosing armor piecing, high explosive, or air burst depending on target. The gunner sits in a small armored dome behind the gun which allows him to switch from the periscope control, or radar, to a broader more active view. We use hydraulics to power almost everything so the gunner has a joy stick that lets him rotate and aim the 40 much quicker than a manned crew. It's very similar to the dorsal and ventral gun positions on the new B-29 aircraft that is being developed.

And last we have acoustic mines that can be released from the wings and left in the path of any ship following us."

Lt. Cmdr. Archer asked the next question, "If your pressure hull is the same size as the *Satyr*'s how do you intend to get that many people in it?"

"We do have more room in our hull for passengers than a conventional sub, but admittedly not enough room for 100 more people. What we have are pressure hulled towing shells rigged with lights, a lot of bunks, and what we call a life support system. The Navy wanted us to also look into transporting troops. The life support system includes a CO_2 absorber unit that is made more efficient by using a fan and a permeable sheet that rotates through a vat of sodium hydroxide or calcium oxide to capture the carbon dioxide. This results in some heat which can be transferred to either the interior of the shell for heat in cold water or through a heat exchanger into the surrounding water. There is also a tank of LOX, liquefied oxygen, to be used in replenishing the oxygen used by the inhabitants. Once on the surface a set of vents and blowers can be used to exchange air just as in a normal sub."

"You expect to safely move people in these shells?" Admiral Miles asked.

"Admiral, it wouldn't be my first choice for travel, but considering the threats to these people's lives, especially if Allied aircraft start bombing Peenemünde, safety is somewhat relative. The CO_2 scrubbers have hand cranked backups, two trained crewmen will be in each shell to operate all the systems. An intercom system keeps us in contact with the shells. There will be a chemical toilet which can be pumped overboard if necessary with interlocked controls to keep anyone from flooding the shell. Water and survival rations onboard. Each shell has an external battery with enough power to last through a trip two times longer and can be recharged when underway by the *Manta*. The crewmen, as a last resort, are able to release the shell from the tow and float it to the surface where it becomes a life raft. A small radio transceiver can act as a beacon. The scientists and their families won't enjoy the ride, but the alternative is probably death."

"It sounds like you have more duration underwater than *Satyr*." Oakley stated.

"Yes, we can operate on batteries probably three times longer than you can and at higher speeds. The life support system allows us to stay submerged for two weeks if necessary. With Sir Miles blessing I can install a small life support system on the *Satyr* that will triple the time you can remain submerged and we have a streamlined pod that we can fasten to your hull that will double your battery reserve." Max avowed.

Sir Miles asked, "How long will it take you to install these devices?"

"Admiral, I have a secure covered dock in Glasgow. We can do the conversion in two weeks. The rescue may not come for another month, we have the time if we start soon."

"Max how do you expect to get that behemoth of yours' through the Oresund Strait? *Satyr* was lucky to get through and return and that was probably helped by the fact that the Germans thought no sane submarine commander would even attempt it. Present company accepted of course," Admiral Miles said with a nod to Lt. Oakley. Oakley nodded back, acknowledging the statement and wisely keeping his own thoughts to himself.

"*Manta*'s pressure hull is more of a flat ovoid than round and her draft is only slightly greater than *Satyr*'s. Because of her shape I've added more ring elements so her test depth exceeds a combat sub. Most importantly [2]Fabian Tamm is eager to repay a debt, and if it skewers the Nazis without being too provocative, that just adds some sauce." Max answered.

Sir Miles nodded in agreement as the two junior officers wondered who Tamm could be and how he could help.

[1]*Thailand was also then known as Siam. Both names were in use during this period. Siamese women may have caused some confusion with Siamese twins, hence Thai was used. SMkIII*

[2]*Fabian Tamm was Chief of the Swedish Navy before and after WW2. SMkIII*

Chapter 18: Mouse on the roof

Reports of Lt. Robin Jarvis, Susan Brodeur, and Lysette Malois

April 25, 1943, 03:00
The roof of the Plans Repository, Peenemünde, Germany

SUSAN BRODEUR, ALSO KNOWN as *La Petite Souris*, had just gained the roof of the Plans Repository. She did a quick reconnoiter of the roof with a pencil thin beam from a small flashlight. There was a roof access, however her inspection concentrated on the surface around it. She was looking for signs that the roof was regularly visited. The surface was slightly pitched toward the rear, allowing for water runoff and she made a mental note to urinate down a plumbing drain vent before daylight. It would not be wise to give some guard a shower from a drain scupper or gain the interest of a guard dog. She found no sign that anyone was visiting the roof, no scuff marks in the tar around the scuttle, no cigarette butts or signs that anyone was using the roof to catch a quick smoke, no bottles that might have indicated a recreational use for the roof. No antennae that might need to be adjusted. Relieved she found the intake air vent and folded her tarp with the dark gray side out so that it didn't cover any tar stripes while staying adjacent to the vent. She crawled along the perimeter, stopping on each side to slowly advance her head over the parapet and look for guards. None were in sight. Apparently the Germans felt that the perimeter security and the buildings vault like construction were sufficient security. There would be an occasional patrol through the area, but nothing to worry about at the moment.

Susan reviewed in her mind the steps she had taken to get here, a practice she used as a way to insure she had left no evidence behind as well as to steady her breathing, calm down, and remind herself of the steps that would follow. Lysette had led Susan to the edge of the aircraft stand adjacent to several tied down aircraft. She had been impressed with both Lysette's skill on the approach and the near invisibility provided by the ghillie suits. While Susan had been raised in the Alps and had gone with her father hunting roebuck and chamois, she had never seen anything quite like the suit. It was both lighter and more maneuverable than she would have guessed from the appearance. A shroud of fabric with a jungle of rag strips and actual foliage, it blended into any bush, tree line, or grass, and prevented a human silhouette from showing. Once on the tarmac of the stand her tarp provided all the cover she needed as she kept aircraft between her and the hangars and once among the buildings she flitted in silence from one hide to the next. She only encountered one patrol and with her dark clothes she was able to hide by lying in the shadow of a high curb, almost in plain sight, but knowing that she would be overlooked. She found the rear of the repository and squeezed under some low pipes, using their shadow to hide while she made sure she was alone. The loud hum from the generator building would hide any noise she might make, however it could also mask any noise a guard might make in his rounds. Taking a last glance she vaulted on top of the electrical conduit connecting the buildings, then placing her feet against the repository and her hands against the generator building, she swiftly walked herself up, bridging the space between with her body. She slowed as she neared the top of the generator building, found a secure purchase for her hands just below the cornice and then dropped her feet to the wall of the generator building. The rough brick provided plenty of purchase for her toes. Susan slowly lifted her head above the cornice and took her time making sure the roof was empty. The only thing she saw was a number of exhaust pipes and air ventilators. The sound from the diesel generators was deafening.

Susan quickly scuttled over the cornice and crouching behind the parapet scanned the route she had followed to the building. No activity was detected. Farther out in the fields surrounding the airfield she could detect no lights or activity. Lysette had probably made good her retreat. Once assured that she was still unobserved Susan stood on the cornice and jumped up and out to the higher repository roof and once over that cornice she knew that she was safe as long as she kept her head below the parapet surrounding the roof.

She would check the scuttle to determine if it was alarmed, then drop the microphone down the air vent and see if she could hear anything. After relieving herself down a plumbing vent she methodically started her tasks. She wanted to be ready to crawl under the tarp well before any aircraft started their morning flight. *"I hope they are all going to sunrise service for Easter and then stay in their cups the rest of the day. I'll have to stay an extra day to make sure the routine wasn't changed for Easter. Dried fruit, dried meat, and water aren't much of an Easter dinner, but the taste of screwing the damn Germans should make it more palatable."*

Chapter 19: Go BIG

Field reports and narratives of Marie Malois and Vincent Fuller

April 27, 1943, 05:00
An Abandoned Farm 8 Kilometers from Peenemünde:

"WELL DONE LADIES, I'm happy to see you back in one piece," Vincent Fuller greeted Lysette and Susan as they came down the cellar ladder.

"I'm afraid I have mostly bad news," Susan replied.

"Sit down, we still have some hot coffee and fairly warm eggs from those courageous old hens that nest in the hay loft. Eat first, then tell us the bad news," Fuller said while pulling a cloth off of the table.

"Fresh eggs, Mon Dieu, I'm famished." Susan quickly shared the plate of eggs with Lysette, who demurred for only an instant before attacking her plate.

Twice Susan started to explain only to have Fuller hold up an immense admonishing hand to stop her. He would simply point to the table and then calmly sit back. Finally finishing her plate by using a German field ration cracker to chase the last morsel, Susan sat back and offered a discrete but welcome belch. "Thank you. Were you the chef Willy?"

"Yes ma'am. I'm sorry I didn't have more to offer."

"It was wonderful. Now Vincent, can I tell you what I found out?"

"Please do."

"As I said it's mostly all bad news. It turns out that at least two people are in the repository at all times. In the morning, starting around five thirty, several more come in, apparently to sort and prepare each set of plans to go out each morning. Next the main guard house calls every hour to check on the staff. When they aren't busy the guards will talk and gossip for ten even fifteen minutes at a time. They are worse than old hens. Too bad we can't record all of their gossip. The guards know more about who's doing what to whom than a gaggle of washerwomen."

"Not what we wanted to hear," Lt. Jarvis exclaimed.

"It gets worse. There is a scuttle, but it only opens from the inside and using that trick Willy told me with a compass it seems to be wired to an alarm."

"What trick," Marie asked?

"I held a small compass up to the side of the scuttle and slowly crawled around it. I got more attraction where I expected to find hinges and the latch. I also found a variation that went from a positive attraction to a negative on the latch side. Willy said the compass would react that way to an electric field."

"It sounds like the system breaks a connection when opened," McCabe stated.

Vincent agreed, "Likely a DC circuit, so it probably runs off a battery which keeps us from just killing power to the place."

"I do have some good news. The intake vent would allow me to enter and the phone and alarm circuits seem to come up through the roof and enter a circuit box before going down the side of the building."

"Small favor, however I think we can give up on a surreptitious entry and having time to accomplish anything," Fuller stated.

"We'd have better luck just knocking on the door and asking for the damn plans," Lysette added.

Fuller suddenly looked at Lysette, one large finger shaking and pointing toward her and his mouth open as if words wouldn't come. Words soon rushed forth, "Exactly! A brilliant idea Lysette. I don't care how often Hiram says that Marie's the smart one; you've pegged it this time."

"Father says no such thing," Marie exclaimed! "Oh, OH! I see what you mean. We go big."

"We don't go big. We go absolutely huge!" Fuller added.

"What on earth are you two talking about?" Jarvis asked. She turned to look at McCabe and Lysette only to see dawning comprehension and smiles. Jarvis turned to her lover, "You just gave them bad news. I heard you."

Susan nodded in agreement, "I am as lost as you are. What are you fools talking about."

"We're going to ask for the damn plans. In fact, they will beg us to take them," Marie said.

Fuller started enumerating factors. "This will take some time. The Brits will have to run a major bombing raid and we'll have to alert the Nazis that it's coming."

Fuller turned to Lysette, "How big is the ferry, will it handle at least a truck or two, the scientists and their families?"

"Stop", hissed Jarvis. "Please lay it out for two very confused people."

Fuller relented, "Very simply we have to coordinate a major air raid by the British and manage for the Germans to discover it before it arrives. We disguise a load of men as soldiers, probably Waffen SS, and send signals telling Peenemünde staff of the upcoming raid. We tell them to secure all the plans, the scientists and their families, load the whole shebang into trucks, head for the ferry and take it over, we head out to sea and transfer to the *Manta*"

Jarvis was nearly at her wits end, "What in the Lord's name is the *Manta*? Where do we get the soldiers to portray Waffen SS? Why Waffen SS? Why are we betraying a British bombing raid?"

"Robin, slow down. I'll go through it slowly. It won't be as easy as I'm making it seem, however it is doable," Fuller said. "First, the *Manta* is a large submersible freighter capable of taking all the plans and the scientists and their families. Max Larsen's shipyard built it as an experiment to provide a safer method for bringing supplies from America."

Susan interrupted, "Max Larsen, the same Max who brought us here, he is part of Larsen Shipyards?"

Vincent waved aside Susan's question, "Max is Larsen Shipping and Larsen Shipyards, owner and lead designer. He calls in me or Ernst Dietsch when he wants one of his wild hares to actually work. There is a lot more to Max than you can see, and as big as he is you can see a lot. Now let me finish my own wild hare. We get soldiers from the SOE, Special Boat Service probably. They have a bunch of large Teutonic looking men and enough of them speak German to pull this off. They have more experience at this sort of thing than any other group available. Third, the Waffen SS has specialized in acquiring scientific and technical materials from all the countries that Hitler has overrun. I believe a Captain Skorzeny has been at the lead in bringing new technology back to Germany. It follows that they would be the most logical personnel to handle the plans and the foreign scientists. We will have to coordinate a night raid by the British. If it is betrayed at the right time there will be time for the Germans to save their information and scientists without having time to deploy additional anti-aircraft weapons. German radar would pick up any raid as it comes over the channel anyway, so there wouldn't be much difference in defense. If we show up at the right time the Germans will do their best to make our gathering of plans and scientists a success."

"How do we get the SBS here," Susan asked?

"The same way we take out the materials, with the *Manta* We don't really need more than a dozen. Susan we may have to get you into the repository again on the night of the raid to insure access to the building. Could you take out some of the personnel?"

Susan looked distraught, "I don't know. I would try, but I don't know."

"Susan, can I fit through the vent," McCabe asked?

Susan appraised the young man, "Take off your shirt." Bill's ears turned bright red, but he took off his shirt. Bill was lean rather than thin and his ropy muscles were surprisingly evident. "Pull your shoulders together as tight as you can. Yes you should make it, we may have to paste your ears to your head, but the rest of you should make it. How well do you climb?"

"I've seen him climb, he should be able to follow your lead," Lysette answered.

"I've climbed high steel and I'm good in trees. I haven't done any mountain climbing."

"By high steel you mean a large building under construction, a skyscraper, like in New York," Susan asked?

"Yes Ma'am."

"You'll do," Susan assured him.

"Bill are you sure about this," Fuller asked?

"Yes sir."

"What if the Nazis actually send some SS," Marie added?

"We will have to intercept them. A job for you ladies, although I would imagine Max and some of his crew would be happy to help."

"Where do you get your trucks," Robin asked?

"Thank you Robin, keep asking questions and our feet on the ground," Lysette answered. "There are plenty of trucks on the site, but I don't believe the guards would swallow a bunch of SS troops showing up on foot."

"How big is this sub freighter and how close in can he get, or can we find a dock where he could unload say one staff car and a bunch of motorcycles with side cars. A bunch of motorcycles around a staff car always means someone important. Then whoever is the supposed commander requisitions the trucks he needs," Bill suggested.

Vincent nodded approval, "I like that thought and the psychology of showmanship would enhance the act. Ream out the mufflers so everything's louder and add some fancy lights. Dazzle them."

"I usually act alone, but I have done some jobs with a large group a few times. Either copying plans or opening doors to get people inside. I like Willy's idea," Susan added.

"We don't need to go much further in planning now. Let's get this off to Osgood and his merry men and see if they can choke it down. I know Max would love to try this. When is our next transmission window? And we need to boil this down to the shortest transmission possible and still convey all that we need. Bill, start loosening up your fingers, you're going to have to tap like mad," Vincent declared to the group.

Chapter 20: Friends and FUBARs

OSS logs and reports from Brig. Gen. Hiram Snowden and Ernst Dietsch

April 30, 1943, 08:00
Col. Osgood's Office

THE OCCASIONAL RUSTLE of pages being flipped was the only sound as the three men read their briefing folders. Every so often one or the other would stop, jot some notes in the margins or in a convenient tablet and then continue reading. Col. Osgood's intercom buzzed, "Colonel, Lieutenant Colonel Brewster needs you in communications," Osgood's secretary requested.

"Tell him I'll be right down." Osgood turned to the other two men, "Hiram, Ernst, if you need anything, more coffee, whatever, call Sgt. Futch, I'm sure she can take care of any legitimate request. You'll notice that I'm looking at you Ernst, you try turning on that silver tongue of yours and Sibyl's liable to yank it right out. I don't want the best secretary I've ever had being deviled by you."

"I'll be good, I'm always good, in fact I've been told a time or two that I was downright wonderful!" Dietsch answered while holding his hands up in the attitude of prayer, an absurdly beatific expression beaming at Osgood.

Mumbling low imprecations, Osgood left for communications.

Hiram Snowden smiled at Dietsch, "I don't need you deviling Albert either. Are you through reading?"

"Yes for now. I don't know whether to laugh or cry. This will either work or be the Grand Royal FUBAR of all times," Ernst said while closing his folder. "When is Max supposed to be here and who else is coming?"

Hiram answered, "Max is being flown in from Scotland in a Lysander and should be here before noon. After lunch or possibly at lunch, Colonel Stewart Menzies will join us, he's head of MI6 and one of the sharper minds you'll meet in this war. He can provide the Special Boat men if he thinks this has a chance to work."

Dietsch shifted the conversation, "Have you heard how our friends are doing? I haven't had a chance to write and I've been moving around too much for their letters to catch up."

"I received a fairly long letter from [1]Dr. Wolf last week so I can bring you up to speed," Hiram said. [2]Tom has been working overtime on some new drugs, a new class called antibiotics that are supposed to fight infections. A Scottish boffin named Fleming discovered the drug and Tom is trying to come up with a better way to mass produce it and make it viable for safe storage. In his spare time, he and [3]Merlin Bourland are helping the FBI prevent sabotage in the Chicago area. Tom and Merlin's contacts amongst the shadier denizens of Chicago are being used to find any Axis spies or even sympathizers along the docks or in industry.

[4]Beryl is staying at the mines in Colombia, training Reyes and helping the Colombian government fight off any German or Japanese espionage. You know about Max and [5]Londa's daughter don't you?"

"Yes, Max said she'll be named Maria Zaragosa as no one can pronounce or even has time to say her native name and that should help hide her connection to our group. And Londa was pretty blunt in telling Max that she wanted his child, but was not interested in marriage or more than a continued platonic relationship."

"[6]Juan Miguel is still in North Africa, once the Germans are routed he'll be moving into either Iran or Saudi Arabia to help get more oil flowing. I hope he has a chance to get into some ruins, but I doubt he'll get a chance to play much. Rumor has it that he and a certain female Russian [7]spy have hit it off. They hope to get together after the war."

Ernst let out a low whistle, "Juan's in love! Good for him; after Samira disappeared I didn't think he would ever find another woman. Hell, I never thought he would ever even try. I hate to say this, but why fall in love with one of Stalin's damn agents. I know we'll end up fighting those bastards before long."

"I pray Juan has a better outcome this time, and I hope you'll refrain from attacking the Russians until the Nazis are defeated," Hiram added. "Of course you know that Max's [9]Verna is in London, up to her elbows in surgery. How two people who started out convinced of each-others ill worth, fall in love so deeply is astounding. You do know that she just lost her third brother, Marchand was the captain of a Canadian freighter that was carrying munitions in the North Sea. Torpedoed and basically disintegrated by the explosion."

"No I hadn't yet heard, Max has been at sea and I've been working with Barnes Wallis night and day. My God, that just leaves Alex in Canada taking care of the Deveraux companies. Verna must be devastated. Does Max know?"

"I sent a message and a briefing folder along with the Lysander pilot. Max may detour to see Verna before he comes here."

"I've been going over the notes from the Polish workers; the Fire Drake lead engineer has to be Alexis Voronstov. I met the Count right after the first war. He lost his entire family to the Bolsheviks. He has apparently joined the Germans in order to take his revenge. I haven't talked or corresponded with him in fifteen years. I would never have taken him for a Nazi sympathizer. I think he looks at them as a means to an end," Dietsch said while waving the briefing folder at Snowden.

"How good is he as an engineer," Hiram asked?

"Too good, a forward thinker fueled by hate, but with an excellent and logical mind. We can't underestimate his abilities."

"In that case let's get back to work. We'll have to be sure Vince gets his hands on Voronstov's designs. Now though, how is Max going to get a staff car and a bunch of motorcycles into the area? Waco gliders maybe, how to get them in without being seen I haven't a clue." Hiram picked up his folder and a pencil and once more started taking notes.

[1]*Dr. Herman C. Wolf Sr. (Progenitor)/* [2]*Dr. Thomas George Fixx (Progenitor)/* [3]*Merlin Bourland, Vincent Fuller's father-in-law/* [4]*Beryl Maria DeLeon Fixx (Progenitor), Dr. Fixx's wife and their son Guatemozin Reyes Morales/* [5]*Londa was the leader of the Guardians, who in the 1940s were still guarding the area around the Lagos Aguabonita and the gold mine under it. Londa's true name is not easily translatable to English and Larsen's approximation was so far off that he started calling her Linda Lou which eventually evolved into Londa. For the younger generation; Lagos Aguabonita simply means a freshwater lake. The lakes actual name and location are never published.*
[6]*Juan Miguel Arroyo (Progenitor), oil geologist and archeologist. /* [7]*The Russian spy was Myra Yegenev, the mother of Natalia Yegenev-Arroyo/* [8]*Samira Suryal al-Misri, an Egyptian Coptic Christian who loved Arroyo and was the mother of Farouk Arroyo. Samira was forcibly separated from Arroyo by her family and it is believed that she was murdered by her family in a so-called honor killing. /* [9]*Dr. Verna Mina Deveraux (Progenitor), Maxwell Larsen's fiancé at this time. SMkIII*

Chapter 21: Verna and Max

Dr. Verna Deveraux Larsen and Dr. (then Nurse) Nancy Lynn Cuny

Hammersmith Hospital
April 30, 1943, 11:08

DR. VERNA DEVERAUX was talking with Corporal Damien Ballinger, British Army, nineteen years old, lying in bed recuperating from stomach wounds received in North Africa. Verna was one of the surgeons who had untangled the Gordian knot of intestine and adhesions left from the rough initial treatment Ballinger had received in the field. Verna found Ballinger's continual good humor in the face of undeniable pain and a long convalescence a source of inspiration and calm.

She was alerted when his eyes widened in surprise and some apprehension as he looked past her toward the door of the ward. Verna turned and saw her fiancé looming in the doorway. Larsen, dressed in dark blue coveralls without insignia, his wide solemn face, heavily ridged brow, graced by his perpetual scowl were enough to give a platoon dread, much less a wounded man-boy wondering how he might protect the doctor with whom he had fallen in love. Damien was both relieved and disappointed when Dr. Deveraux strode quickly to her ogre and was enveloped in his arms. Her arms around his neck, her body cradled in his arms, she broke into quiet tears; anxieties and a myriad of losses soothed by the giant who was slowly swaying side to side, like a father settling a young child.

[1]Nancy Cuny, a young, very tall, American nurse, walked up and slowly led Max to a vacant office. Neither Max nor Verna seemed to notice as Nancy turned a small desk lamp on and then exited, closing the door behind her.

"Let me finish checking your dressings and drains Corporal," Nancy said as she approached Ballinger's bed. It always took him a moment to understand her, a combination of a West Texas drawl and a speaking rate, half the speed of the British, always caused a moment of confusion.

"Who or what was that. I'm sorry, but I think I've just seen Beauty and the Beast and not a single Brother Grimm around," Damien said.

"Who would be more appropriate, although I can appreciate the what. That, Corporal Damien, is Maxwell Larsen, Dr. Deveraux's husband to be. He's some kind of merchant captain and just in from the North Sea. And for your information the good doctor recently lost her third brother to the war."

Ballinger instantly looked contrite, "I had no idea, I'm sorry. Should I have said something to her?"

"Corporal Ballinger, please don't worry. Let me thank you. The doctor has told me that being next to your cheerful presence is like a balm. Darlin', you just keep being your cute little self and get well, that's all you need to do." Nurse Cuny said as she readied to go to her next patient.

"Little!, well maybe next to you Sister Cuny I am, and thank you for the kind words," Ballinger thought as he watched the nurse walk away.

Thirty minutes later Max and Verna came out of the office. "I hate to leave you, but I'm overdue for my meeting," Max rumbled.

"Go on. Our duty is to the living, especially when they're our good friends. There will again be time to cry and remember later. Do you have a place to stay? I'm afraid I share my flat with a nurse and another doctor," Verna responded.

"The two of us have a place to stay. Admiral Sir Miles has access to an 80 foot Air-Rescue boat that was converted to ferry Lord High Muckety-Mucks up and down the Thames. He says it has a large stateroom, a discrete steward and an excellent cook. And I had the foresight to bring some frozen steaks and produce from the *LaDonna*. The Brits have laid a car and driver on for me. What time do you get off? My driver will pick you up, run you by your flat if you need anything and then deliver you to the boat. I'll be there in time to clean up before dinner. The war can stop for us for at least one night."

"Seventeen hundred, you impossible man, I love you so much," Verna said as she pulled Max's head down for one more kiss. "Go save the world, but don't you dare be late."

"Yes Ma'am. I'll be there."

[1]*Dr. Nancy Lynn Cuny, MD, later married to Lysette Irene Malois. Cuny had put off her final year of medical school working toward her MD, to volunteer as a nurse early in England's war. SMkIII*

Chapter 22: Bluff and raise

OSS logs and reports from Brig. Gen. Hiram Snowden, Ernst Dietsch, and Maxwell Larsen

April 30, 1943, 13:20
Col. Osgood's Office

"WELCOME MAX, I'm glad you could make it," Col. Osgood said as Max entered the office. "I have some news for you from Dr. Melton Miles, he's chief of surgery at Hammersmith and Admiral Sir Miles younger brother; I'm to tell you that Verna has the next two days off, several surgeons have volunteered to share her duties. Dr. Miles will be most disappointed in you if Dr. Deveraux shows up even a minute before then."

"Thanks Albert. Would you get me Dr. Miles address so I can send him a thank you note and a case of steaks?"

"Consider it done, Sibyl will have it for you before you leave. Now let me introduce you to Colonel Stewart Menzies, head of MI6 and the man we must convince to loan us some SOE troops."

Col. Menzies stood to shake hands with Larsen. "Captain Larsen it is a pleasure to meet you. I have a report on my desk that was sent over from the Admiralty. Frankly I thought it was a bit ridiculous about how you singlehandedly destroyed an E Boat and her crew. Seeing you I now believe all the hyperbole."

"Please, call me Max. At the time I believe luck was a much bigger factor than hyperbole." Larsen next greeted Brig. Gen. Snowden and Ernst Dietsch and then the men sat down around a table that had been brought in for the conference. A knock on the door was followed by Sgt. Futch carrying in a tray of mugs and a coffee pot.

"Thank you Sibyl. Will you tile the door, I don't want any interruptions for a couple of hours."

"Yes Colonel. No one will bother you." The trim WAC turned and closed the door behind her.

"How well can she use that little .38 she carries," Larsen asked.

"How did you see that? I know she carries it and there is a .45 in her desk drawer, but I didn't think anyone would notice the .38. And to answer your question she can use either one with either hand damn well. How she shoots accurately with that snub nose .38 is beyond me. I would have to shove it into someone's gut in order to hit them." Osgood answered.

"When you've had as many people as I have wanting to promote your demise, hideout guns become much more evident." Max answered.

"Speaking of hideout guns, how are we going to hide a dozen or more SBS men, a staff car and a bunch of motorcycles? Were you able to read the report I sent you?" Snowden asked Max.

"Yes, I read it on the flight from Glasgow. I think the answer is so obvious that I drew a picture." Max pulled a folder from his attaché case and placed a photo in front of Snowden.

As the other three craned to see the picture Hiram burst into laughter, "I know you're not kidding, but this seems a little extreme even for you." The picture was a photo of the *Manta* with large swastikas penciled onto it.

Max stood up and leaned over the table, his fists planted squarely in the middle, "Hiram, Colonel Menzies, Albert, you need to think about this. Peenemünde, the home of Nazi Secret Weapons, the port and docks have been bringing in and shipping out rockets and jet engines and things we know nothing about. The islanders have seen all sorts of weird stuff and I'm sure threatened every which way from Sunday to keep their mouths shut. We show up with the *Manta* all decked out in German Navy insignia and giant swastikas, add a menacing Kriegsmarine captain, a Waffen SS colonel, hopefully with dueling scars and a swagger stick, add a bunch of really mean looking hombres literally dressed to kill. We pull up with the quad-40 turret up and rotating, horn blaring and maybe a siren wailing.

"Who amongst the people in Peenemünde are going to say, "Hey stop. You can't tie up here and unload a staff car and motorcycles with side cars and mounted machine guns." No and no, the sinister SS Colonel tells the harbor master that no one is to approach the submarine and no one is to let anybody else know we are here. Have Vincent and the twins take out the phone and telegraph wires just before our appearance. Let the islanders know that we have temporarily shut down their communications. Jam the hell out of their radios. Put men on board to commandeer the ferry. And let the Germans at the test site know that Colonel Goose Step and his un-merry men are coming to get the papers and scientists and by Hitler's stinkin mustache they better have everything ready. Put them all on the ferry and head to sea in case someone finally figures out that we're not kosher and transfer everything to the capsules, then run like hell with the *Satyr* waiting to eliminate any interference.

"Last the Pathfinders and every bomber England has available blow the site off the face of the earth. What's not to work?" Slowly Max straightened up and sat down.

Ernst Dietsch slowly began applauding, a devilish grin spreading across his face. Dietsch's applause finally seemed to wake everyone up. They had been engrossed by Max's unusually fervent presentation until they were on the edge of their seats and leaning into the table.

Colonel Menzies straightened up, then stood up and reached across for Max's paw. "That has to be the daftest and most improbable scenario I've ever heard. Sign me up. The reward is worth the risk. I just hope I can find enough equally daft volunteers because I only give all of you a thirty percent chance of living through this."

Hiram and Albert were exchanging looks. Ernst began feverishly drawing in his notebook and quickly turned it toward Larsen. "Is this what you were thinking of for the car and cycles?" The sketch was of a submersible freight pod with the clam shell streamlined fairing open and the hatch descending like a loading ramp of an LST.

"Yes, that should do it. We can ballast up or down to align the ramp with one of the floating docks, a munition pod should hold all the equipment. The remora can push it into the dock. We'll add four or five hundred pounds of explosive, a timer, and leave the pod behind us when we clear the dock. I want all the speed I can get when we leave. We want to be well past the range the Germans think a submarine could make before they start searching; if they start searching. I'm hoping a very large bombing raid and maybe a few strikes at their naval bases will slow any search."

"Max, what's your main worry," Hiram asked?

"The Baltic is basically a very shallow slightly salty lake. I can't go deep and I'll have to be careful not to run aground. The Germans mostly have *Schnellbootes* and minelayers there now since they bottled up the Red Fleet in the Gulf of Finland. Probably more mines in the gulf per square mile than anywhere else in the world. Getting in or out is a problem, too many choke points. We may need a couple of *Satyr*'s sister ships waiting near the entrance to cover our escape. Colonel Menzies, do you think you can get a squadron of Beaufighters up to harass the Hun when we're ready to run the gauntlet?"

"If you can get that far I can assure you a slew of Beaufighters when you are exiting the Baltic. Coordination with all the parties will be difficult, but I think I can convince Bomber Command and the fighter squadrons that it can be done."

"We'll hug Sweden as much as possible, their neutrality leans a little too much toward the Germans, pretty understandable that, but they still don't like warships in their territorial waters. I've already contacted Admiral Tamm through my own channels, our reps met in Iceland last week to confirm our agreement. He's willing to not only look the other way, but maybe schedule some patrols in the strait that will help mask our entry and exit. All of course in the name of protecting Swedish neutrality." Max added.

Hiram asked, "Max, is there anyone in any navy that you haven't befriended at some time?"

"Very few actually. I've shared a meal or two with Donitz and I've known Canaris for years. I use to play chess with him on occasion. I've also turned a couple of his agents who tried to join my workforce over to the FBI."

"I think the hyperbole hypothesis I inferred earlier tonight just got closer to theory," Col. Menzies said.

Col. Osgood leaned over to his intercom, "Sergeant Sibyl Virginia Futch, please bring glasses for all including yourself and my best bottle of scotch. We are about to bedevil Hitler's stinking mustache."

"I'll drink to that," Max declared.

"No you won't. You'll raise the glass and pretend. Just pass it to me and I'll enjoy it for you," Dietsch said.

Chapter 23: Hiding Dragons

Count Voronstov's Compiled Daily Reports and Reports from Major von Stulpnagel

May 12, 1943, 12:00
The Railyard in Rouen, France

"KLAUS, YOU HAVE done a magnificent job. I can't believe how you managed to coordinate the building of a thousand *Drachenspringteufel* much less getting the *Feuerdrachen* installed. Where have you put them all," Count Voronstov asked?

"Alexis, the imprimatur of Göring can work wonders, and enough of the regular army and our arms manufacturers are still happy to help a von Stulpnagel. Not all are happy with the Nazi party, yet none wish to see Germany defeated. Combine that with your simple and effective design and the Fire Drake jack-in-a-box is a reality. We still need another three hundred and with the competition for materials and workmen on those last three hundred will probably take longer than the first nine hundred," the major replied. "We have two hundred and fifty of them cached here in Rouen, four hundred more in Amiens, and two hundred and fifty in Calais. I am worried about the ones in Calais as they are close enough to the sea to be in range of naval guns, however that is the most likely site for the invasion. The others can be shipped by train, barge, or even trucks if necessary and delivered to wherever we need them."

Count Voronstov was beaming, "Well done sir. They should make you a colonel at least."

"I doubt that will happen, but thank you for the compliment Herr Graf. We still need to get more of the units under cover. We've been storing the units in various hiding places, disued train tunnels or a copse of trees and using camouflage netting to hide them. We cut new roads to the old roads during the night, then cover the new roads with brush and haystacks before daylight. Per your suggestion some of the houses overlooking the water in Calais have been gutted, a *Springteufel* installed and a false front reconstructed similar to the original. However you said that the launch sites should not be more than ten meters above the beach and there are limits on the number of houses suitable. We have also dug into some of the lower sections of the bluffs and have installed a *Springteufel* and then covered up the front of the box. They can be deployed in less than four minutes if the crew is sharp."

"How goes the training," Voronstov asked?

"Let me show you. I've set up training centers at each town. The training is in the forest, where we have cleared an area and then set camouflage netting over the area. Even if the enemy takes aerial photos he might wonder that something is going on, but they won't know what is happening. The training area for Rouen is a few kilometers from here; my driver can have us there in ten minutes."

"Excellent Klaus, I am anxious to see it. All my years in exile are culminating with the advent of the Fire Drake. I only hope that the next three hundred can be used on the Eastern Front. Stalin's fortifications will be the next to crumble."

May 12, 1943, 12:47
The Fire Drake Training Site

Major von Stulpnagel and Count Voronstov stood ten meters from a large metal box. The box was some thirteen meters long and three and a half meters wide and high. A *stabswachtmeister* (an artillery sergeant major or warrant officer class1) was timing a group of eight young German *soldatin* advancing on the metal box under the direction of an *obergefreiter* (senior lance corporal). As the sergeant major shouted "go" the soldiers burst into rapid but, well ordered action. Two men opened the doors at each end of the box, two more pulled an ultraviolet projector on a tripod from the front and moved twenty meters upwind of the box. Both of them checked a windsock to make sure of the wind direction. The remaining soldiers quickly opened the roof which split longitudinally down the middle and sprang upright. Next the walls lowered flat to the ground and four of the six jumped to each corner of the base. Handles were inserted into apertures in the floor and under the command of the corporal the handles were turned causing screw jacks to level the platform. As they leveled the pad the remaining soldier and one of the projector operators extended a long telescoping metal tube with a wide slot in top another fifteen meters from the front of the box. Once the two reached the end they unfolded braces from the front and middle of the extension and drove attached spikes into the ground, anchoring the tube as well as providing a half meter of elevation at the end. As they finished the two joined the others who were folding down the Fire Drake's wings and securing them in place. Next the corporal extended a control box with a wire umbilical that attached to the missile. The corporal called the men to attention and made sure that they all saw that the main switch was in the off position. Two *obersoldats* (private first class) plugged wires into the solid rocket boosters attached to the rear of the missile. As soon as the wires were in place six of the soldiers ran and placed themselves behind the corporal with their backs to the Fire Drake and kneeling on the ground, hunched over and covering their ears with their hands. The projector operator turned his UV projector on and placed his eye to the low power telescope used to aim the projector. Sighting on a flag three hundred meters down range he raised his hand indicating that he had acquired his target and the corporal activated the main switch. The soldier shouted out the compass course of his target and the corporal repeated the course before turning a dial on the control box that would both start and align the missile's gyro compass. When a greenlight illuminated indicating that the sensors had acquired the ultraviolet illuminated target he uncovered the safety switch and stabbed it. The warrant officer clicked his stopwatch and shouted out the time; "three minutes and twenty-seven seconds."

Count Voronstov burst into applause while advancing toward the soldiers, "Well done gentlemen, well done indeed!"

The soldiers beamed in appreciation as the warrant officer came up to the men, "Very good. Anytime under four minutes is exceptional. Go ahead and power down the missile and repack it. One more drill under four minutes and you will be ready to man a real dragon."

Major von Stulpnagel approached the count, "Of course the practice model is not armed, the warhead is simply filled with sand to the same weight, the rocket boosters are dummies and the tanks for [1]*T-Stoff und Z-Stoff* are filled with water. I saw no reason to risk lives and materials by using a functioning missile."

"Quite right Klaus. I agree that an armed unit presents a palpable risk. I am impressed with the training. I particularly appreciate the caution shown by the corporal and his men to insure the master switch is off before arming the boosters. The few seconds lost are amply rewarded by a more secure and effective operation."

"Thank you Herr Graf. When the senior noncoms went over the procedure to arm and fire the dragon, they presented an excellent argument for the current procedure. They also felt that if anything went wrong and a premature firing caused an explosion and subsequent loss of personnel, the other operators would be reluctant to fire their own missiles. The range to the flag is of course much too short, however it is the best we can do and still disguise the operation."

"Thank you Klaus, I am much relieved to see that you have an excellent handle on this part of the operation. I will return to Peenemünde with one less worry. I'm flying to Berlin to rejoin Lt. General Erlich and we will continue back to base together. Have you had any problems? I was serious about you being promoted to Colonel; having more rank can smooth your operation," Voronstov said as the two returned to the major's car.

"Don't worry Alexis. Both General Erlich and the Reichsmarshal have made it clear that I am their direct representative. No one has questioned my authority although there are a few who wish to take my position. No one is such a fool though as to hinder the operation."

[1] *T-Stoff is highly concentrated hydrogen peroxide and Z-Stoff, calcium permanganate, is the actuating catalyst used in several German rocket designs. SMkIII*

Chapter 24:   North of nowhere

**Log of the *S.S. Caroline Maverick* and narratives from Ernst Dietsch,
Hiram Snowden, and Maxwell Larsen**

May 11, 1943
Thurso Bay, Scotland

"WELL MAX, I DON'T think you could find a more remote, out of the way location than this. It's not one of those mythical faerie towns where time never changes and it disappears when you leave? My grandmother told tales of a town in Germany when I was just a kinder back in Luckenbach. Do the locals know about the war? I mean number two, not number one." Ernst Dietsch complained as *LaDonna Johnson*'s tender brought them into Thurso's harbor.

"I'm pretty sure time doesn't actually stop. I am willing to bet that it seems to go a lot slower here than London or Glasgow. Thurso has a railroad, it's as far north as you can get in Scotland and Colonel Menzies assures me that the probability of an Axis spy in the area is below zero. I'll have to ask Hiram how a probability can go into negative numbers, make him use that math degree he got from Duke," Larsen replied.

"You mean Trinity College don't you? We can't let Hiram forget how old he is. When he went there it was still Trinity."

Max chuckled, "You really can't miss an opportunity to needle Hiram, can you?"

"Never ever. I'll ask your question when I get back to London and ask him if Trinity taught algebra with an abacus when he went there. How soon will you be finished on the *Satyr*? And why didn't you do this somewhere else," Dietsch asked? The two men were let off at the pier and continued walking into the town.

"We can't risk any hint of the *Manta* getting to the Germans. Those pictures in the files are the only ones not locked up in my personal safe at the shipyard, and at least two of the Mother Hens are in the outer office twenty four hours a day, even on holidays. I pick up the files after every meeting and they're either in my satchel at my hand or locked away in my office on the *LaDonna*. All communication coming out of Thurso is monitored by MI-5, whether phone, telegraph or mail and all the ships in the harbor and two land stations monitor for any radio traffic. This is the most secure port in the British Isles.

Last, everyone knows everyone and most are related. The Germans would have had to plant a sleeper family a hundred years ago to have anyone willing to spy for them.

I was able to house the *Satyr* in the [1]*Caroline Maverick* while in the lee of one of the outer isles without even being in port. No one will see her being refitted and when it comes time to disguise *Manta* we'll do that out in the isles also. And in answer to your first question, about a week from now, give or take a day."

"How are you going to paint that much out at sea? The *Manta* sits so low in the water that any wave action at all will ruin a paint job and she's too big to get in your floating dry dock."

"It's easy Ernst; the welders on the *Caroline* are cutting out all of the symbols from sheet steel and painting them there. All we have to do is align them and tack weld them to the boat. The symbols will be painted with that anechoic paint her hull is covered in, touch up at the weld points when they're finished welding and we're done in a half a day."

"Optimist." Dietsch grudgingly proclaimed. "Who was Caroline Maverick, or LaDonna Johnson for that matter? I can't believe these are all old girlfriends as none of your ships are named for any of the ladies you've been involved with since I've known you."

Larsen's countenance darkened momentarily, then with a shrug he turned to look Ernst directly in the eye. "Miss Johnson was a teacher who loaned me books and left me lessons that I could hide from my grandfather. I would sneak out once he was in a drunken stupor, retrieve the lessons and leave my homework for her to pick up. If it hadn't been for her I would have never known that there was a world outside the brush thickets of our little community, or any emotions besides hate and fear. Indeed you might say she inspired the *Manta* for she introduced me to Jules Verne and Conan Doyle and other adventure writers. Miss Johnson's favorite authors were definitely not those you would imagine of a spinster school teacher."

"And Caroline," Dietsch asked?

"A woman who was kind to me. She died when I was barely four years old." Max turned away and Ernst knew better than to ask any additional questions.

Over the years Dietsch had slowly gathered small bits and pieces of Larsen's life story. While he considered Max to be his best friend, he doubted that Maxwell Bledsoe Larsen had any legitimate claim to that name. Some great sadness or horror lay in Max's past. He had probably grown up somewhere on the Texas coast, he had no formal education, yet was one of the smartest and most widely read persons Ernst had ever known. If you could find a book on a subject that Max was not familiar with, he would devour it in a day, two at the most, and be ready to challenge the author on obscure points, or utilize the knowledge as if he had been using it his whole life. His constant fight to free subjugated people, especially Negroes hinted at some deep and personal past tragedy. Dietsch now had two new clues, bits he could exploit, but which he never would. Max would tell him when he wanted; until then Ernst would abide.

If anyone knew the full story it was Verna Deveraux. Ernst had once teased Max whether he was going to propose to the young Canadian doctor. A very somber Max replied, "Not until she knows all the truth and then we'll see if she will still have me." Verna apparently now knew the truth and the two were engaged, but the truth had left Verna more somber and quiet than any of her friends had ever seen. She also became much more protective of Max. Ernst felt that if ever a person lived who could protect himself, it was Maxwell Larsen, and Verna's response simply added more questions for Dietsch to ponder when he returned to London on the train.

[1]*S.S. Caroline Maverick is a fast, self-propelled floating dry dock using a unique catamaran style hull and owned by Larsen Shipyards. SMkIII*

May 14, 1943, 10:43
Saint Andrew's Golf Course

Four guards surrounded a large barn that normally held maintenance equipment. While each was at least thirty yards from the building they could still hear a periodic and disturbing shout of "*Heil Hitler*" exploding from twenty voices. Orders were given and acknowledged in German. "*Alle zusammen, wieder bitte,*" and again the Nazi salute rang out. "Please, once more and all together." *Oberst* (Colonel) Wilhelm Raeder (Major Ian MacDougal) commanded as his soldiers once again shouted out while raising their arms in salute. The colonel turned toward an older man, short with thinning hair and a normally cherubic face and in German asked, "Are we sufficiently menacing Wally?"

Wally, Waldo Yardley, Britain's home answer to Charlie Chaplin and Buster Keaton, was sitting in a director's chair and nodding up and down, "As a group you scare the water from me. I want to listen to all of you individually, especially Sergeant Brown, he needs to let his inner monster out a little more. Overall you're nearly ready. Colonel Raeder you and your men will be moving up to Thurso in Scotland tomorrow. We have a secure area and several instructors to help you while you wait. No one will speak English again until you return to England."

As the troop marched out, legs kicking in lockstep Waldo turned to two men in civilian dress who had been standing in the back of the barn. "General, what do you think?"

"Mr. Yardley, I am impressed, you've done an amazing job. My German was learned late and I don't consider myself fluent, but they are the picture of Hitler's elite." Brigadier General Hiram Snowden proclaimed.

"I quite concur and I have spent time in Germany portraying a native on more than one occasion before the war." Colonel Menzies added.

"A picture is exactly what we are building. I and several of my fellow actors and directors here in England are a little long in the tooth and gimpy to contribute on the battlefield, however we have studied German film and especially their propaganda films by Leni Riefenstahl and the posters and propaganda sent out by Goebbels' Ministry of Public Enlightenment and Propaganda. We are producing a picture that the Germans themselves expect to see, indeed desperately want to see of the Waffen SS. Combine this with the directives they think will come from Berlin, the time constraints imposed by the approach of the bombers, and you should have a willing cooperation from the locals. The instructors you have provided, Colonel Menzies, will assure that there are no gaffes by these brave men. Something as simple as looking in the wrong direction crossing a street, right left right instead of left right left, or answering a question asked in English. My job is to make sure that the Germans wherever you are going will want to believe in you."

"Have all the vehicles and equipment arrived," Snowden asked?

"Yes, five Zundapp KS 750s with sidecars and one without a sidecar. MG34 machine guns are mounted on the side cars. There is also a Type 166 Schwimmwagen, their amphibious patrol car with a MG42. I must tip my hat to whoever came up with the idea of more lights and louder exhaust pipes. Bloody brilliant! We have several artificers working on them and we have enough spare German equipment that we can add rotating beacons as well as twin headlights to compliment the standard shielded headlight."

Menzies had the next question, "Have they been able to practice with the vehicles? It wouldn't do to have someone stall or flip one of the damned things over."

"Yes, much to the ire of the head groundskeeper. They mostly work at night, with the shielded lights only, to avoid attention. There will be a field on a sheep farm near Thurso which should allow for any additional practice they might need," Yardley answered.

"Wally, I'm sure I speak for Colonel Menzies as well as myself when I say that you and your cohorts have done a magnificent job. It's a shame that one of the most important productions you've ever been involved with will never be filmed and will only be played once," Snowden said as he shook Yardley's hand.

May16, 1943, 03:00
Helsingor, Denmark (Under German occupation)

"Right on schedule. Regular as clockwork these last few weeks. Do you think they do it just to show off? Our ships won't traverse the strait except in daylight." The German soldier watching the narrowest part of the strait between occupied Denmark and neutral Sweden was referring to a Swedish patrol traversing the strait. Their navigation lights brightly lit as if daring the Germans to fire at them.

His officer answered, "Yes, they're demonstrating that this is their home waters and they have some advantages over us. Also I'm sure old Fabian Tamm, Sweden's naval chief is using it to restore some pride to his men as well as asserting Sweden's neutrality."

"Why don't we stop them," the soldier asked.

"Both Germany and the Swedes want to preserve the fiction that they are neutral. If it makes Tamm happy to risk his ships in the middle of the night running from the Baltic to the Kattegatt and back, then it is to Germany's benefit to let them preen. Besides, why antagonize Sweden. They still have the third largest Navy in the Baltic and we have enough on our plate with reverses in Russia and Africa."

"And the fact that the *Sverige* has eleven inch guns and we have mostly antiaircraft weapons and a few fifteen centimeter heavy howitzers on hand is of course not a factor in commands thinking," the soldier added.

The officer replied with a begrudging grin, "Of course not, I'm sure our artillerists would gladly take on the Swedish ships if ever required. For now though in honor of the strictest neutrality, we will watch Her Swedish Majesties Ships *Sverige* and *Remus* continue to make their nightly rounds and hope they don't run aground and block the channel."

Chapter 25: Meet U-2547

Logs of the *Satyr*, Caroline Maverick, and *Manta*

June 12, 1943 12:00
One mile SE of Stornoway off the Isle of Harris, Great Britain

THE *SATYR* AND CAROLINE MAVERICK were anchored in the lee of the Isle of Harris. One on either side of the *Manta*, whose mottled gray green hull resembled a rocky reef much more than a submarine. The illusion was heightened by several men walking on the wide flatly curved hull. A crane arm suspended over the sub from the Caroline and the occasional flash of a welder gave lie to the illusion as two large swastikas were attached to the wings and a designator number U-2547 was attached to the deck on both sides of the raised blister that contained *Manta*'s quad-40. "You're sure that number isn't in use Max?" Hiram Snowden asked as they watched the work from the *Caroline Maverick's* bridge wing.

"It's at least a thousand past any U-boat number known so far. Hopefully anyone trying to look it up will write off their inability to find it as proof that *Manta*'s a highly secret X-craft." Max turned from the railing and ushered Hiram in to the bridge. A tall, lean older man was talking on the ships phone, his long gray hair and beard were indications of age, but a spry walk as he replaced the handset and advanced toward Max and Hiram demonstrated that age had not yet penalized his activity.

"Max, the boys should be done welding in another fifteen to twenty minutes. Allow another fifteen minutes to daub on some of that rubberlike paint where we ground it off for the attachment points and your boat there will be ready to submerge and take her place in the Nazi navy. Paint that's activated and hardens in salt water, now that's a trick."

Max made quick introductions, "Hiram, let me introduce Captain Benjamin Crabtree, the best ship handler and jack of all trades it has been my pleasure to know. Ben, this is Brigadier General Hiram Snowden Esquire. Hiram's firm handled the patent application and award for that new lifeboat fall you built last year."

"Nice to finally meet you Hiram, even nicer since I started receiving those royalty checks. Now maybe I can retire early from this penny pinching miser taking up all the space on my bridge." Crabtree said as he shook Hiram's hand.

Max jumped in before Hiram could reply, "Retire early! You would have had to retire twenty years ago you old reprobate just to retire normally. Methuselah retired earlier than you."

"Ben, it's good to finally meet you." Hiram declared, "Max has bent my ear for years about you and your wife. Is it true that either of you can outshoot Max?"

"Outshoot Max? Well on a good day we might, on a bad day we'd whip his ass to a fare thee well. Janelle with her pistols and me with a rifle although the other way around Max might take us," the captain responded while one arm affectionately attempted to reach Max's far shoulder. "You're too damn big to hug, it's like petting a longhorn steer, only not as lovable."

"If anyone here is going to pet me on this ship, it will be Janelle, she'd at least be polite to me or the steer."

"Steers aren't nearly as grumpy as you Max; and they damn well don't send us to this forsaken cold ass port in a town where half the people don't even speak English, much less American."

"Scottish Gaelic is what most of the people speak. However let me assure you that if you say something rude in English or American the locals will understand and you'll have someone's stick up the side of your head before you know it," Max warned. "Let's get back to our mission, how many in our crews speak German?"

Crabtree started counting, pulling in fingers as he mentally reviewed his crew; "better question is how many could pass for Germans. I'm assuming that Ardison or Fau will not be chosen." Ben was referring to Ardison Mitchell, a large black man and the *Manta*'s first officer, and Chen Fau, second officer and navigator.

Max grinned at Crabtree, "A fairly safe and accurate assumption, although Ardison comes over the radio sounding like the announcer for the [1]Shadow only deeper and his German is much better than mine, he sounds like Prussian nobility."

"Max, I figure we have at least eight on the *Caroline* who can pass for Germans, two more if they don't have to say much more than "Yes Sir". Three more on the *Manta* and if I remember the crew correctly on the *LaDonna* maybe five more. The Navy folk on board *LaDonna* are a cipher to me, I haven't met them yet. How many do you need and what jobs will be undermanned if you take them? Our ships don't have much in the realm of extraneous crew," Crabtree declared.

Max deliberated for a moment, "Five ratings and a boatswain to take over the ferry. The extra Boat Service soldiers can direct the scientists on board and guard the dock. Four more to help the twins interdict any Nazi troops that may be sent to intercept the scientists if the Germans smell a rat. That group shouldn't have any contact with locals so we can put the less Germanic individuals in it. I want two in the group who are good with explosives. I'll make up the packs they need to close the road. They'll just have to put them where they belong and connect the detonators. I understand that Lt. Jarvis has been trained as a saboteur and we know the twins have equal or better training so if we only have one of our men trained they should still be all right.

"As far as needed crew, *Caroline* will stay here in Thurso so you can strip her down to minimal crew needed to get her underway. *LaDonna* will be on the fringe of the action, fast as she is, she's still not a match for destroyers that will be screening *Manta*'s escape. We can take the four from her without hurting her ability to protect herself. Leave the Navy personnel on her. I've met them and I don't see any reason to use them for duty on shore. Their good sailors and fight the ship well, but our men have fought together on land and sea often enough that I see no reason to mess with the mix."

"All right Max, I'll write up a list matching personnel to tasks and also how that affects operation of the ships. *Manta*'s crew is fairly small and specialized so most of those probably should stay where they are."

"Thanks, Ben. I'll leave that to you, just copy me on what you decide." Max and Hiram moved from the ordered noise and industry of the bridge back out on to the bridge wing to watch the work and continue their conversation.

Max turned to Hiram, "Now comes the waiting and getting into position. I think we've gotten about all the help we can expect. I doubt that you, Osgood, or Menzies can get us much more than you have. SHAEF has gone out as far as we can hope for questionable return. Spreading the resources between the U.S. and Great Britain kept the price from being too high for any one player."

"Don't forget your own contribution Max. I know that other than supplying the guns and other weapons, Uncle Sam hasn't paid for the *LaDonna* or the *Manta* yet. Much less the cost of bringing the *Caroline* over here or any of your crew costs. Can Larsen Shipping or the yard afford all this," Hiram asked?

Max nodded slowly," Things will be a little tight for a while. You know my finances as well as I do. Some of your corporate lawyers are working with my staff to raise the margin on the shipping I've been providing. I was a bit more generous than I should have been when I first started negotiations. The accountants have the numbers to prove it and the War Board's already approved the raise. I never begrudge research and development. The design and engineering that Ernst and Vincent helped with will pay off in the long run and your patent experts believe some of the new patents will definitely bring in long term rewards. I can always fall back on our friends or just borrow the money from you for the duration. We have enough mutual interests and shared investments that our fortunes are fairly incestuous. Worse comes to worst I still have a bit laid aside."

Snowden laughed," don't borrow money from me or Ernst; Tom and Juan Miguel will give you better rates. I'm pretty sure I've never heard a Wall Street maven call finances incestuous, those asses probably can't spell it even if they practice it. You're right of course, our money is pretty well tangled together and now with the rest of you falling in love and getting married and having children I think we need to work out a more stable relationship. We've all discussed it off and on, and our fortunes have been intertwined as well as our lives. When Tom and Beryl's three children were kidnapped and only Reyes was saved it truly brought home just what our fortunes could cause for good and ill. Antonio and Victoria's death was the hardest time in my life. Retribution was not enough. We can't let that happen again."

Max was quiet and Hiram looked toward him in time to see him straightening a guard rail that had been warped by the confluence of memory and legendary strength. Somewhat embarrassed by this display of passion, Max looked out toward the sea for a moment. "Old friend, I agree we need to not only get our finances arranged, we need to lessen our footprints. Like the *Manta*, we need to be harder to see, reduce our notoriety, our more obvious wealth. We need to use that wealth not only to protect our children, but we need to train and guide them in using it for more than just ourselves. We've all seen or been the victims of man's greed and hatred. We've all benefited from mankind's love and charity, from knowledge and the wise use of it. Our lives have to represent more than a quest for ourselves, we owe it to mankind to strive for its' betterment and to fight oppression wherever we find it."

"Max, I concur with all you say. Ernst and I will start accelerating the process, move from theorizing to implementing. We have a long road ahead of us and it takes one step at a time. I suggest that our first step should be to the ward room for coffee. It's still too damn cold and damp for me to be happy. We stay out here talking and I'll get all maudlin and teary eyed and scaring the crew. Generals aren't supposed to be sad and worried. Right now we need to whip the Axis and stop the current oppressors."

"Amen Hiram, amen." The two turned toward the bridge and entered the ship.

[1]*The Shadow was a pulp fiction hero in a radio serial featuring a mysterious crime fighter, trained by Tibetan mystics and who had the power to "cloud men's minds". The announcer, spoken by actor Frank Readick Jr., was famed for his deep sinister voice and the opening phrase, "Who knows what evil lurks in the hearts of men? The Shadow knows." SMkIII*

Chapter 26: Pieces all in play

Log of the *Manta* and narratives from Maxwell Larsen and Vincent Fuller

August 15, 1943, 03:00
200 yards offshore of the beach on the island of Usedom on the German Baltic

SHROUDED SIGNALS WERE again exchanged. The beach that had already witnessed two previous clandestine intrusions was invaded once again. This time a British cockle was freed of lashings from the deck of a fifty foot long submarine. The small aluminum craft was unfolded from its collapsed state. A brief hiss as an inflatable collar puffed out around the rim of the hull, an addition added by artificers onboard the *Caroline Maverick*, enhancing the small boat's stability in the surf and guaranteeing that it wouldn't sink with its load of four men, weapons, and explosives. Oars were quickly put to use and the little craft was soon coasting to a stop on the sand of the beach. The four men jumped out and the various packs and canisters quickly placed beyond the reach of waves. One man, a head taller than the four crewmen took their place in the boat and as he shipped the oars two of the original occupants turned the craft around and helped launch it through the first few low waves and on to its return journey.

On shore the men shared the cargo and silently followed two slim figures up a tidal wash and into the obscurity of the dense forest. The outgoing tide erased their footprints and the shore was once again devoid of any human presence.

Offshore the small boat gained the sub and was quickly collapsed, the collar deflated and the cockle once again lashed in the lee of the entry hatch. The tall man gained the sub's interior and carefully closed the hatch. "She's tight, let's go." Vincent Fuller squatted and turned, unable to stand in the close confines of the sub's control area.

In the dim red light suffusing the cabin a man nearly as large as Vincent turned from his seat at the control station. His teeth flashed a large white greeting in a very dark face. "Vincent, good to see you, it has been too long. Grab a pew," he said while pointing to a cushioned seat next to him. Ardison Mitchell turned back to the controls, deftly submerging the remora and setting course for the *Manta*

"Ardison, you're a sight for sore eyes. How have you been?"

"Well my friend. Busy as a whore at Mardi Gras. I understand this circus is your doing. If I die in this charade I plan to haunt you and all your family."

Vincent finally squeezed through the confines and sat next to Ardison while scanning the instrument panel, his pilot's eyes quickly discerning course, depth, speed and in lieu of fuel gauges the linear meter showing battery reserve. "Haunt away as long as you promise to sing something cheerful to my family. Frankie says she prefers your singing to Bing Crosby."

A deep laugh came from Ardison, "Vincent, let go my leg. Nobody sings better than Bing. Your lovely wife is simply enamored by my good looks rather than my admittedly wonderful voice."

"Ah Ardison, your voice is eclipsed only by your good looks and modesty."

"Vince you speak truth! I just get prettier every day. Lord knows it's a burden, but I'll shoulder it, yes I will." Ardison's steady hands adjusted the course and then engaged the autopilot, a design of Vincent's that held the craft on course using a gyrocompass, pressure gauges for depth and an innovative magnetic bubble level keeping the sub aligned much as an aircraft pilot following a bank and turn indicator. "We'll be with the *Manta* in about an hour. There's some towels in that locker next to you and a bag of sandwiches." A thermos of coffee was opened and two mugs poured, the aroma of a very dark roast with chicory filling the close confines.

The two men occasionally interrupted their conversation, looking out the two forward ports filled with immensely thick and strong glass, armored on the exterior with strong bars of stainless steel preventing anything larger than a softball from damaging the ports. An occasional flash of phosphorescence was all that could be seen. The powerful lights that could be used when maneuvering loads were dark, speed was reduced to six knots to keep noise from signaling the sub's presence to any German ships in the area. The subs bulbous bow and brutish outline belied the speed it could produce. The pressure hull encompassed only the front third of the underwater tug. The aft two thirds was comprised of batteries and electric motors encased in shells filled with mineral oil. Air tanks and bladders under the fairing provided buoyancy control. The counter-rotating screws were inside a duct that could be swiveled for directional control and the prop blades adjusted for pitch. It was an underwater tug, dependent on its mother ship for power to recharge batteries, yet powerful in action.

An hour later Mitchell slowed the remora, turned up the amplifier for the hydrophone and then engaged the sonar depth sounder for a brief moment, the rotary display of the sounder flashed that the bottom was eighty feet below them and the depth gauge showed sixty feet above them. "This should be the area, right depth at least and both Max and Chen Fau went over current, tide and course for both in and return trips. *Manta* will have heard us and should send a signal." Two pings followed by one ping sounded both through the hull and the hydrophone. "They have us, two followed by one means forty five degrees to port from our track and they should be within three hundred yards." Ardison advanced the throttle slowly while coming toward his new course. He turned the red glow of lamps off so that only the instruments themselves showed by their luminous dials. Both men strained looking forward through the ports.

"There at eleven o'clock and a little low," Vincent said pointing toward a dim red flashing light in the murk.

"Got it," replied Mitchell. He corrected his direction and depth and was rewarded by a white light shining steadily above the red flasher. The remora slowed as it approached the lights, the dark gray-green mottled hull of the giant submarine was nearly invisible, the increasing glow of the white and red lamps revealed a tunnel to the right of the main hull where the starboard wing joined the pressure hull. The interior was white and funnel shaped, barely making way Ardison guided the remora into the tunnel, clamps rotated into sockets in the tug's fairing, locking it into the *Manta*. An annular ring descended and locked onto the hatch coaming, then a blast of air evacuated water from the space through check valves built into the coamings sides. As Ardison started shutting down systems a metallic knocking was heard on the hatch. "Ok Vince, you can open the hatch now, we're home."

"I like the VASI light set up, if you're too low do you get a steady red under the flashing red," Vincent asked?

"Yes, similar to a visual glide slope for a landing field. Max didn't bother with a double white signal if you're too high. Most of the time we dock when the *Manta*'s on the surface, we can't get too high."

Vincent spun the wheel and stepped back as the hatch was raised from outside, avoiding the pint or so of water that splashed to the deck. As he started to climb Max's hand appeared in front of him, Vincent reached up locked on and was suddenly pulled up through the hatch and subjected to a bear hug and back pounding. "Enough Max.

Damn let me breathe." He was deposited a few feet away from the hatch and greeted by a rare grin on Larsen's face.

Max turned and gave another un-needed assist to Ardison, "I thought I told you no hitch-hikers."

"I tried to leave him behind, but when he started to whimper and quiver his chin I couldn't help myself."

Vincent rejoined, "I may have whimpered, but I never chin quivered." He dropped his voice another impossible octave, "I did bat my eyes and Ardison swooned. I snuck in before he could recover."

"You promised not to tell, now no one will respect me ever again," Mitchell countered.

"Enough. I give up, I disrespect both of you and I'm sorry I started that. Welcome aboard Vincent. We need to start getting you ready for your part, show time in two days. It's time to prepare for Peenemünde." Max said as he headed for the hatch leading into the main hull.

Chapter 27: Circus acts

Narratives of Marie and Lysette Malois and
Lt. Robin Jarvis

08/15/1943, 06:00
An Abandoned Farm 12 Kilometers from Peenemünde

THREE EMPTY RATION CANS set up on a wooden crate, lit by a dim flashlight, and backed by a rick of moldy hay, were waiting for additional holes to be punched in them. Three rapid coughing sounds were heard as the cans jumped off the crate. "Not bad Willy, not bad at all," Lysette said from the opposite wall of the barn.

"Can I get down now?" Corporal Bill McCabe asked as he hung upside down from a rafter. His feet were in a loop of rope that extended over the beam, then back down to wrap in a spiral around both legs, his torso, and then his right arm to be clenched in his right fist. Bill's left hand held Vincent Fullers silenced .22 Colt Woodsman with which he had once again successfully vanquished the trio of ration cans.

"Mai ouis," answered La Petite Souris. "You appear to be most formidable my young friend. Ration cans will be shivering in terror at your approach. Hopefully all the ration cans will have evacuated before we go in tomorrow night."

"I would make a very rude gesture if my hands weren't so full and the memory of Sister Agnes' ruler so close," said McCabe as he eased his grip on the rope and used the friction of the rope around his body to lower himself to the floor. He immediately policed the shells ejected by the gun.

"If you take a piece of pipe or wood dowel that's about an inch and a half thick and wedge it in the shafts framework you can take a couple of turns around it with your rope, you can use that to belay your descent rather than your leg. I am worrying you'll get a loop around your neck and kill yourself," said Able Seaman Aloysius O'Flannery from his observation spot in the loft. "Happy I'd be to show you how to rig it."

"Good idea Aloysius. You can show Willy how to set it up down below. Sun's coming up and we need to disappear," answered Lysette as she collected the cans. "Willy there may be a future for you in the circus after the war. That really is impressive shooting. I can get you together with the Toepperweins when you get back home."

"Who are the Toepperweins? I've got the rope, were you going to use the broom?"

Lysette grabbed the broom from next to the trapdoor, "I'll sweep, everyone down below so I can erase our tracks. Adolph and Elizabeth Toepperwein are a husband and wife team of trick shots. They do some phenomenal demonstrations. Lord help anyone foolish enough to challenge Plinky at skeet. They travel all over the country demonstrating for Winchester. I've met Ad and Plinky a few times when they gave lessons at the Ranch school."

"Somehow the thought of hanging upside down and plinking at tin cans for a bunch of school kids or Boy Scouts does not really grab me as future employment," McCabe responded as he followed Brodeur and O'Flannery down the ladder to the lair below.

Lysette finished sweeping and followed her cohorts below. The trap door eased down, the old wagon following, and soon the only things moving were floating dust motes picked out by sunlight entering through gaps in the eastern wall.

In the basement the four were joined by Marie, Lt. Jarvis, Arthur Dietel AB, Rajko Baltzar AB, and Boatswain Gerard Arcenaux. The four sailors were members of an elite crew employed for Larsen Shipping's less well known and more martial endeavors. All had been victims of repressive governments, ethnic rancor, or racial injustice and they welcomed any chance to strike a blow for freedom. Many strange paths had led them to join Max in his quest towards freedom for all.

Chapter 28: Subterfuge

Log and notes from OSS records and narrative of Brigadier General Hiram Snowden

08/16/1943, 05:30
Col. Osgood's Office

SGT. FUTCH CAME IN with a tray holding a large vacuum bottle of coffee and service for four. "Do you ever leave," Hiram Snowden asked?

"Actually I rarely do. I talked the master sergeant in charge of the building into designating an office down the hall as my confidential file room and then the sweet man had some of his guards move a bed and wardrobe into it. That and a rather lavish WC that is attached give me the best and most private room I've had since I joined the service. The files are safe and I have a bathroom the likes of which few people back home in Arkansas have ever dreamed. The previous occupant was apparently a rather flamboyant poofter as the Brits say and could apparently well afford to remodel the office at his own expense."

"He must be rather put out to have lost his office. Where is he now?"

"According to Leftenant Markham the gentleman was one of the first to volunteer and died fighting a protective guard action during Dunkirk."

Snowden shook his head, "sorry to hear that. The battlefield is the great equalizer. Thanks for the coffee Sergeant."

Sgt. Futch left the room as Col. Osgood and Col. Menzies entered. "Colonel Brewster will be here in a minute or two. He was collecting the latest intercepts and any new traffic from our people," Col. Osgood told Hiram.

Hiram looked up from where he was pouring coffee into several cups. "Good to hear. Stewart do you think we've blown enough smoke up the Abwher's skirts to get the response we want?"

"Yes Hiram, I do. Between leaks through [1]Garbo, the [2]Red Orchestra in Germany and Switzerland, and a few well-choreographed and egregious slips of the lip in certain pubs, we should have the Huns scurrying about getting plans and their personnel ready to vacate Peenemünde."

"You haven't overdone it I hope. Be a shame for them to evacuate before we get there."

"No General, our man [3]Griffin says they think they have a few more days than they actually will. We should be able to combine maximum preparation with instant confusion and acrimony to get our timing right."

"Griffin is this Polish scientist who feeds you data? You're sure of him?"

"Griffin has been reporting on the German rocket experiments almost from their start. I have the utmost confidence in him. The Polish intelligence service was one of the premier services before the war. Their misfortune was being tied to a moribund government and ineffectual legislative process left from the Sanacja movement that guaranteed political ineptitude and inaction."

Menzies continued, "Group Captain Alan Filson will be joining us shortly. He is Air Marshall Harris' representative and will be coordinating the bombing raid with us here. Hopefully we can make sure our people are out of range before the bombing starts."

"How many aircraft are they calling for," Hiram asked.

"I believe it will be some six hundred bombers, which should come out to somewhere near eighteen hundred ton of bombs. Quite outside the efforts of your group in Peenemünde, Griffin's reports and what we've learned of their new rockets have convinced the powers that be to end Peenemünde's effectiveness for once and all."

"Good Lord, six hundred bombers should do it. I pray that our subterfuge doesn't increase their losses," Osgood said.

"Let's hope they continue to expect the raid three or four days from now instead of tomorrow night." Hiram added.

"We just need to be sure that our "warning from Berlin" is cut off before the base commander can question it. The disinformation we leaked of the new glide bombs that can home on an operating transmitter seems to have decreased some of the extraneous radio chatter along our bombers routes into Germany. Peenemünde's operators will hopefully exercise undue caution accordingly. If by chance the aerial photos post raid show some transmission antennas down we can resume a whisper campaign about the success of Albert's fictitious glide bombs," Menzies said.

"Max plans to unleash a small pod with a powerful transmitter as a decoy against our supposed secret weapon. Not only will the radio noise alert us to the start of our commando raid, it will also render moot any Nazi attempt to transmit or receive in the area, a case of rather studied serendipity." Snowden said. "Unfortunately we won't be able to contact *Manta* until they shut down and blow up the decoy."

"Whether it goes off perfectly or not at all the bombers will strike. The operations window is very narrow. Let us hope they can get everything we want through it," Menzies concluded.

[1] *Garbo was the code name for Juan Pujol Garcia, who became one of the most effective double agents working for the Allies during WW2. He was instrumental in deceiving the Nazi High Command on the landing site for D-Day. SMkIII*

[2] *The Red Orchestra was a group of Russian clandestine radio operators in Germany. Many were rounded up and executed in 1941. Some continued to act through 1943 and the group continued on as Red Orchestra 3 in Switzerland through the end of the war. SMkIII*

[3] *Griffin (Paul Rosabud) was a German scientist who spied on the German rocket program for the British. Menzies portrayed him as a Polish scientist to the OSS as an additional layer of protection for his agent. SMkIII*

Chapter 29:   August 17, 1943

Combined Reports of Lt. R. Jarvis, L. Malois, Maj. I. McDougal, V. Fuller, M. Larsen, and Log of the *Manta*

08/17/1943, 03:00
The roof of the Plans Repository:

LA PETITE SOURIS and Cpl. McCabe were standing on the roof of the generator building, just a few feet from the wall of the repository. Once again Susan was checking their back trail and once again they had penetrated the base without alarm and Lysette had made her escape back toward the barn. "Now for the easy part," Susan said as she pointed toward the parapet of the repository a few feet higher and with a three foot gap between the walls of the two buildings.

"I'm all for easy," McCabe panted quietly while looking down the side of the building they had just scaled. "Ladies first," he whispered with a flourish toward the adjacent roof so gallant that even Errol Flynn would have approved.

Susan gave a low laugh then vaulted up and out, catching her hands on top of the parapet and continuing into a forward roll that finished with her standing on the repository roof while a silent pirouette left her facing McCabe. Brodeur returned McCabe's gallant gesture with an extravagant curtsy. Gathering his legs under him and swinging his arms, Bill gave a mighty leap propelling most of his body onto the repository roof, but catching his shins just below his knees on the parapet, causing him to face-plant into the weathered tar of the roof and causing much more noise than Susan expected. Rushing forward the diminutive burglar grabbed McCabe's legs and silently pulled them onto the roof. "Are you all right?" She whispered while keeping an eye on the roof scuttle.

McCabe rolled onto his back, pulled the silenced .22 from his shoulder holster and aimed it toward the scuttle. "Knocked the wind out," he gasped while taking great slow breaths of air. "All right in a minute. Do you think they heard?"

"We'll know soon enough," Susan replied. She went to the scuttle and put her ear against it. Listening for several minutes while the young airman recovered, first sitting up and then rolling onto his knees. "I think we're good. A gramophone is playing rather loudly, otherwise it's quiet," Susan finally said. "Don't do that again. Think about what you are doing my young friend."

"That's the problem. I thought about missing and falling three stories and landing on all the piping down below. Your style looked much too difficult so I felt just jumping as hard as possible would work better. Remind me to practice leaping onto roofs before ever trying that again."

"And I will promise not to show off again. Hook into their phone and radio system and let's get under the tarp before it gets light."

"Yes Ma'am, "said Bill as he scurried to the circuit box on the roof and began unfastening the cover.

16:42:
The Baltic near Peenemünde:

"PREPARE TO DROP PODS two and three." echoed the intercom throughout the *Manta* and the three manned pods in tow behind. "Fau, you agree?" Max and Chen Fau, the two best navigators on board were bent over a backlit glass topped table on which a large scale chart of the waters within 20 nautical miles of Peenemünde was taped.

"Yes, we're eight point four nautical miles northeast of the harbor entrance to Peenemünde and one nautical mile northwest of *Griefswalder Oie*. Shallow enough they can hug the bottom and deep enough that no ship in the area can foul them." Fau lay down the dividers and parallel rule he had been using. "You're sure these new anchors will hold? They seem awfully light."

"The bottom is good firm sand, just what they were designed for. I was surprised when I read the test results from the Naval office so I called one of the engineers that I knew and he said the Danforth anchor is all it's cracked up to be. They were looking for something light, safe and simple and they came out on top of the competition. As long as we get the pods headed into the little bit of current and they leave enough scope between the front and rear anchors it shouldn't be a problem. Add that the pods will be lying on the bottom and they shouldn't move at all," Max replied.

"You're the boss, captain sir, on your head so be it," Chen Fau said while giving an officious looking bow to Larsen.

The officious bow was met by an upraised finger from Max and a nervous chuckle or three from Vincent Fuller, Ardison Mitchell, and Maj. Ian McDougal. Max took the mic for the intercom, "Pods two and three are you ready?'

"Pod three ready Captain," came from one of the two crewmen aboard the third pod.

"Pod two ready Sir," echoed from the second pod.

Max addressed his helmsman, "All ahead creep slow, maintain course."

The helmsman repeated the order and pressed the lowest of a row of double switches just above a double red light marking all stop on his control panel. The helmsman was seated at a station more resembling an aircraft cockpit than a ships helm, facing forward and on the boats centerline. The controls were integrated into a wheel on a column and rudder pedals on the floor. The *Manta's* controls mimicked an aircraft's controls. Powered hydraulics moved the control surfaces allowing one man to control the boat in all aspects. Two green lights appeared as the red lights went out, denoting that both of the screws were going forward at the slowest possible speed.

"Pod three deploy aft anchor now." Max was keeping an eye on course and speed and the repeaters showing angle for the various control surfaces.

"Pod three anchor deployed, releasing line," the rear most pod in the string answered. "Three hundred feet out. Setting anchor now." The aft pod locked the wire rope spooling off a hydraulically powered drum between the pressure hull and the ferro-cement fairing. "Strain gauge showing in the green."

"Pod three drop tow and release forward anchor now," Max ordered.

"Dropping tow, forward anchor away, now. " The intercom went dead as the tow umbilical to pod three was detached.

"Clean separation Captain," the talker at the signal board reported to Max. A single tone sounded over the hydrophone, "Pod three reports maneuver successful, Captain."

A relieved sigh went through the *Manta's* bridge. Max looked away from the instruments toward the small group of officers trying to stay out of the way, "Oh yee of little faith. The pod will be setting the forward anchor by reeling in on the aft line. They should signal right about now." Max looked at the ships clock on the bulkhead above the helm. He waited a minute, "Riiight about now."

Twenty seconds later his prognostication was rewarded with a second single ping. "Pod three anchored Captain," came the redundant confirmation from the talker.

This time no one on the bridge could refrain from a simultaneous release of air held too long in apprehension. Grins were shared all around. "Your faith appeared to be starting to sweat a bit there Captain," Ardison observed and Max just smiled and shook his head.

In a more relaxed manner than the previous action, "Pod two prepare to deploy anchor," went out over the intercom and the action was repeated.

18:10:
The Island of Usedom on the road to Peenemünde
between Karlshagen and Trasseheide
A HAND SNAKED OUT of a small culvert that ran underneath the road. Grasping the edge the hand was followed by Rajko Baltzar. Dressed all in black, including a knit cap and face paint he became just another shadow as he pulled a string of explosives through the culvert until its entire length was mined. A length of duplex wire attached to a detonator was rolled out as Baltzar backed into the trees that bordered both sides of the road. "The culvert is ready," he said to Lt. Robin Jarvis who was collecting different runs of wire as they were brought into her hide between the forest and the coast line.

"Got it. Just two more to go," she said while adding the new wires to a board with several different sets of contacts, all fed through a rotary switch that had yet to be connected to a German field telephone generator.

"East forest," Marie said as she and Aloysius O'Flannery crawled into the hide and extended their wire reel to Jarvis. They had planted explosives on fifteen large trees along a hundred yard stretch of forest on one side of the road. Burlap bags of gravel, camouflaged with pine branches, were covering the explosive, providing that the charge's force would be directed into the tree while also providing shrapnel that would spray the road area. A matching set of explosives had already been installed along the west side of the road by Lysette and Arthur Dietel, after which the two had moved on towards Karlshagen, north towards Peenemünde. "We passed Gerard on the way back, he should be through setting the charges for the telephone and telegraph services in a few minutes," Marie added as they watched Jarvis add their wires to her board.

"Very good, if any troops are sent to Peenemünde they should come from Wolgast or Molschow and this is the only road that connects them with the airfield." Jarvis finished checking and tightening her terminals.

19:08
A [1]F4 1000ft AGL, 60 miles south of Peenemünde

The F4 long range reconnaissance aircraft had been modified to carry some special radio equipment. Using a directional antennae similar to a radar antennae it first transmitted a message to Peenemünde. The message played out using a carefully made punch tape designed to mimic the hand of a Wehrmacht operator often tasked with important traffic. Once the message was acknowledged the plane turned toward Wehrmacht HQ. As soon as the operator heard the static roar of the floating beacon deployed by the *Manta* to jam radio traffic around Peenemünde he started a second tape mimicking a Peenemünde operator and sent off a message to the German HQ. The message artfully stopped mid-word and the operator turned off his radio to guarantee no further transmission would betray the OSS fabrication. The pilot jettisoned the directional antennae and headed back to England, soon too high and too fast to worry about interception by German forces.

[1]*The F4/F5 was a modified P-38 fighter, sometimes unarmed and unarmored with an extended nose that could carry aerial cameras and their operator, or in this case specialized radio equipment. With external tanks these craft had a range exceeding 2200 miles. SMkIII*

19:12
Peenemünde Base Headquarters
Office of Oberst Herman Krupp, Base Commander

"Colonel Krupp, urgent message from Berlin," shouted a young lieutenant bursting into the colonel's office. "The British bombing raid is set for tonight!"

"What, we were supposed to have several days more time to prepare. Are you sure, Lieutenant?" The Colonel was sitting at his desk, his tunic undone and boots off going over some of the interminable paperwork until the lieutenant's abrupt entry.

The young communication officer waved the radio telegraphy report at his commanding officer. This was the most urgent dispatch to ever pass through the lieutenant's office and he was taking full advantage of the excitement. "Yes sir, it came in from the right direction on the correct frequency. Un-coded due to the urgency of the message. Here Sir," he said as he handed the missive to his commander.

"Have you confirmed it?"

"I tried to sir, my operator confirmed it was a HQ operator's hand, but if you will look at the last paragraph it says that the English have developed a glide bomb that automatically homes in on any transmitter. They say to load our German scientists into the Junker 52s and send them under radio silence to Berlin immediately. Plans and the foreign scientists will be loaded onto trucks and embarked on the ferry. Transport will meet them at the port and we are to follow a *Standartenfuhrer* Wilhelm Raeder's orders."

"What transport? I've no report of any large ship in port. Lieutenant get me some confirmation now," Krupp bellowed.

"I don't know about the transport sir. Headquarters has gone off the air and all radio traffic is being jammed by a new radio source in the middle of the bay."

Just then there was a knock on the door and the captain of the guard contingent entered, "Sir, a large *untersee* boat has just surfaced in the bay and is entering our harbor. All radio traffic is being jammed and our phone and telegraph lines to the mainland have gone out. The boat is nothing like any of us have ever seen."

Colonel Krupp decided it was time for action and quickly started issuing orders. "Captain, get to the port and find out what is happening. Lieutenant, get Major Eichenroht in here as quick as you can and contact the airfield, Have them ready the Ju 52's for immediate flight. The internal phones are still working, yes?"

"Yes, sir. The base phones are still working. With your leave sir," the captain answered as he headed for the door at a near sprint. The lieutenant followed, slowed only by his desire to salute and giving that up as a waste of time.

The colonel picked up a base phone, "alert the gunnery officer and have him contact me soonest," he barked at the switchboard operator. While waiting he once again read through the directive, *"who is this SS colonel? Damn Himmler has his fingers everywhere and this standartenfuhrer has probably had his nose up Himmler's ass forever. Why couldn't they stay on the air long enough to confirm and what's happened to the equally damned phones? Abwehr screws up the intelligence and now all the shit falls on us and I'll be buried under all of it."*

Colonel Krupp's reverie was interrupted by the entrance of Major Lyle Eichenroht. "Major, I need you to act with all due haste. Apparently the British are bombing tonight instead of next week. Have your men round up all of our German scientists and load them aboard the Ju 52's and get them headed to Berlin. The foreign scientists and their families are to be loaded onto trucks along with the plans from the repository and sent to the ferry. And Major, do me an immense favor and make sure [1]Magnus von Braun is onboard the first plane out. I don't want his big brother, that prima donna of an SS want-to-be, crying to Himmler that we didn't save his little brother. Thank God that Wehrner, General Ehrlich, and Voronstov are already in Berlin."

"Yes, sir, Colonel. I'll be sure baby brother is safe.

[1]*Magnus von Braun was an organic chemist and younger brother to Wehrner von Braun. Magnus worked on both fuels and guidance systems in the German rocket program. SMkIII*

Chapter 30: Chutzpah and charades

**Log of the *Manta* and reports from Max Larsen and
Vincent Fuller**

August 17, 1943 19:21
Peenemünde Harbor

THE PEOPLE OF PEENEMÜNDE were not easily impressed. For years
they had been witness to the forefront of aeronautical technology.
Experimental jet and rocket aircraft had filled the local skies. Rockets
had screamed toward the sea and guided missiles of various design
had flown and exploded in the area. But now a leviathan had erupted
onto the surface of the port unlike anything even the most imaginative
of inhabitants had dreamed. The *Manta* announced its arrival with
siren and horn blasting, German naval battle flag flying as the blister
on top opened revealing the lethal quad-40 cannon raising up and
swiveling like a hunter searching for game. A hatch opened on top and
a squad of Waffen SS in mottled camouflage battle dress appeared.
Bristling with Schmeisser MP40 machine pistols or MG42 machine
guns, and every man weighted with multiple grenades they were a
small, but formidable force. Behind them stalked a colonel, a very large
and brutish Kriegsmarine captain, and a tall civilian dressed in a black
leather overcoat and slouch hat pulled low over his eyes. The last man
reeked of the *Geheime Staatspolize*i, Himmler's dreaded secret police.
 As the giant submarine nosed into the dock with the greatest
depth a second sub surfaced headed into the adjacent dock. This
submarine was long and thin and as it neared the dock the forward
part of the sub opened as if it intended to swallow the pier. A hatch
opened in the revealed pressure hull coinciding with an immense roar
as multiple engines started and revved loudly. A section of the hatch
deployed forming a ramp onto the pier and the cacophony increased
as a half dozen motorcycles roared onto the dock followed by an
amphibious staff car, a *schwimmwagen*. All the vehicles were manned
by more Waffen soldiers and had numerous lights flashing as they
proceeded in formation to the landing next to the giant submarine.
Two crewmen followed the mass of noise up the ramp where one of
them opened a small hatch and set some controls then swiftly closed
the compartment and leapt to the dock as the ramp lowered and the
main hatch closed. The shell closed restoring the pod to its initial

streamlined configuration and the entire submarine slowly backed and submerged until it was out of sight.

By now the port captain had made it to the main dock as well as the sergeant of the small guard contingent normally deployed. They both offered salute to the colonel who wasted no time in returning their salute with a loud "*Heil Hitler*" which was immediately robustly echoed by all the Waffen soldiers. The local guards returned a surprised and feeble echo of their own while staring at the immense ship that had so surprised them.

The colonel started barking orders, "Sergeant, deploy your men to the perimeter of the port, no one either civilian or military is to be allowed in the area without the express consent of myself or U-2547's captain. Port Captain," he said as he turned to the nervous official, "have everyone removed from the ferry. My men and sailors will take over its operation until we leave. No one is to approach either ship on pain of death. My men have orders to shoot to kill anyone unauthorized to approach. None of your men have been authorized and this includes you two. Am I understood?"

The sergeant and port captain immediately raced each other in agreeing to the order.

The Colonel unbent a little at this show of cooperation, "I have orders from Reichsfuhrer Himmler himself to secure the plans and foreign scientists from our experimental base here. All communications out of Peenemünde have been severed until we have accomplished our orders. Your radios will not work and this is for your own good. Is there any official from the town here?"

The bewildered port official looked around, but the only city officials he saw were two local police officers who had come to see what was happening. The port captain pointed them out and the colonel beckoned to the two men. As the two briefly hesitated the colonel snapped his fingers and two of his men swiftly marched to the policemen and ordered them to report to the colonel.

The two hurried forward, fear growing on their faces as they approached. Their apprehension was not helped by the sinister scar on the left side of the colonel's face, the obvious contempt of the brutish submarine captain for the port and its inhabitants, and the cold indifference and pale menace of the black clothed Gestapo agent. Col. Raeder addressed the apprehensive policemen, "You will go immediately to your superior and clear the streets between here and the base. I am bringing important cargo here from the base and I don't want a car, truck, cart, or person in the way. Any traffic on the road during my return will be considered a hindrance and my men will blast it out of the way. Go now, run, your life depends on this," the colonel ordered while pointing to the senior of the two officers. The frightened policeman broke into a run as the officer turned to the second. "Assist the port guards in securing the harbor. Now! Go," he bellowed though he was only talking to the second policeman's back as the terrified man ran to the port guards.

Soon all the motorcycles were manned, the men in the sidecars racking their machine guns assuring themselves of the weapons readiness and the colonel and Gestapo agent were in the back seat of the amphibious staff car as a driver and guard manned the front. Lights flashing, sirens wailing, and the thunder of unbridled exhaust reverberating off the streets and buildings the convoy headed for the airbase test site.

Meanwhile a small contingent of sailors and Waffen SS took over the ferry. A single guard was placed at the gangway to the U-2547 and one more at the entrance ramp to the ferry, their authority menacingly reinforced by the ever watchful gun emplacement of the *Manta*'s slowly rotating quad-40.

19:32

As the port quieted the only action seen was the ordered mill of soldiers and sailors preparing the ferry for departure. The Kriegsmarine captain had retreated to a small bridge deck, barely a wrinkle on the brow of the giant submarine, where he was joined by an officer and a white coated steward serving steaming mugs of coffee to the two officers. Speaking in German the two officers were quietly conversing. "So far so good. Is Ardison on his way," Max asked?

He was answered by his junior officer Lars Anderson, who though a chief on board the *Manta*, was flaunting his blonde Nordic good looks as U-2547's second officer. "Yes Max, he should be releasing the pod in the channel those two schnellbootes will need to traverse if they are to interfere with our op. We had more weight allowance available in the pod than we originally planned so there is now two thousand pounds of high explosive awaiting our acoustic signal."

"That should put them out of business when we leave. Hopefully they won't deploy before our departure. Looks like the boys have the ferry armed and ready." Max declared while making a curt gesture towards the ferry. On board the ferry, exhaust was coming from the stacks as the engines were fired. On the bridge wings two MG42 machine guns had been deployed on the bulwarks.

The intercom chimed and Lars scooped up the handset. "Sonar reports remora enroute to the pickup point. I hope there's no trouble getting the twins and their crew embarked," Anderson said as he hung up the interphone. A grim nod was Larsen's only reply.

On board the remora Ardison had finished placing the pod in the channel and had disconnected from the service socket in its back. The two arms that were deployed to attach to the pod and which also allowed the remora to control the pods hydraulic buoyancy controls were retracting into the bow of the submersible tug. Ardison left the harbor, carefully avoiding the islets of *Peenemünder Haken, Struck und Ruden*. The remora headed for the Baltic and the waters just east of *Karlshagen* to rendezvous with the team interdicting any German troops that might reinforce the guards at the base.

Chapter 31:   Audacity and fear

Log of the *Manta* and reports from Lysette Malois,
Max Larsen, and Vincent Fuller

August 17, 1943 19:41
Peenemünde Base Headquarters

COLONEL KRUPP HAD never seen as lethal a group of soldiers as those now surrounding him. Their attention turned outward as if guarding the SS colonel and the intimidating Gestapo agent from Krupp's own soldiers. Krupp had been an administrative officer his entire career, too young for World War 1 and his Krupp name gaining him advancement not in accordance to his abilities, he was overwhelmed by the deadly efficiency presented by the Waffen SS troops. His discerning eye told him that the ribbons present on the SS colonel's tunic denoted combat experience and ability far beyond his own. The dark unadorned simplicity of the Gestapo agent's clothing bespoke of someone without need for the pretension so often displayed by Himmler's henchmen. The sound of a Junkers 52, its triple motors straining as it left the field allowed him to demonstrate his own efficiency. "Colonel Raeder, the last of our German scientists are taking off even now," he said while pointing to the southbound aircraft.

Colonel Raeder glanced at his wristwatch before a grudging "well done" escaped his throat. "Krupp, how long till the plans are on board the trucks?"

"Colonel, we were originally told that we would have several more days to prepare. My men have been putting them into boxes as quickly as possible."

A grim deep voice emanated from the tall sinister Gestapo agent, "Perhaps I can speed their task. I will select those plans best capable of aiding the fatherland while emphasizing the haste necessitated by eminent attack."

Colonel Krupp tried to hide a small shiver. The voice had sounded to him like the deepest organ note of a funeral dirge. "Herr...," Krupp hesitated as he realized he had no idea who the man was, his name, rank, or even place in the operation. All he had as a guide was the deference Colonel Raeder had displayed toward the man. An occasional quiet word passed between the two and this was the first time Krupp had been addressed by the somber giant.

Vincent Fuller turned to Col. Raeder and said, "I will go to the repository now. Make sure we make contact with the other men we have deployed." Vincent's indifference to Col. Krupp was beyond disdain. Krupp was of no more import than an insect beneath the Gestapo agents boot.

Col. Raeder signaled his men and four broke off, surrounded the agent and headed for the repository at a brisk walk for the agent and a slow jog for the soldiers.

The Schwimmwagen roared to life as its driver started up the machine and one soldier leapt to the seat of a Zundapp motorcycle with side car and the two headed at breakneck speed for the main gate. "They will make contact with some of my commandos who are interdicting the road beyond *Karlshagen*. I will allow no interference with the reichsfuhrer's wishes. Now Krupp take me to the scientists' barracks. We must be sure their families come with them or we could lose our hold on their services."

Krupp managed a weak "Yes Sir" acquiescing command to his brother officer while striving to keep up with the rapid trot of the SS officer and his commandos.

19:52
The road near *Karlshagen*:

The German staff car and its attendant motorcycle slowed as they saw a small pine tree half blocking the road. They came to a complete stop as two black clad figures stepped out of the trees and waved them down. Lysette and Art Dietel exchanged a few words with the two SOE men. Turning over the amphibious car to Lysette, the two rolled in the dirt on the side of the road, fired a few careful rounds into the sidecar, then mounted the motorcycle and roared back down the road with the soldier in the sidecar shooting the MG34 machine gun randomly into the woods.

With Lysette behind the wheel the sturdy car turned and ran back toward the ambush site. Lysette closed the exhaust cutout which had previously augmented the cars presence and the loud roar was muted to a normal tone. "This should get us out to meet Ardison once we set off the explosives."

"I hope it's a bit more seaworthy than it looks. I doubt if this thing was designed for the open ocean." Dietel said.

"*Schwimmwagens* have a pretty good rep; guess we'll find out. Worse comes to worse we have those small rafts you brought in and the remora can come into fairly shallow water." Malois responded.

19:58
German barracks in Molschow:

"Captain Moeller, Major Frerschaften sent a courier from Wolgast, they are also unable to reach Peenemünde by phone." reported Igor Moeller's sergeant as he came into his officer's quarters.

"Did the major say anything about this damn noise on the radio?" was Moeller's curt response.

"No sir. He says that his people are trying to reach headquarters and the radio shack puts the disturbance in the bay outside Peenemünde's harbor. Major Frerschaften has sent a courier south towards Anklam in an attempt to get outside the disturbance and find a radio with which to contact headquarters. Sir, he wants you to take your men to the base there and see if anything is wrong. The major has already left with a platoon from Wolgast and they should be ahead of you already.

"Very well, have my men get ready, I'll go with them and we'll take one truck and the [1]Puma. We may be able to catch up to the Wolgast folk before Peenemünde."

"Yes Sir," the sergeant said as he hurried out to alert the soldiers.

[1]*The Puma (or Sd. Kfz. 234) is a German armored car or reconnaissance vehicle with a top road speed of 56 mph. Weighing over 12 tons and with 8 wheels it was designed with an air-cooled diesel engine which helped its success both in the North African desert and the cold winter steppes of Russia. It has both a 2"cannon in a turret and a 0.3" MG34 or MG42 machine gun. Technically very advanced for their time these machines influenced future reconnaissance vehicle design for decades. SMkIII*

Chapter 32:   Audacity doubles down

Narrative of Vincent Fuller

08/17/1943, 20:15
Plans Repository, Peenemünde

"SIR, ARE YOU SURE you have permission to view all these plans?" The plaintive wail of *Oberleutnant* Guenther, tasked with securing the plans from his personal fiefdom, echoed off the hard masonry of the repository's walls. His anxiety was fueled by his sense of ownership, his lack of control over the process, and the sense of enmity radiating from the overly large Gestapo agent. "Vampir" he had heard one of his men whisper as the pale giant dressed in black had stalked into his domain. Lastly, while tall at six feet, the lieutenant was unused to being looked down at both figuratively and literally, exacerbating his dislike for the man. "*I don't like this bastard, I don't like his choosing which plans to protect. What does one of Himmler's lackeys know of aeronautics? God, I wish there was some reason to stop the damn vampire.*"

Fuller continued to ignore the repository's guardian as he designated which boxes of files were to go to the trucks. A pile of boxes containing lesser designs were gathering in one corner of the room, to be taken if time and space allowed. A small commotion was slowing the line of soldiers conveying boxes to the truck. He gestured to where two of the local soldiers had tangled their slung rifles while passing boxes down the line, "Sergeant, fix that," again ignoring the lieutenant while addressing a large and grizzled noncom from his own guards.

The sergeant bellowed in German, "You fumble footed slack witted disgraces to the Fuhrer's Army, stack your weapons over there." The commando pointed to a wall next to the rejected files. The sergeant waded into the local soldiers, cursing, tugging, and pushing until they were all disarmed. Then he efficiently reordered the line, including one of his own men who passed his machine pistol to one of the other commandos before joining the line. Once again the boxes began moving out to one of the three ton Opel trucks waiting outside.

Waiting in a tee of the air ducts, Corporal McCabe and Susan Brodeur faced each other from opposite horizontal branches of the duct system. Between them was the terminus of the vent that fed the room now occupied by the various parties involved in removing files. They had severed all the communication lines and then abandoned the roof after their headset was filled with the screech of the floating radio beacon U-2547 had deployed in the bay outside the harbor. Ostensibly the beacon was to decoy any Allied glide bombs while coincidentally preventing German radio communications in the area for several miles around. McCabe had loosened several of the screws holding the louvers in place and was sure a brisk hit would easily drop it to the floor. He had his feet already in a loop of the rope and Brodeur held the bitter end with which to control his descent. The silenced .22 ready, McCabe was silently beseeching all the saints to which catechism classes had ever introduced him, that the gun would not be needed.

Meanwhile *La Petite Souris'* whiskers were alerting her to pending trouble. She quickly zeroed in on the first lieutenant's discomfort. After watching him for another minute she waved to get Bill's attention, then pantomimed keeping an eye on the young officer. McCabe nodded and as he watched he too became convinced that the man would be trouble.

The pace of the boxes increased as Fuller became more adept at choosing the collection and the sergeant urged on the young soldiers. Disaster came as the commando in the line turned toward the soldier handing him boxes just as the local soldier felt the box slipping from his grasp, it caught the commando's right forefinger bending it backwards with an audible snap that stopped all motion and focused all eyes on the commando. "Jesus, mother, damn fool," burst from the supposed member of the Waffen SS. The loud burst of English startled everyone and started a lethal chain of events. Lt. Guenther immediately began pawing at the holster flap securing his pistol. The commando whose finger had broken unleashed a massive uppercut with his left fist against the offending soldier, dropping him to the floor. Two of the three remaining commandos jumped into the fray against four other local soldiers. A quick witted Peenemünde corporal leapt toward the stacked arms and the remaining commando stepped to the door of the repository and quickly closed it before the personnel outside could see the mounting fracas. The vent louver crashed to the floor as McCabe dropped headfirst from the vent. The lieutenant had finally freed his pistol and was bringing it to bear on Fuller when three coughing sounds were heard and three small holes appeared in a line along the lieutenant's sternum, neck, and forehead. One of Fullers long arms flashed out catching the German corporal in mid leap. The German gasped as an immense hand encircled his throat, cutting off not only his cry of alarm, but the blood flow through his carotid arteries. The German struggled in a vain attempt to remove Vincent's hand and soon passed out. Vincent was aware of more coughing sounds as McCabe slowly rotated at the end of the rope. As targets came into his sight the pistol continued to cough. Between McCabe, the commandos, and Fuller all the local soldiers were soon dead or unconscious, with the unconscious ones quickly having their throats slit by the efficiently savage members of the SOE.

Silence reigned as the Allies took stock. McCabe was slowly lowered to the floor as Susan eased him down. She appeared shortly thereafter, sliding down the rope and taking in the grisly detritus littering the room; she paused a moment, then ran to a wastebasket. She stared into the basket for a moment, gagging a bit before she straightened up to ignore the still empty wastebasket and return to help the men pull the bodies out of site of the outside door.

Vincent had a quick word with his sergeant who went to the door and outside, closing the door behind him. One of the local soldiers came over to discover why files were no longer coming out. The sergeant leaned into the man and whispered conspiratorially to him, "One of your men tried to set the archive on fire, we were able to stop him, but he had a suicide pill. A spy or just crazy as a loon, I don't know. You trot off right now and get Colonel Raeder and your base commander and have them come here as quickly as possible. Quietly now, we can't know if there's more of the damn traitors and we don't want to alert them that their man has failed." The young soldier quickly ran off on his errand.

08/17/1943, 20:30

Col. Raeder and his commandos came at a run to the repository trailed in the distance by Col. Krupp gamely demonstrating his lack of conditioning with his red face and staggering gait. Behind them Major Eichenroht was shepherding three Opel trucks carrying the foreign scientists and their families. Raeder sprinted into the repository and the door was immediately closed and guarded by the sergeant. He motioned to one of his fellow commandos who came over and after a few words quickly set the remaining commandos to guarding the trucks and the repository. Krupp staggered up and when he tried to enter the grizzled sergeant denied him entry, standing firmly in his way and ignoring his entreaties.

A few minutes later Col. Raeder strode out and immediately began issuing orders. Six commandos were sent with three motorcycles to escort the foreign scientists to the U-2547. They roared off to the port and Maj. Eichenroht was told to wait. Rounding on Krupp, Raeder unleashed a short and venomous tirade, "Krupp, your oberleutnant attempted to set the repository on fire. How many other traitors do you harbor? Remove your men from the trucks carrying the files. I will only trust my own men to drive them. Now! Move you puking bag of fat!" Krupp, now completely un-manned hesitated but a moment and Raeder again erupted, "Major Eichenroht, take Krupp into custody, disarm him and follow my orders. Disperse your men to cover the perimeter. Quickly now!"

Eichenroht moved instantly to follow Raeder's orders, his men were securing the bewildered Krupp when the motorcycle dispatched earlier to make contact with the "other commandos" came speeding into the area, siren wailing, lights flashing, exhaust cutout wide open. It careened into a slide as it stopped near the group. The soldier in the sidecar jumped out while the machine was still moving, the small windshield on the sidecar starred by gunfire while more bullet holes in the metal tub attested to a battle. "Colonel, we were ambushed near Karlshagen. Allied commandos, they disabled the car. We barely escaped. I believe they were British or possibly Danes. They were between us and our men to the south." The soldier's dirty face and clothes, and numerous shell casings littering the floor of the sidecar gave credence to his testimony. As if to emphasize his report a series of large flashes were seen from that direction, soon followed by the sound and thump of explosions.

All the men were startled, the locals at the thought of an attack and the Brits by the knowledge that the interdiction force had been engaged and German forces were headed in their direction.

Raeder gestured to the sergeant guarding the door with a hurry-up motion and the man immediately went inside. A minute later two of the commandos appeared carrying a file cabinet wrapped in a blanket. They were followed by another carrying a large heavy box and both objects were quickly stored in the last truck. The three commandos replaced the local drivers who were directed to join the perimeter guards by Maj. Eichenroht.

Suddenly several shots were heard in the repository and the sergeant came running out the door, "They have a bomb. Run for it!"

He was followed by the Gestapo agent, coolly firing his pistol through the doorway, then ducking to the side just in time to avoid the bright flash and flame erupting from the doorway as an explosion occurred inside. The agent scrambled to one of the trucks and leapt onto the running board as it took off toward the main gate. The other trucks followed and the remaining commandos followed with the motorcycles, quickly overtaking the trucks and providing a protective formation ahead of them.

Eichenroht started issuing orders; a force of guards to deploy against the Allied commandos to the south, the base fire brigade to try to put out the fire, and the incarceration of the near catatonic Krupp. The fire brigades actions would be doomed to failure as Fuller's combination of thermite grenades carried by the commandos, solvent used to clean mimeograph machines, and highly flammable nitrocellulose film stock resulted in a conflagration that would destroy the remaining files, the repository and the bodies inside.

20:15
Guard Contingent at *Anklam*:

The courier listened as the lieutenant in charge of the radio station finally received a response from Wehrmacht HQ. As the Morse code came over the receiver the lieutenant paraphrased for the couriers benefit. "Whatever it is HQ knows nothing about what is going on. Peenemünde apparently declared they were being attacked and then they went off the air immediately after. Go back at your fastest, contact Major Frerschaften and get us a report back here if the radio and phones are still out."

"Yes Sir," the rider answered. With speed of the utmost importance he planned on taking some back logging trails that would save him many miles. He would have to unmask his headlight, but speed was of more import than stealth. Kicking his BMW motorcycle into life he left a tail of dust and flying gravel behind him.

Chapter 33:   Roadblock

Narratives of Marie and Lysette Malois

The Island of Usedom on the road between Karlshagen and Trasseheide on the road to Peenemünde:
August 17, 1943, 20:33

THE SOUND OF engines preceded three trucks carrying forty soldiers and Major Frerschaften to augment the guards at Peenemünde. He had been unable to contact the base by phone or radio and had ordered these men and a second smaller cohort from Molschow as a precaution. He should have taken different precautions sooner.

Lt. Jarvis set her controller for the explosives in the culvert, "second truck is following too close for their own good," she whispered to Marie Malois who was manning the generator. "Ready? Now!"

Marie spun the handle on the field phone generator and the road came apart. The first truck flipped end over end as its momentum carried it past the erupting culvert. Soldiers were thrown from the open back, the fuel tank erupted into a flaming Catherine wheel. The second trucks windshield and cabin dissolved in a torrent of stone, instantly killing the driver and Major Frerschaften. The front axle, shorn of tires fell into the trench and for a moment it looked like this truck too would flip over, going nearly vertical before falling back onto its rear wheels. Fewer soldiers fell out of this truck, it having a stout canvas cover bowed over the truck bed. The third truck driver had left more room between his truck and the leaders and was able to drive off the road and come up to a survivable stop against the trees lining the road. The sergeant up front ordered his men to take up guard positions along the road, while he and the driver advanced to look for survivors.

"Now," shouted Jarvis while switching to the next contact. Again Marie spun the generator and again the world erupted. For a hundred yards multiple trees on both sides of the road fell toward the road, with a lethal shower of rock shrapnel in advance. The saboteurs burrowed down into their foxholes as the deadly chain of explosions marched down both sides of the road.

A half mile further back Captain Moeller responded to the chaos ahead, "*Mein Gott!* An ambush, God be thanked we didn't catch up to them." His driver slowed the 12 ton *puma* as quickly as possible. Coming to a stop he looked to his captain for directions. The truck behind them carrying a dozen soldiers had also stopped and the lieutenant in charge came running up to the armored car. Moeller quickly gave orders, "Stay behind with your men, scatter them along the road and don't let them bunch up, kill your lights. We'll go ahead and reconnoiter."

The *puma* advanced without lights and one soldier running ahead to guide the driver along the roads edge, they came around a bend in the road to see a scene of immense devastation. All three trucks were still burning, the road impassable for over a hundred yards with uncountable large pine trees covering the roadway. Moeller saw two young soldiers crawl from the remains of the second truck only to be cut down by a smash of small arms fire from the eastern side of the road. The captain immediately directed both gunners to target the flashes of gun fire erupting from back in the trees. His machine gun operator was the first to react, sending a stream of rounds into the area. With a tracer every third round from the machine gun delineating his target the gunner on the 2" cannon opened fire. The first round impacted the remains of a tree trunk sending shards of wood toward the group of saboteurs while the second exploded on a tree being used for protection. None of the saboteurs had heard the armored car arrive. Their ears still ringing from the explosions that had decimated the first force they reacted quickly to the attack. Arcenaux and O'Flannery responded, but their MP40s were never designed for the range or armor confronting them. They were rewarded with a few sparks as their rounds bounced off the *puma*'s armor. Both men dove back down into their foxholes as the MG34 responded to their action with a far more deadly return. Marie began crawling along the line of tree trunks and foxholes that protected them. None of the men could hear her shouts to retreat back to the schwimmwagen. As she contacted O'Flannery and Arcenaux and started them back into the forest, Rajko Baltzar opened up with his Mauser rifle from the farthest end of the line. Firing the same ammunition as the MG34, his shots had much more effect causing Moeller to close the hatch as several rounds ricocheted off the turret. The small group melted back into the forest. The light from the burning trucks unable to penetrate more than a few yards into the gloom prevented Captain Moeller from determining the number of enemies he confronted. The cannon sent a few more rounds into the woods before Moeller ordered a stop. He made the hard choice to disengage, getting to Peenemünde was more important than punishing whoever had attacked the major's convoy. "Reverse out of here, there's a logging road a kilometer back that will allow us to get around this blockage."

He detailed one of his men to stay and hide in the western forest and observe the battle ground. "I'll send a few men to help you. I believe the bastards have retreated. When the others get here, use your best judgement and try to help any survivors. If you can track the saboteurs try to keep a couple of men in contact with them."

Back at the waiting truck he found not only his men, but an exhausted courier who relayed the orders from HQ. Moeller detailed a lance corporal to lead three other soldiers to the ambush site. Next he turned to the courier, "We will head for the test station and see what we find. Follow us at a distance; if we are attacked turn around and make best speed back to Anklam and report what you've seen." Then he turned to his driver, "Klaus, head for the logging road. There's not a moment to spare. Let's see what the puma can do now that its claws have been bloodied." Followed by the truck with the remaining soldiers both vehicles accelerated to the next confrontation.

Chapter 34: Escape

Narratives of Marie and Lysette Malois

The Island of Usedom 1.6 km east of the road between Karlshagen and Trasseheide enroute to Peenemünde:
August 17, 1943, 20:45

THE FIVE SABOTEURS ran out of the forest and on to the logging road that led to the beach. Rajko Baltzar was carrying Lt. Jarvis whose left thigh had been impaled by a large wood splinter. O'Flannery was limping gamely along, assisted by Marie and Gerard Arcenaux. Art Dietel ran up to the group from the waiting Schwimmwagen and carried Jarvis the rest of the way.

As the crew crammed into the car the lieutenant cursed mightily as her leg was bumped, "pull that damn piece of wood out of my leg!"

"No, leave it," Lysette countered. "We don't know what veins or arteries that big splinter may be occluding. Art, throw some sulfa powder on it and wrap it with a lot of bandages. Make sure it can't move. When we get to the *Manta* Chen Fau and Max can take care of it. What happened on the road?"

Marie answered, "Three trucks with troops, maybe thirty or forty men, we took care of those, but a second force was behind them. Some sort of armored car, not sure which kind, opened fire on us. Machine gun and a small cannon. That's what did the most damage. Robin's leg and Aloysius bouncing off a couple of trees. I think they backed away from there, but we didn't hang around to find out."

Aloysius continued, "The cannon wasn't all that fucking small. We ought to have had a bazooka or some [1]panzerfausts to take it out."

"Al, you pantywaist, just like an Irishman to bring fists to a gunfight and then complain," Arcenaux countered. "Now pipe down we're coming onto the beach. I hope this Hun amphibian is all it's cracked up to be."

Lysette was driving, concentrating on speed, stealth, and a careful entry into the water; not a combination inherently compatible. As she entered the water she started lowering the propulsion unit, and as she felt the car begin to float she engaged the prop. The sturdy little car started through the water, surprising all of them with its ability.

"Are we overloaded?" Rajko asked. "There are only seats for four."

Lysette replied, "It's supposed to take four soldiers and all their equipment plus a little more. Art and I stripped the spare tire, shovels, everything but the bilge pump out of it. The only thing we added was a few of those one man life rafts the air service uses. Let me concentrate on driving, these were mostly designed for flat water. I don't want to take waves too fast and bury the bow. If you have any extra weight you might toss it out now. We definitely aren't going to fight anything much bigger than a row boat."

Arcenaux chuckled, "Remind me to tell you a story about Max and a schnellboote if we make it to the remora."

Art Dietel, who was holding Lt. Jarvis on his lap piped up. "Lieutenant, if we have to lighten load I'll be happy to help you remove your clothing, just in the interest of survival of course."

"Great idea Art. Marie I'll be happy to add my efforts in that endeavor," said Rajko who was similarly situated with Marie Malois.

"Gerard, I don't hear you volunteering to help divest me of my raiment," O'Flannery said while sitting atop the bosun.

"I'll just heave your whole ass in the water as a gallant gesture to preserve the modesty of these blushing maidens," the bosun said. "Lysette are we on course?" he asked in an attempt to change the subject. The last thing the sailors' leader wanted was to report how two of his men lost their testicles aboard a German staff car afloat in the Baltic.

"Near to it anyway. I doubt this compass has been adjusted since it left the factory. It's in major agreement with the stars as best I can tell," Lysette answered. "What do you think our speed is?"

"Six knots should be close. My feet are still dry which is good. This damn thing works pretty well. We should be near the remora in another fifteen minutes and Ardison should hear us on the hydrophone. The remora doesn't have sonar other than a depth sounder, but he can hear what's in the area," Gerard answered.

Fifteen minutes later they slowed, Lysette kept just enough head way to avoid being swamped by a wave. "Did we overshoot? Should I turn around?" a nervous Lysette asked.

"Hold the course," Arcenaux counseled. "Ardison will come in on the reciprocal and he may be late. He wouldn't know the exact time we left so he will be listening. The farther from the German shore the better."

Five minutes later a blinking light signaled them from a hundred yards ahead on their port side. Lysette quickly responded with her shrouded flashlight and was rewarded by a confirming blink code. Soon the remora could be seen creeping up on them. A dim red light came up through the hatch as it opened, soon obscured as Ardison Mitchell's upper body was revealed. "Come on in, I missed you on the way in and we need to be gone."

Lysette soon had the amphibious car alongside the remora. A few brief words of explanation and first O'Flannery and then Jarvis were gently lowered through the hatch. The remaining crew were soon aboard, last was Lysette, who unable to access the external bilge drain to scuttle the staff car, set the schwimmwagen on a new course back toward shore, setting the throttle to high and stepping into the ocean as the car started off. Quickly swimming the few yards to the submarine she was soon inside and dogging the hatch, shivering and sitting at the base of the ladder in the cramped confines of the remora.

Marie was administering a syrette of morphine to Jarvis while Dietel was arranging support for her leg on an adjacent seat. O'Flannery had the remaining seat and Marie was soon giving him an injection as well. "You might as well be comfortable," she said to the objecting Irishman. "We'll probably be blown out of the water sooner or later."

"Marie, throw Lysette a towel. There are some coveralls in there also. Once you're through acting doctor you'll find a sack of sandwiches, some apples and coffee in the locker." Ardison offered. He turned back to his helm, diving the tug and advancing the throttle to full as he set course for the rendezvous with the *Manta* and her pods.

[1]*Panzerfausts (literally armored fists) were German one shot anti-armor weapons analogous precursors to an American LAW. A large caliber shaped charge was used with a 30 to 50 yard range. Once used the aiming tube was often discarded. SMkIII*

Chapter 35: Their ill-gotten gains

Logs of Peenemünde Test Site captured after the war; narratives of
Vincent Fuller and Maxwell Larsen

August 17, 1943, 21:30
Peenemünde Harbor

AS THE LAST three trucks from Peenemünde ground to a halt next to the ferry ramp, Vincent Fuller jumped down from the running board he had occupied for the entire trip. A sailor brandishing a headset and microphone waved him over. A long cord plugged into a protected jack recessed in the hull of the *Manta*. Fuller donned the headset, the microphone was attached and had a mouth piece that fit over the lower part of Vincent's face. This kept extraneous noise down while also preventing anyone from reading his lips. "We need to get out of here. The twins set off their explosives, so someone may still be headed in our direction."

On the *Manta*'s bridge deck, Max Larsen sporting a similar head set agreed. "We heard the explosions; the scientists and their families are on the ferry. We can back two of those trucks onto the ferry and pull the plans while underway. The third truck we'll have to empty on the dock and load it onto this boat. We also have eighteen hundred tons of bombs headed in this direction and about an hour to get out of here."

"I'll get everyone moving down here. We need to get the ferry on its way. If we have to fight our way out of here we don't want them exposed." Fuller turned and Col. Raeder was at his elbow. A few words passed and the commandos started backing the first truck onto the ferry. "Max, we had some problems at the depository. I don't know how long our story will hold up. Can those S-boats range us?"

"Not from where they're tied up and Ardison sank the pod in the channel they will have to use to reach us. I'm sending some extra sailors out to help with the plans. Right now I'm only keeping the quad-40, a couple in the control room, and the engine room manned. Ramrod your end and if we see something before you do we'll sound the horn."

Max turned to Anderson who was already on the intercom and starting men out onto the dock. "Go down and keep those plans moving. Tell The Mouse and McCabe to head for the wardroom once their boxes are carried in. Also tell the mate on the ferry to dump those trucks as soon as they're emptied and out of land observation. Any extra knot he can make will help." Anderson sketched a quick salute and vanished down the bridge deck hatch only to reappear a minute later at the main hatch, accompanied by eight more sailors in German naval attire. *"They're too damn pretty for submariners, hopefully any Germans will put it down to this being an experimental project of Himmler who likes his troops to look like recruiting posters."* Max refilled his coffee from a thermos and then began speaking into the intercom. Aft of the bridge deck the periscope extended and started looking back down the road to the test site with an occasional quick survey of the port and the two S-boats still tied up to their dock.

Five minutes later the second truck was onboard the ferry which immediately left the loading area, turned, and headed out through the harbor.

21:43
Peenemünde Test Site Main Gate

Captain Moeller and his men pulled up to the main gate where they were greeted by Major Eichenroht. Capt. Moeller waved a quick salute as he jumped from the puma which was briefly acknowledged by Maj. Eichenroht. "Igor, how did you get here? There is supposed to be a group of Allied commandos south of us. Did you see the men I sent to stop them?"

"Lyle I ran into your men, I also exchanged a few shots with some saboteurs. I told your men to proceed with caution. Maj. Frerschaften was ambushed along the road. Most, maybe all of his troops were wiped out and the road's impassable. We came around using a logging road. What's happening here? Where's Col. Krupp?"

Maj. Eichenroht quickly laid out all that had happened on the base, in the background smoke and flame could still be seen emanating from the plans repository.

"My God, I wouldn't believe it if I hadn't already run into the saboteurs. Frerschaften sent a courier to Anklam and I made contact with him while on my way here." Moeller waved for the courier who had come in a minute after the puma and the truck with Moeller's remaining soldiers had arrived. The courier soon relayed the message from Wehrmacht Headquarters.

"*Scheisse!* I don't know what is happening, but we best head for the docks. Those damn SS troops should have a better explanation than just saying Himmler told them to grab all the plans." Eichenroht's words were back dropped by a large gout of flame and smoke as the roof of the repository fell in.

22:10
Peenemünde Harbor

"Captain, an armored car and a few trucks are coming down the road from the test site. Also a runabout is bringing an officer over from the S-boats." the control room talker reported to Max Larsen.

"Copy, I see the armored car. Sound the horn one time and alert the engine crew we'll be needing full power soon." Max waited for the horn to finish its blast and then began talking to the Bofors gunner. "Quad-40 target the armored car, armor piercing. If I tell you to fire take it out. Then switch to HE for the trucks."

"Quad-40 copies, AP on the armored car, HE for the soldiers."

By this time Fuller had regained the headset, "What do we have Max?"

"Armored car and three trucks headed our way fast. S-boat officer coming to visit. How much longer for the plans?"

"Last two boxes headed in now. I'm pulling our guards in or do you want us to block?"

Max didn't hesitate, "Bring them in on the hop. The 40 can deal with any interference."

Fuller pulled off the headset and threw it to the sailor. Shouting to the commandos he soon had them running back to the sub.

Max took a look through the Big Eye before unplugging it and stowing it in a watertight compartment. *"That's a Major standing in the hatch of the armored car and he doesn't look at all happy."* Larsen turned back to the intercom, "Control room, I'll conn the boat from the bridge deck. Be sharp, we'll be hauling ass. Sonar, be ready to set off the pod at my command. Now all back slow, tell me when the boat is tight."

"Aye all back slow. Board is green but for your hatch Sir."

"Very good." Max eyed the dock as they pulled back. "Guns, we'll be starting our turn soon, stay on the armored car."

"Quad-40 aye, stay on the puma. Captain I recognize that model. Two inch cannon and a thirty cal machine gun."

Max checked the situation, he now had room to maneuver, "Helm, starboard screw, forward one quarter speed, port screw maintain back slow. Rudders amidships." The helm responded back and Max was keeping one eye on the puma and one on the boat. As the boat rotated around like no other warship could, Max began running both screws forward, now using rudders as well as engine power to start the *Manta* into the harbor.

"Max, I'm keeping an eye on the armored car with the periscope. I'll let you know if they're about to start something," Vincent said over the intercom. "So far the cannon's tracking off to starboard."

The armored car began sounding its siren and horn, obviously attempting to get U-2547's attention. "Still tracking well starboard," Fuller intoned again. Suddenly the puma's cannon fired, the round hit well to starboard and skipped off across the harbor.

"Guns, take them out," Max commanded and a short moment later the puma disintegrated as a dozen rounds of 40mm armor piercing decimated the armored car. A brief pause as the automatic loader switched the quad-40's feed to high explosive, then the trucks began to dissolve, the first hit with the remaining four armor piercing shells which penetrated the truck, most going through to impact against buildings further down the road, one shot hit the engine which was stout enough to detonate the round, blowing the front of the truck apart. The other two trucks fared no better as the high explosive rounds quickly blew them apart.

"Cease fire." Max said. There was no reason to cause further harm to the town and its civilian population. "40, target s-boats."

"Copy. Captain, I don't have a shot on the s-boats yet."

"Then they can't shoot at us either. Keep them targeted. Vince anything new?" Max watched the runabout carrying the naval officer from the s-boats make an abrupt turn and go racing back toward its berth.

"Max, looks like the s-boats are firing up their engines and the gunners are manning their anti-aircraft guns. Those are twenty millimeter, probably wouldn't hurt the pressure hull, but they'd chew up the fairing shell and the fuel tanks, batteries, and buoyancy chambers."

"Got it Vince. We'll be most vulnerable when we cross the mouth of the channel and only their forward guns can hit us then. Hope they don't send a torpedo down the channel at us. Helm all ahead full, maintain present course. Adjust depth down three feet. Let's give them a smaller target and make a bigger wake while we're at it." Larsen could feel the *Manta* accelerate as the big diesels roared and the sub ran through the harbor. They were soon doing twenty five knots and still accelerating and the bow wave smoothly flowing over the subs curved hull accentuated the wake which was soon wreaking havoc among the small craft moored in the harbor.

"S-boat starting down the channel," Vincent reported.

"Sonar stand by, on my count, ready?" Max kept watch on the S-boat. Huge clouds of black smoke was erupting from them, the diesels still too cold to be efficient, yet Max knew that even at its best speed the *Manta* would still be no faster than the torpedo boat. "Sonar, five, four, three, two, one, Now."

The acoustic signal flashed to the pod. For a moment Max was afraid he was too late, but then a massive explosion lifted the S-boat out of the water, breaking its back. At least one of the four torpedoes on board detonated in sympathy to the massive shock wave and the one hundred fifteen foot long boat disintegrated. The fast moving submarine was rocked and shoved sideways by the blast. Max had ducked down and had his hands over his ears and his mouth wide open trying to equalize the pressure on his ears to little avail. All he could hear was a massive ringing as the nerves shrieked in protest to the overstimulation. He looked up to see the second torpedo boat overturned and washed up onto the shore. Max regained the headset and put it on. He could hear what he thought might be a voice, but he wasn't sure. He started giving orders, hoping someone could hear him. "Helm, steer ten degrees right. Chen Fau report to the bridge deck, I've lost my hearing, you'll need to take the conn." *"Someone can hear me, we're coming up to the new course. I've got to get with Vince and Ernst, see if we can't find better hearing protection. Damn, Verna's going to be pissed if I've gone and ruined my hearing."*

He was relieved when Chen Fau came through the hatch. Fau shouted into Max's ear and Larsen thought he heard mumble something mumble conn. Fau glared at him, gave him the OK sign and pointed to the hatch as he put on the headset. Larsen nodded, it made sense for him to get out of the way; his Chinese compatriot could navigate as well or better than Max, no sense in staying in the way up top.

Chapter 36:   Attack on Peenemünde

Logs of the *Manta* and *Satyr*

08/17/1943, 23:00
One mile northwest of Griefswalder Oie in the Baltic

[1]TOWARDS PEENEMÜNDE the sky was filled with searchlights, flak, and the occasional sight of a heavy bomber momentarily caught in the flash of explosives or the beam of a searchlight. A near continuous rumble and flash of exploding bombs betrayed the destruction wrought on the experimental base. Aside from two lookouts the sight was wasted on all the men trying to load plans and scientists with their families into the two pods.

The sailors aboard the two pressurized shells hearing the signal from the *Manta*s sonar had unshipped the anchors and inflated the bladders that provided positive buoyancy to the pods. Once on the surface they had opened hatches and set light stanchions and ropes to guide the former prisoners as well as keeping them from falling into the sea. Some of the prisoners debarking from the ferry hesitated to descend through the pods' hatches. The supposed Waffen SS commandos allowed no one to slow the line going below. The interiors were surprisingly well lit and the tiers of bunks lining both sides of the hull were incongruously covered with brightly colored blankets, some even had stuffed animals ready to comfort young children. The sailors were polite, showing the bewildered scientists and their families where to go. The smell of coffee and baskets of fruit and pastries on a table attached to the stern bulkhead helped propel the flow of refugees.

A much more hectic scene was taking place on the deck of the giant submarine where a line of commandos and sailors were passing file box after file box down into the hull. Inside the boxes were being rapidly stacked into spaces normally used for berths.

In the control room of the *Manta*, ship's officers and some of the conspirators were gathered. Max Larsen, his hearing returning by the moment, had a headset on allowing him to communicate with "Colonel Raeder" who was keeping an eye on the procession of file boxes. Max could also talk to the two pods, the boats radio and sonar compartments and the gunner at the quad-40. "Nothing showing on the radar receiver so the Germans haven't found us yet. We're not transmitting," he quickly assured Vincent Fuller who had doffed his

Gestapo garb for a roll neck sweater and dungarees. "We can hear their transmissions before they can see us. And with all the noise German sonar operators will have a hard time hearing anything. Any S or R boats out there are using their AA guns on the bombers. Not too worried about that as most of their stuff is too short of range. The [2]R-boats carry a thirty seven millimeter that might be effective, but at night it's not likely they'll do much damage."

Fuller replied, "Let's hope the bombing raid will hold all their attention for the next few hours. The radio jamming pod should be detonating in a few more minutes. Hopefully the Nazi's will be afraid of our radio hunting glide bombs and stay off the air. You know that's a pretty good idea, I'll have to actually build some when we get back."

"Cut Albert Osgood in on the profits, the idea was his to start the rumor," Max replied.

Max's headset came alive with some welcome news, "Last box going down the hatch now and the two pods are full and buttoned up," Major Ian McDougal, now shed of his Col. Raeder persona, reported. "The remora has just arrived and is maneuvering the first pod to its umbilical."

"Max replied, "Thanks Ian. I'm glad they made it back. Sonar reported them at the same time as you did. All this noise makes it hard for us to hear other ships as well. Have your men come down below and we'll make some space for them."

"Copy that Max. I detailed a couple of my noncoms to each pod to assist your sailors in case there is a [3]quisling among the scientists. My men are starting down now. As soon as your sailors have both pods attached I will inform you and then beat a hasty retreat into the *Manta*"

"Very well Ian, don't fall off now please. Report to the control room when you're down below," Max replied. "Conn to Sparks, current status on the radio buoy?"

"Captain, still on, but the signals getting weaker, batteries falling off a little quicker than we planned. It's due to blow up in about twenty seconds."

"Conn copies, as soon as it dies listen for the *Satyr*, she should confirm her blocking position as soon as the jamming stops."

"Conn, Bosun, the second pod is attached, deck crew headed down now."

"Thanks Anderson, good work." Max turned to his bridge crew, "As soon as the remora is secured we'll be making our run, all four engines and rigged for surface action, let's make as much distance towards Sweden as we can before sunrise."

A round of affirmation came from the helmsman, the quartermaster at the navigation station, and Max's second, Chen Fau.

Max, while retaining his headset, switched on the interphone speaker so the entire command crew could hear any further communications. Soon the board was green but for the designator for the quad-40. The blister was still open and the gun still deployed, the operator was inside the pressure hull seated in a glass half dome, a repeater for the radar was in the center of his control board, dark now with the radar off. An optical sight was in front of his face and his seat was synchronized to the gun, both swiveling together to align with any target.

The remora's designator showed her locked into her cradle as the talker confirmed the join. "All ahead half, fine pitch at start," Max said, referring to setting the adjustable props to a finer pitch, giving more power' but trading off speed until they had the tug and tow moving easily. Once assured both pods were trimmed properly and no problems were found Max had the helm slowly bring the power to full, the pitch coarsened, the twinned green lights marching up each side of the helm station and soon six green lights displayed on each side. There were two unlit lights in each row designating emergency full and the penultimate B/W setting which stood for "Balls to the Wall" and had not been used since the initial sea trials. B/W used not only the four huge diesel engines, but added the battery powered electric pumps to the hydraulic drives. While effecting a twenty percent gain in speed over emergency full, it was not an effort that could be sustained for more than a day before exhausting even the *Manta*'s massive battery reserve. Once clear of any obstacles or reefs the *Manta* went to B/W, her surprising speed being the best safeguard against a German search.

At thirty two knots, the *Manta* and its precious cargo was headed for the Falsterbo Peninsula of Sweden and the narrow entrance to the North Sea and hoped for freedom.

[1]*The British bombing raid on Peenemünde, designated Operation Hydra, took place over the night and early morning of August 17-18, 1943. For the first time a master bomber was used for the main force. It was commanded by Group Captain John Searby, CO of 83 Squadron. Some 40 British bombers out of 596 heavy bombers were lost along with their crews. An estimated 800 civilians, mostly prisoners used as slave labor were killed along with a few scientists working on the V2 rocket program. SMkIII*

[2]R-bootes were minesweepers used by the German Navy. About 135' long and slower than an S-boote, they were armed with 37mm and 20mm cannon. SMkIII

[3]Quisling referred to any residents of German occupied countries who collaborated with the Nazis. The name came from Norwegian Fascist Vidkun Quisling who headed the puppet government of Norway under the Germans. SMkIII

Chapter 37: *Satyr* sows confusion

Log of the *Satyr* and German Naval Reports

08/18/1943, 13:30
The Baltic Sea 30 miles NNW of Peenemünde

"FINALLY A SHIP, even if it's one of those *sperrbrecher* hermaphrodite obscenity of a target, dead ahead." Lt. Oakley said while peering through the *Satyr*'s periscope. He was referring to a German makeshift minesweeper, which was a converted merchant ship. Heavily armed as an anti-aircraft platform, the ships main task was to run ahead of a German fleet and set off any mines in its path. Earlier *Satyr's* hydrophones had barely picked up the strange muted roar of the *Manta* rushing towards Falsterbo and the Oresund Strait. "We'll come around to its port and try for the props and rudder. They fill those ships' holds with flotation. They've lost dozens to mines, but they're hard to sink. We'll try to cripple it and make sure it catches a glimpse of us and our new numbers before we retreat," Oakley said to his number two.

"Aye Captain. Hopefully they won't recognize us for an S-class. The turtleback aft with the new battery reserve and the blister the Caroline welded onto our bow makes us look like no boat I've seen before. That and our new paint job should do it." The *Satyr* now sported a large U-2547 and swastikas on both sides of the conning tower.

Several minutes later the aft section of the minesweeper jumped out of the sea as a British torpedo exploded, destroying both the props and rudder. The ship instantly was changed from hunter to hunted, and searchlights stabbed out into the sea surrounding it. Several spotters called the bridge reporting an apparent broach of a submarine and the confusing symbols and unusual appearance. The minesweeper's captain radioed in both a distress call and that his ship had been attacked by a German Navy submarine of unusual design.

Chapter 38: Thank you Admiral Tamm

Logs of the *Manta* and *Satyr* and narratives of M. Larsen, V. Fuller, and M. Malois

August 18, 1943 02:20
Approaching the Falsterbo Peninsula and the Oresund Strait

THE *MANTA* HAD finally slowed from its rush across the Baltic. Falsterbo was to her starboard side and she was silently proceeding at quarter speed, barely awash and on electric motors only.

"I hope our ride is here. Thankfully August water levels are some of the highest of the year," Max said quietly to the control room. Only crew were in here now, Vincent and Major McDougal had moved to the wardroom. Max didn't want anyone but his regular crew in the control room. Ardison Mitchell was on the bridge deck with one lookout. The Big Eye night glass was in its repeater mount. Any sighting that Mitchell made above, the repeater would show the bearing at the navigation console. Chen Fau was using the periscope to get more readings off the points of land to the *Manta's* starboard.

Earlier Chen and Max had removed the chunk of wood from Jarvis' thigh. They had stopped most of the bleeding, packed the wound and put in a drain. Further measures would wait until they were out to sea or had rendezvoused with a British ship. Chen Fau had been a medical student in China before running afoul of a tong allied with the Nationalist government and Max had studied and learned extensive first aid through the years. The stark necessities inherent in deep-water sailing, mining, explosives use, and guerilla warfare had given him more exposure to trauma than many doctors.

"Conn, sonar, we have a target to the northwest. It sounds like *Sverige* and *Remus* are turning, prepping for their nightly run through the strait."

"Copy sonar. Ardison, have you got her spotted," Max asked?

"Max, *Sverige* is starting her run and *Remus* looks to be her usual half mile behind. I'm centering the Big Eye on *Sverige's* stern."

Max checked the repeater and looked toward Chen who was relaying bearings to the quartermaster. The quartermaster was keeping track of their position with a wax marker on the glass overlay. "We're clear of the point and have enough depth to mate up," the quartermaster confirmed.

Max too had been checking the positions shown on the chart. "Fifteen degrees to port, ahead to half," he told the helm. *Manta* sped up and with some coaching from Chen and Ardison slipped into the slot between the two Swedish warships. "Speed down to one quarter, follow the repeater. Ardison will keep it on *Sverige's* stern. Sonar, Ardison, call the speed, keep us in position."

"Aye Captain, I'll stay on the Swede like a bull following a heifer in heat." Ardison confirmed.

"Chen, keep your bearings coming. Can you still see them if we bring the periscope down a bit, I don't want the Germans see it occlude a light on the Swedish shore. Too bad they aren't under blackout."

Chen lowered the scope while nodding affirmatively to Larsen.

Keeping an eye on the depths shown in the chart Max called to the Chief of the Boat. "Chief we can come down three more feet. That should leave us one to two feet to spare. Bring her down very gently."

"Gently it is sir," the COB answered while slowly adjusting ballast by pumping air from the buoyancy bladders back into the high pressure tanks. A minute or so later he advised Larsen, "She's down three and holding."

"Thanks Chief, nicely done. Ardison, how does she look?"

"She looks good, *Sverige* is keeping her speed right where we need it and *Remus* has moved up a bit closer. Between the three of us it looks like a fairly normal wake for two surface ships. The only problem is our feet are starting to get wet. If you need to go lower let us know so we can start swimming to Sweden. Those Swedish girls are going to love me and Rajko," Ardison said referring to Rajko Baltzar who was the lookout.

Max let a short chuckle escape before answering, "The Swedish ladies will stay safe for now, and we won't get any lower. You just make sure we hold our position on *Sverige* and don't let *Remus* run up our stern. I don't want to have a destroyer stuck in our ass"!

"Aye aye sir," Mitchell responded while he continued to keep the Big Eye riveted on the Swedish ship.

"Can you believe Churchill wanted to run one of their old battleships through here and into the Baltic," Max said to Chen while he studied the chart.

"How could that be accomplished? No British battleship has a shallow enough draught to even look at the Oresund," Chen said in disbelief.

"He was going to lighten her up by having most of the minor guns removed, some of the main guns removed and welding hollow sponsons onto each side. He would have nearly tripled her beam. Fortunately the Admiralty finely convinced him that it was simply not feasible. She'd be impossible to protect while they returned her guns to her and the German air arms and subs would have had a field day. It would have made more sense and been no more suicidal to just bring it in to the narrows off Helsingor and just sink her there. She would have clogged up the strait for a damn long time."

Chen kept giving the quartermaster bearings and wondering how any country survived its leaders. *"I would disparage Churchill if he wasn't so much better than Hitler, Stalin, Chiang Kai-Shek, or Mao."*

Chapter 39: Kattegat ahead

**Logs of the *Manta* and *Satyr.* V. Fuller, M. Larsen,
M. Malois and L. Malois**

August 18, 1943, 05:00
Entering the Kattegat from the Oresund Strait

"SO FAR, SO GOOD!" Max said to Ardison Mitchell as Manta's exec came into the control room. "Menzies reported that *Satyr* hit a German mine sweeper and they showed enough to have the Germans thinking we're still in the Baltic."

"I hope they don't pay too much for their impersonation. Can they get out now that they've poked the hornet's nest?" Ardison asked.

"They plan to lie doggo for two days; possible now with her additional batteries, CO_2 scrubber, and LOX tank. Meanwhile we may contrive to be seen later today to take the pressure off of Satyr. *Sverige's* Swedish night train will be running for another week and *Satyr* will be able to come out under their cover." Larsen answered. "If you're ready I'll turn her over and catch a bit of sack time. No reports of any Germans along our course from any of the British subs out here. Hold her at three quarters speed for now. Sun will be up shortly and we're going to submerge to stay out of sight. Colonel Menzies should have some [1]Beaufighters up by now and they should keep an eye on the German ships or aircraft in the area. Osgood has some Lightnings coming out this way to help with any German aircraft."

"Get some rest Max, you've been up for at least two days if not more. I've got it for now. I plan on coming up to periscope depth every once in a while so the radio shack can hear any new reports while we take a quick look."

"Sounds good, keep it a little random so we don't set up a pattern." Max said around an impressive yawn that elicited sympathy yawns throughout the control room.

"Go random yourself out of my control room before you send the entire crew to sleep." Ardison said while shooing Max out.

Larsen stopped in the ward room where Chen Fau and Lysette were caring for Lt. Jarvis and Seaman O'Flannery. Jarvis was asleep on a cot with Susan asleep on a deck mat next to her. The wood splinter had come perilously close to her femoral artery. Neither Chen Fau nor Max had attempted to examine it too closely. It wasn't bleeding and they didn't want to risk injuring it further.

Fau was listening to O'Flannery's chest; tapping slowly in different areas as he moved the stethoscope's pickup around. Chen finally straightened up and noticed Larsen in the entrance. "Percussion shows Aloysius has some blood building up in the pleural space around his left lung. I'm starting him on some oxygen and I'll put a drain in. He's having trouble breathing and I don't want any extra pressure on his heart."

Max came up to the cot holding the Irishman, "Al, sorry about your injury. We'll do what we can and as soon as we get to the *LaDonna* or a British warship with a surgeon I'll get you transferred."

"'Tis' but a scratch. Chen Fau's better than any fancy hospital or fluoroscope anyways." O'Flannery labored to reply.

Max yawned again before asking, "Fau, you need my help?"

"Not at all. Lysette is more than capable enough to assist. What I do need is for you to get some rest before we get jumped on by the entire Nazi navy."

Max just nodded and headed toward his small cabin near the control room. He was asleep seconds after he fell into his bunk.

August 18, 1943, 12:26
Nearing the Skagerrak

Hair still dripping wet from a quick head dunk in his sink and a towel around his neck Max came into the control room. Ardison and Vincent were conferring over the chart table and at this time *Manta* was some seventy feet below the surface. "Problems?" Max asked as he entered.

"One or two." Ardison answered without looking up from the charts. "Reports have the Germans sending some surface ships towards the Kattegat from Kristiansand and from further up the northwestern coast of Norway. Mostly S-bootes and a few R-bootes. We're just loafing, hoping they won't slowdown and listen properly until they get closer to the strait. We will be making our turn here into the Skagerrak in about a half hour."

Vincent Fuller added more bad news, "The last radio transmission we received before submerging stated that the Germans are sending out several flights to hunt us. Mostly Heinkel [2]HE115s and some Messerschmitt [3]Hornets. They probably don't have any idea where we really are, but it's not that big an area and by now they know they've been snookered."

"Anything else?" Larsen asked while toweling his hair dry.

"Yeah, as a matter of fact there is. Sonar heard a German sub about an hour ago, headed in instead of out and he says from the way the sound changed he thinks it came about and tried to follow us. We sped up a couple of knots to above what most German subs can make submerged. We may have lost him unless he decides to surface and run on his diesels. If he does that he could close up on us some, but he'll also get a lot noisier." Mitchell added.

"Vince, what's your take on the aircraft?" Max asked while he came up to the chart table and checked *Manta's* position.

Fuller answered immediately, "The Hornets just came in service this year and can damage us badly if they catch us on the surface. Twenty millimeter cannons and .50 cal machineguns, also they can carry bombs, though not torpedoes. What really scares me is that some are configured with a two inch autocannon, similar to what was on the Puma armored car we killed back in Peenemünde. That could put some serious hurt on us. They're faster than a Beaufighter and will even be able to mix it up some with the Lightnings. Our other threat is the 115s. They're pretty slow and three .30 cal is all they carry in offensive machine guns, but they have a lot of range, loiter time, and a three man crew with better viewing capacity that's more likely to find us, and topping that they can carry torpedoes. They have the capability to destroy us if they get a good target."

Max took a moment to think, "Ok, we'll head up in a bit and see what we can hear on the radio. Any problems with the scientists?"

Ardison answered, "All quiet so far. They know the truth now and nobody's asking to go back. The crew checks in every fifteen minutes. Most of the kids are asleep, a few claustrophobes are responding well to brandy, same for an overly anxious adult or two. The scientists are some of the worst; they're busy figuring how much pressure at what depth can crush the hulls, how long the oxygen will last, what's the probable strain on the umbilical tethers. You know, the usual problem with engineers and eggheads when they aren't in their own bailiwick; more nervous than a cat at a rocking chair convention."

Max chuckled, "Engineers, Lord bless their hearts. Right Vince?"

"Well, if something does go wrong at least you'll have a bunch of people trying to find a solution to the very last." Vincent rejoined.

"And I've got a couple of sailors in each pod who will actually fix the problem by instinct and practice instead of some algorithm." Max replied.

[1]Beaufighter: The Bristol Type 156 was a twin engine heavy fighter bomber. It was used as a night fighter due to its ability to carry the large and bulky early radar equipment. Later it was used in ground attack and anti-naval roles. Heavily armed with 4 x 0.8" (20 mm) automatic cannon in the nose and up to 6 x 0.30" machine guns in the wings they were also capable of carrying a torpedo. Wing guns were sometimes replaced with 8 x 90 lb. rockets or 2 x 250 lb. bombs. Top speed was 303 mph with a range of 1,470 miles with a crew of 2.

[2]Heinkell HE115: A twin engine seaplane with a crew of 3 and good range. Armed with 2 x 0.30" forward firing machine guns, one crew served; 1 x 0.30" machine gun again crew served at the back of the cockpit, and 2 fixed 0.30" machine guns firing toward the rear from the engine gondolas. Several German designs used fixed or remote operated machine guns firing toward the rear to discourage enemy fighters. Top Speed 179 mph and range of 1,700 miles.

[3]Messerschmitt ME 410, the Hornisse (Hornet). Land based twin engine heavy fighter/ reconnaissance/ high speed bomber. Crew of two. Armed with 2 x 0.8" auto-cannon and 2 x 0.5" machine guns fixed in the nose and 2 x 0.5" machine guns facing rearwards in remotely directed blisters on each side. 2,200 lb. internal bombload or they can carry a 2" BK5 autocannon in the bomb bay. Top speed 391 mph and range of 1,050 miles.

Chapter 40: The Hunted

Log of the *Manta*, M. Larsen, and V. Fuller

August 18, 1943, 14:00
The Skagerrak, Entrance to the North Sea

"HELM, PERISCOPE DEPTH, use your planes only. I want to stay heavy in case we need to hurry back down." Max said.

"Aye Sir. Periscope depth, planes only." came the prompt reply.

"At least here we can head north into deep water if we have to evade." Chen Fau said with some relief as he marked the chart with their supposed position.

"I'd much rather head west and get some Allied warships between us and the Nazis." Max replied. "Sparks," he continued into the intercom, "be ready to take down traffic from the Brits and make sure the radar alarm is on in case we get painted."

The "Aye Aye Sir" came back with sufficient emphasis to imply that the radio shack knew its job and the captain was maybe a tad tense.

Max took the response with a rueful smile and shook his head, "Fau, remind me to give Sparks a bonus when we get back. Artie both put me in my place and reminded me that if the crew weren't all consummate professionals they wouldn't be on my ship. The last thing they need is for me to be looking over everyone's shoulder."

The *Manta* bristled with antennae and the periscope as it came to the proper depth. Max took a quick three-sixty sweep with the periscope. "Nothing at the moment." He said as he began a second slower sweep to make sure. "Some flashes to our east, closer towards *Frederikshavn*. Might be something going on there. Sonar?" he said into the intercom.

"Sonar here, nothing in the immediate area that's active. Something going on to the east, but I don't think anything heavy being used."

"Radios to conn."

"Go ahead Sparks."

"Captain, we're getting some feed from the Brits, I'll have it decoded in a moment. Also we hear some chatter on the air to air channels. Sounds like the Beaufighters are lighting up some ship east of us and headed our way. Nothing on any of the German radar bands at the moment."

"Copy Art, thanks." Max answered. Angling the head of the periscope up as high as possible he did another turn around looking for aircraft.

Ardison Mitchell came into the control room. "Did a walkthrough and talked to the tows, no problems so far."

Max answered while finishing his sweep for aircraft, "Good. As soon as we're sure we have all the traffic we'll head down again. Fau, what' our reserve?"

The navigator checked the gauges showing battery status. "Eighty percent, she's good for quite a while more."

"Conn, radio room, I have a full repetition of BBC's notices to lonely sailormen everywhere. We're good to go."

"Thanks Sparks. Helm, make her depth one hundred feet, all ahead half." Max ordered. After the helm acknowledged, Max turned to Ardison and Chen Fau, "We'll know a bit more here shortly. I'm guessing we're still ahead of the German search. I'd like to be seen to take some pressure off *Satyr*, but I'm not going to risk the information or the scientists."

Suddenly an alarm rang, "Conn, sonar, torpedo in the water to our port."

Max reacted immediately, "Helm, emergency full, course three hundred magnetic. Weapons, release two mines now. Fau, how close to deep water?" The helm responded by triggering the maneuvering alarm even as he began the course change.

"Deep water in forty seconds at present course and speed. Three hundred feet and increasing to four-fifty or more quickly."

"Probably a Heinkel seaplane, we should be too deep for any German torpedo already. They're hoping for a lucky shot, just like I'm hoping for some luck with the mines." Max said while watching the helm.

"Deep water, we should be good." Chen Fau said.

"Make your depth two-fifty feet. Course three-forty. Reduce speed to full."

The helmsman reacted quickly, the big sub banking into the turn sharply enough to make everyone grab a handhold. Nosing down the helmsman hit the switches for full. The lights blinked once to signal that the engine room was acknowledging the input and when the lights came back on they showed speed at full. A few minutes passed very slowly. "Good job!" Max said as one big hand gave a reassuring squeeze to the helmsman's shoulder. "Now, all back to one quarter. Sonar, anything new?"

"Negative sir. Torpedo stayed on its' original track. Nothing else. The noise from the ruckus to the east has stopped also after one large explosion. Possibly a torpedo and secondary detonation. Something got blown up."

"Copy sonar. Well done." Max said. Turning to Ardison and Chen Fau he shook his head. "How did I miss that damn HE 115?"

"Periscopes aren't meant for air search." Ardison offered. "Lookouts or radar are better and still not infallible and deploying either would have delayed submerging. Chalk it up to luck and we'll brainstorm later on possible fixes. Maybe a microphone on the periscope, might at least let you hear something."

Chen Fau added his thought, "We can make a bit more westing and stay in deeper water for a while. We're safe from aircraft at the moment; use it to head for friendlier skies. They missed, we are in good shape. Take advantage now."

"You're both right. We'll get while the getting's good. Helm, course 280 and come to three quarter speed." Max said. The *Manta* turned toward home.

Chapter 41: Reports

OSS Logs, Narratives of H. Snowden,
A. Osgood, and E. Dietsch

August 20, 1943, 00:35
Col. Osgood's Office

"THANK YOU, YES BRING them right in." Col. Osgood said into the intercom. Moments later Sgt. Futch, still looking fresh and bright even though she had been up and working for eighteen hours, came in with the latest sealed dispatches from communications.

"Sergeant, please call it a night. I'm telling you this for my benefit, not yours. You are much too bright and perky and I feel old and tired just seeing you." Brigadier General Hiram Snowden said. His jacket off, tie undone and feet up on a chair, he was shuffling through dispatches while watching Ernst Dietsch and Lt. Col. James Brewster putting position markers on a chart pinned to the wall.

"Yes Sir, just as soon as I know everyone is safe." Futch said as she left the room.

"Hiram, your aura of command is just scintillating tonight. Are all your orders obeyed so adroitly?" Ernst asked.

"You've infected and subverted the poor girl you little mechanic. My God she's starting to act like you." Hiram replied. "Do we have an answer for her?"

Col. Osgood looked up grinning from the latest sheaf of information, "Yes we do. Latest dispatch has the *Manta, Repulse,* and *LaDonna* together in the shelter of the Orkneys. Scientists and their families are being transferred as we speak and they have several thousand pounds of plans. By God they did it. No fatalities although some wounded. Absolutely amazing."

"Sergeant Futch!" roared Hiram. "In here now."

Wide eyed, Sgt. Futch came through the door. "Sir?"

"Sibyl, you may go to bed now, all are safe. If you would be so good as to bring that bottle of Albert's best scotch from the safe, I hope you will join us in a toast before you retire." Hiram beamed.

Sgt. Futch's "Yes Sir!" hung in the air as she sprinted for the safe. When she returned all the men were standing by the desk, grabbing each page of the dispatch as Osgood finished. Col. Menzies came through the door unannounced while Sgt. Futch filled glasses.

"Sorry I'm late. I take it by your expressions and that really excellent brand being so generously poured, that there is good news." Menzies said as he joined the group around the desk.

177

"The best of news Colonel, the very best." Snowden said as he passed a glass to the British spy chief.

"To the brave." Hiram said as he raised his glass. His words were quickly echoed by all and the scotch was downed lamentably quickly.

"Let's pour one more round that we can savor a bit more while we total up the action." Hiram said.

Sgt. Futch, tears of joy streaming down her cheeks, poured one more round. "Excuse me sir," she said to Col. Osgood before hugging him fiercely.

"Good night Sibyl," Osgood replied gently, "and certainly you are excused. Please don't come in until noon at the earliest."

"Yes Sir." Sgt. Sibyl Virginia Futch replied as she walked to the door, one hand firmly in charge of her glass and the other wiping tears away.

"So, James, Ernst, have you got the tallies from the North Sea?" Hiram asked while moving over to the chart.

Lt. Col. Brewster pointed to the Baltic. "Recon photos show considerable damage to Peenemünde airfield. How much was destroyed in those bunkers is still hard to answer since we don't have a firm idea of what all was in them. I'm afraid that considerable destruction occurred in the areas housing workmen. Most of them will not be Germans. Slave or forced labor from conquered people. We won't know more until possibly we hear from Colonel Menzies' agents."

Ernst took up the narrative, "In the Baltic one of those merchant conversion German minesweepers was put out of action. It's still afloat so the Germans will probably tow it close to one of their ports and simply use it as a flak battery, probably run it aground at high tide and just let it sit. In the Skagerrak the Beaufighters took out at least five S-boats, two R-boats and badly damaged one Type 36 destroyer, the Z-35, an A model. It was later sunk by a British sub, *P-236, HMS Scimitar.* Colonel Menzies, when you get an opportunity would you please instruct our navy in how to name ships. You Brits do it so well. We're naming subs after unimpressive fish, grunion, skipjack, perch. I've always believed more martial names enhance the ability to fight."

"Mr. Dietsch, as a rose is just as sweet a ship's name has nothing to do with the bravery and commitment of its personnel.

However I would be disinclined to serve on say the HMS Pansy." Menzies replied.

"Ernst, the report and then you go to bed. I must be tired as you're almost making sense." Hiram said.

"Yes Hiram. Sorry for digressing. Two Beaufighters were lost, several others damaged, but they managed to return to base. One Lightning lost, however the Nazis lost four Hornets and at least six of their seaplanes. As far as we know the *Satyr* is still operational. I don't believe she is due to exfiltrate the Baltic until tomorrow night late."

"Thanks Ernst. Colonel Brewster anything else?"

"No General, at least nothing that can't wait until later tomorrow, excuse me, later today. We should have a better report then after gun camera film is checked and all the squadron reports are in."

"Thank you Colonel. Colonel Menzies do you have anything to add?"

"At first light I'm headed up to Thurso in a Lysander. I have room for two more."

"I'm going to pull rank and take one of those seats, thank you. Albert, Ernst who goes?"

Col. Osgood answered, "I have another operation going that will keep me here, besides Ernst will be frantic to get a look at the plans, not to mention seeing the twins, Vince, and Max."

"Thank you Al. I would have hated to have to steal a plane to get up there if you had bumped me."

"Gentlemen, I'll be around to pick you up at 06:00 sharp. Let us hope that our effort and our losses are well repaid. Frankly just obtaining the scientists and engineers who are familiar with the German projects should more than repay us in lives saved." Col. Menzies said as he readied to leave.

"Stewart, thank you again for making this possible. We'll see you at six." Hiram said as he walked Menzies to the door.

Chapter 42: *LaDonna* Rendezvous

Logs of the *Manta* and *LaDonna Johnson*, V. Fuller, M. Larsen, M. Malois, L. Malois, V. Deveraux

August 20, 1943, 01:20
3 Miles West of the Orkney Islands

HMS REPULSE, SS LADONNA JOHNSON, and the *Manta* were hove to in the lee of the Orkneys, busily transferring scientists and their families from the transport pods used to rescue them. Both surface ships had dim floodlights illuminating accommodation ladders against which the pods were fastened. Sailors from all three ships were assisting in the process. One boy of five, pic-a-back on a sturdy sailor, was loudly urging his steed to go faster. The boy was speaking Polish and the Jack Tar carrying the boy spoke only English, but he understood the boy just fine, speeding up until almost ramming the person ahead and then rearing back and giving a most passable imitation of an impatient horse. "That boy was afraid to say one word when we were embarking his family at Peenemünde." Vincent said while observing from the *Manta's* bridge.

"And in two days he's relearned that life can contain joy as well as fear. And you know what; joy is much more fun than fear." Max replied. Once we have all the personnel on board the destroyer and *LaDonna* we'll start loading the plans. Have you had a chance to look at them?"

"Yeah, I marked a few boxes back at the repository that I wanted to concentrate on first. Damn but the Germans have come up with some beautiful stuff. Their jet engines are a bit ahead of the Brits and even farther ahead of our engines. Metallurgy and reliability will be the big problem with them. All that power means a lot of heat, makes me think that ceramic coatings might help. They have some air to ship and air to air missiles that are starting to cause problems. Fortunately the guidance systems are still the weak link, the controllers are an easier target than the rockets."

"What about the fire dragon that Ernst and Hiram were exercised over?"

"Max from what I've read so far that bastard's a real bitch. They call it a fire drake, *Feuerdrachen*, same thing. Self-guided, so all the operator has to do is paint his target with an ultraviolet light beam that we can't even see without special filters. The operator can be well protected on shore or even I would think you could mount a projector on a U-boat's periscope and aim it from somewhere away from the launch site. In fact I guess you could have multiple projectors from different places guaranteeing the result if any one light is destroyed. What's worse is there is little defense for them. They fly in ground effect so they're no higher than 15 feet above the ground or water."

"That's bad. During the invasion all manner of small craft, destroyers, LSTs, you name it, will be in toward shore. If a battleship or cruiser is targeted they can't even use their AA. Depressed enough to target the missile they would decimate any ships inshore. Even the inshore ships would be unable to fire." Max said while watching the last few scientists head up the ladders. "Any idea where they'll place them. Specific I mean, obviously the damn things will be used against the invasion."

"There are some shipping papers, hopefully we'll find more information as we go through all the material. They definitely need to be a priority." Vincent answered. "I see your boys are getting ready to take Robin up to *LaDonna*. How's she doing?"

"Running a bit of a fever, keeps insisting that she can get up and walk. She's one of those people that morphine doesn't make them sleepy, just pain free, restless and a bit goofy. I'm going to head down and make sure they have her strapped down tight. Hopefully Susan can keep her calm; I'm less than happy about her wound. Too close to the femoral for peace of mind." Max started toward Robin's stretcher and the sailors tasked with delivering her to the Q-ship. Vincent decided to tag along.

As they drew near Robin could be heard complaining to the sailors, "I truly am just fine. It doesn't hurt a bit. I'm quite sure that nice Mister Chen fixed everything. Now be good boys and let me walk."

"Enjoy the ride Robin," Susan said nervously, "How often do you have four handsome men willing to carry you up the stairs?"

"Ah Mouse my dear, I believe there was a time at Cannes one summer when I had five or six carrying me up some stairs. But really my leg is fine, I'll show you." Robin said as she tried to strain her leg from under the wide straps securing her to the stretcher. "Oh! That feels odd." She said as her face blanched and her head fell back onto the stretcher.

"Max!" Susan yelled.

Max leaped forward and one big hand clamped down on Robin's upper thigh, blood squirting between his fingers. Robin let out a weak moan as Larsen increased the pressure of his grip. "Quick, set her down and lose the straps. Vince a tourniquet now! Meyers run up and alert the bridge, we're supposed to have a surgeon on board. Tell them to meet us in the infirmary." As the straps were released Max held Robin up enough for Vincent to get one of the stretcher straps around the thigh tight against her groin. A quick loop and a large pocket knife for a windlass soon had the gush of blood slowed. Cradling her in his arms Max charged up the accommodation ladder toward the infirmary, one sailor racing ahead to clear the way.

"Make a hole!" Max bellowed as he entered the passageway leading to the ship's surgery. Sailors quickly leapt out of the way while dragging a few wide eyed ex-prisoners with them.

A clatter was coming down a companionway stair that lead from the wardroom above.

"Clear way now!" a very loud and authoritative female voice commanded. Nancy Cuny was descending the stair two and three steps at a time, closely followed by Dr. Deveraux.

"Femoral just let go, she was wounded two days ago, chunk of wood in her thigh from an explosion." Max informed them as he ducked through the hatch leading into the infirmary.

"That's Lt. Jarvis, correct?" Verna asked as she flipped on the bright overhead light for the operating table.

"Yes, Robin Jarvis." Max confirmed as he carefully lay her down.

Vince had followed, "What do you need?" he asked.

"Notebook on the desk by the entry, I got all of our people's blood types before I left and combined all matches. Index in front has everyone's name. Find the matching page and it will have everyone with the same blood type." Verna answered as she donned gloves and began removing the bandage covering the wound while leaving the tourniquet in place. "Max, scrub up, you can help. Nancy, start her on some oxygen, then once you have the surgical kit out you're my anesthetist."

The trio worked smoothly and soon Robin was completely unconscious. Max took over monitoring her breathing and heart rate while Nancy prepared to assist.

"I have five matches on board, starting with the twins and three sailors, one more on the *Manta.*" Fuller said.

"Get the twins, one can assist and one can provide blood, the sailors also in case we need a reserve." Verna ordered while Fuller walked to the intercom to contact the bridge and have them announce which people needed to report to the sickbay.

Soon the two compartments were crowded with activity. Chen Fau had come over from the *Manta* to handle any other patients and care for O'Flannery. Lysette was already donating blood with an IV established by Marie who was prepping a sailor as a second donor. Fuller had gotten out of the way, ushering Susan ahead of him to the wardroom. "We need to give them room, even a Mouse takes up too much room in their now." Vincent said to the protesting thief.

"I can give blood, what if something goes wrong?"

Vincent shook his head, "Susan do you know your blood type? You weren't on the list. And right now they don't need any elbows jogged."

"Uh, no I don't. I've only been to a doctor once when I was eight and broke my arm while climbing."

"We'll find out later, right now they have plenty of volunteers available. I asked Marie to send for you the moment it is safe for Robin. Also as soon as they have her stabilized they still have to take care of O'Flannery." Vincent said.

Susan allowed herself to mount the companion way while inwardly cursing Fuller for being both logical and too large to evade.

In the operating room Verna and Nancy were working smoothly together. Clamps, retractors, sutures were quickly and efficiently used and put in place while the first bottle of Lysette's blood was run into Jarvis' veins as quickly as a large bore needle could flow it. In the infirmary next door the first sailor was donating his blood while Marie prepped the second sailor and started his donation.

"Do you need a hand?" Lysette asked from her cot.

Marie took a glance at Lysette's pale face and nearly laughed, "Don't be stupid sister. You gave plenty and I don't need to be picking you up off the floor. Lay back and take it easy."

"Yes Dear." Lysette responded and gladly laid her head back down.

Marie collected the bottle when the first sailor finished. She went to the intercom and asked for the third sailor and told the bridge to send for the matching sailor from the *Manta*. Putting a mask on, Marie took the second bottle into the OR and swapped it for the first. She looked at Max and raised an eyebrow in question.

Max nodded affirmatively and then said for both her benefit and Verna's, "Respirations steady, heart beat has slowed a bit and blood pressure up."

"Good." Verna answered as she and Nancy continued their work.

Twenty minutes later Verna watched as Nancy closed. "You really do beautiful stitches. How much more time in school when you return?"

"I was in my last year. I'm not sure the dean will let me pick back up where I left. He wasn't happy when I left to volunteer; especially as I had a scholarship as well as for another reason. It might not be available when I return."

"Ridiculous. You're already a better surgeon than half of the doctors I work with in England. Where were you going to school?"

"UT Galveston."

"Where?"

Max chuckled, "Verna be careful. Everyone in Texas knows she means the University of Texas. A question like that would cause untold consternation in Austin."

"Well thank goodness I'm not from Texas. It was a grave mistake when you colonists revolted. No proper person in Northern Canada would be so succinct as to refer to their school by its initials." Verna said coolly as her eyes smiled in mischief above her surgical mask.

Nancy looked up to see Verna and Max looking at each other and realized their banter was an indicator of their affection. "Mr. Larsen, how is our patient doing?"

"She's doing fine Miss Cuny. Respirations normal, heart rate still a tad fast and blood pressure low normal. One more pint of blood?"

"A good idea. Doctor? I've finished and the drain's in place. How does it look?

Verna made a show of the inspection as Nancy hung the next bottle of blood, "Nancy dear I believe you are just fishing for a compliment. And you deserve one. Very nice work. Also you shouldn't worry about your med school dean. Between my recommendation and Max's pull with Texas academia I assure you there will be no problem. Correct Max?"

"Well I have to admit being a bit more partial to A and M, but certainly not a problem. Nancy believe me when I say between my and Verna's money we can buy you a hospital of your own. You just helped save someone I respect and have become very fond of and you are about to work on one of my sailors who is also a good friend. You will have a scholarship."

Nancy was blinking back a few tears, afraid to say anything. "Thank you. I'll take the lieutenant out and then cleanup for the next patient."

Verna stopped her for a moment. "Stay with Jarvis while she recovers. Chen Fau will be helping with Aloysius and Marie can assist. Max has a corpsman who will help cleanup. I want to be sure the lieutenant stays put this time."

Max added, "Be sure and let Vincent Fuller and Mouse know she'll recover and let Mouse stay with her."

"Mouse?" Nancy asked.

"La Petit Souris. You'll enjoy meeting her. The smallest and bravest burglar in France." Max replied.

Chapter 43: Truth be told

August 20, 1943, 03:50
LaDonna Johnson's **Infirmary**

THE INFIRMARY WAS dimly lit, a lamp on the bulkhead softly illuminated Lt. Jarvis' bed and a second one did the same for O'Flannery. The sailors who had donated blood had with the assistance of their mates, headed for the ship's mess for soup and tea. Lysette had fallen asleep on her cot and no one planned to wake her any time soon.

Brodeur and Cuny, were next to Jarvis' bed and conversing in low tones. "Should she still be asleep?" Mouse asked.

Sitting in a chair as a polite way to get her head more level with Susan's, Nancy answered, "Yes she should, and she has no reason to get up. We placed a catheter to keep her from having to get up and we'll cut down the morphine. It's better to have her in a bit more pain and lucid so she doesn't try to shake a leg again. Let me show you how to check for capillary refill on her big toe. Whatever you do don't tickle her."

Susan started to give a sharp retort until she saw Nancy's smile. "Yes Sister. I'll be good."

"You love her very much, don't you? How long have you been together?" Nancy asked quietly.

"Seven years. Do you not approve?"

Nancy smiled, "I approve very much. I've known all my life that I loved women. But most of my early knowledge of lesbian life was colored by rural myths, rumors, and so called Christian morals. Alpine, Texas was not a hotbed of lesbian life style. It wasn't until I attended college that I was able to read anything beyond [1]J.H. Kellogg. My God that is an evil man. Anyway, I am heartened to see two women who have remained together and in love even while engaged in war. It truly gives me hope."

"I have no idea who is this Kellogg you speak of, and it sounds like I never want to. I pray that you too will find someone to love. Believe me, you are not alone in your search. Don't give up my dear." Susan said. She turned once more towards Robin and standing on tiptoe brushed some hair back from Jarvis' forehead. "She still has some fever."

"Yes, we gave her a new drug. It's called penicillin. Captain Larsen brought some from the States when his ship came over. She should recover. You will have the task of keeping her in bed for as long as possible."

"I have often kept her in bed for extended times. I doubt though that my usual practices will be appropriate." Mouse replied with a grin.

Nancy nearly shrieked with laughter, biting her knuckles to stay quiet, "Shush, I don't want to wake up everyone. My imagination just received more of a jolt than it needs right now."

From Lysette's cot came a stir as she sat up and swung her feet to the floor, "Good morning, or evening, or whenever it is. Didn't mean to sleep so long and I need to find a head."

"I'll give you a hand." Susan said as she moved over to Lysette. "There's a toilette just across the hall or whatever they call it on a boat. I can stand guard to make sure you have some privacy."

"Thank you Mouse, but I'm fine."

"I've heard that before. Let me help."

Lysette stood up, wobbled for a moment, and then pitched backwards towards the deck. Susan was just in time to get between her and the floor and absorb most of the impact.

Nancy ran over, picking up Lysette with little effort. "Susan are you all right?"

The Mouse jumped up laughing quietly, "It was nothing. Poor girl is worn out."

"I'm so sorry," Lysette said. "Please set me down, I still need to pee."

Nancy stood up, still cradling Lysette in her arms as if she was a young child. "Not a chance dear. Susan would you be so kind as to get the door to the head and if there are any sailors present ask them to be discreet. I don't want to inflict a bedpan on anyone if I can avoid it."

"My pleasure." Mouse jumped across the passageway, banged on the door to the head, and entered without stopping. "Attention, a lady coming in."

Susan disappeared inside and a moment later a sailor in his skivvies and half shaved popped out shaking his head and laughing to himself. He held the door open while waving the two women in. His grin turned to concern, "Do you need help?" His appearance and accent both proclaimed his Spanish heritage.

"Gracias, no I have this." Cuny answered and carried the embarrassed patient in.

The sailor took up a guard position in front of the door. Susan came out and administered a light pinch to the sailor in passing. They both grinned in delight as Susan entered the infirmary to keep an eye on Jarvis and O'Flannery.

[1]Dr. John Harvey Kellogg, 1852-1943 A medical doctor, the inventor of Corn Flakes, a quack, and an ardent crusader against smoking, alcohol, masturbation or even marital sex. Some of his recommendations included sutures to prevent erections and the use of carbolic acid applied to the clitoris as a deterrent to masturbation. He was widely read and edited Good Health periodical from 1874 until his death in 1943. SMk3

Chapter 44: First Look at the Fire Drake

Log of the LaDonna Johnson, E. Dietsch, M. Larsen,
V. Fuller, and S. Menzies

August 20, 1943, 17:25
The wardroom of the LaDonna Johnson

"COME IN CAPTAIN, after all it is your ship." Max Larsen declared to Lt. Cmdr. Archer as *LaDonna's* captain stuck his head in the door.

"I think the ship's owner might question that statement and I am rather heavily outranked by the owner's friends." Archer replied.

The ship's owner quickly responded, "As I am a civilian I consider all my friends to be of equivalent rank, and Rob you are a friend and therefore coequal with the rest of the assemblage." Max said as he waved the young officer in.

"My God Max, you must be sleeping with a thesaurus under your pillow. Join the assemblage Captain. We can use your outlook on how we might defend against this new weapon Count Voronstov has made." Ernst Dietsch said while he looked at some blueprints.

Col. Menzies, Hiram Snowden, and Vincent Fuller were also gathered in the wardroom. The table was covered in folders and pictures. Even as Archer entered he was followed by George Lee carrying a 16mm projector into the room. Arthur Dietel came next carrying a projection screen which he quickly erected against the aft bulkhead. Once finished he left, closing the door behind him, guarding it from further intrusion.

Brigadier Snowden was chairing the meeting, "Stewart, We have several of your lorries carrying the bulk of the plans to Bletchley Park even as we speak. And while I am sure there are some devastating weapons in the batch, I believe this Fire Drake missile is the most immediate threat to any invasion fleet. The scientists and their families will be on a train headed south shortly and I imagine they'll be debriefed and put to work soon. Allied scientists and engineers will be questioning them as well as defense intelligence agents."

"You will have barristers and police taking statements as well I hope." Max addressed Col. Menzies. "Their imprisonment and forced labor is one more crime the Nazis need to answer for. Too bad we probably won't be able to prosecute Stalin and the Communists for their internal pogroms or the U.S. Congress for the internment of Americans of Japanese ancestry."

"Anyone else who needs protection Max?" Dietsch asked his friend. "I hear we're deporting a bunch of Mexican American citizens for the crime of being defenseless against Anglo aggression."

"I shouldn't have started, but yes there are the Americans of Mexican heritage, the Roma throughout Europe, African blacks still being exploited by Belgium, Italy, France, Arabs, South Africans, and some of their own leaders; all the American Indian tribes on reservations in the U.S.; our Negro citizens; and in China the non-Han Chinese. Probably not a country in the world that hasn't made some group a scapegoat for the ruling classes deficiencies. Let me apologize and step off the soapbox. We need to get back to the problem at hand."

Menzies nodded towards Larsen, "No apologies needed Max, you've forgot our East India Company and the messes we've made in Africa, India, Afghanistan and the probable partition of Hindu India and the [1]Moslem Northwest Territories. The sun never sets on all the trouble England has been involved in over the years. I've heard of some of your outside activities and inferred some others over the years. I look at it as more of a series of small retail operations of high quality. Many I've applauded and some deplored and a few times I think good intentions have gone awry. However on the whole I believe you accomplished more good than bad."

"Thank you Stewart. I'll never know some of the results as I expect to be deceased long before all the long term effects are known. Truly though we need to get back to Hitler who is our greatest problem at the moment. Let's just hope that Russia and China don't exceed his evil in the future."

"All right, soapboxes on hold, sins have been confessed and the film is due to roll." Vincent Fuller said. He had threaded film into the projector and started it up. "I believe this is some footage of the first test run of the Fire Drake."

The men watched in silence as the film first showed some shots of the hull mockups and the bunker, it also showed the slaves being forced into the hulls. Next they saw the arrival of Goering and the salutes of the German officers and engineers. Last they had several different views of the missiles accelerating, entering the bunker and then the destruction wrought by the weapon.

"My God," Hiram exclaimed," that would devastate any ship we have."

"How low and how fast was that thing? It would be damn near impossible to shoot it and anything behind it would be riddled by our own defense." Rob Archer said.

Ernst spoke up, "if my stopwatch is right and those bigger hash marks on the ground are at one hundred meters, then it was traveling at over four hundred miles an hour. Slow for a rocket, but still damn fast for a plane to catch and how Voronstov keeps it flying that low and fast has me bamboozled."

"It would also appear that the Germans didn't want any of the workmen to tell tales. How many did they put in the mockups, forty or fifty?" Max said in the coldest of voices.

"I see one problem with their deployment already." Ernst said. "They need clear lanes. Those things would maybe just clear over a [2]Higgins Boat. Also the light projectors will have to be high enough for their beams to clear the inshore craft and sight the larger ships."

"Yeah, that much firepower would be wasted on LCMs. Does that mean they will use them on the [3]LCVPs and LCTs before the Higgins boats are deployed?" Archer asked.

Max spoke up, "Another possible fault. These dragons are self-guided, but if they're homing on a light spot on a hull they can't avoid anything that gets in their way. Vincent, do you know yet what happens if they lose their signal?"

"It looks like they stay on course with a gyro. If the signal disappears they should continue to head for wherever they last saw it. If we have a brighter UV source will that spoof the rocket?"

"Who gets to wave the red flag at the bull?" Ernst asked. "That will not be a popular job."

Hiram cut in, "Gentlemen, I'll leave the technical analysis to you engineer types. Vincent, was there any information on where these infernal devices are stockpiled or sited. Some of your hypotheses will be moot if we can bomb the rockets out of existence. And that's something Colonel Menzies and I can get started on."

"I believe I can help you there General." George Lee said. "Vince turned over all the invoices, bills of lading, etcetera over to me and I and the purser have been making some progress. I can get you in the ball park. Aerial recon can help after that. If I might caution you, take them all out at one time, because as soon as the Germans suspect that we know where the Fire Drakes are stashed, they will transport a lot of them where we can't see or bomb them."

"Thank you George, I agree that we need to take out as many as possible the first time. Knowing that we have no chance of getting them all I'm hoping that we can come up with countermeasures as well. Max, Vincent, Ernst keep working on them. I want to transfer you and the plans and other information to Bletchley as quickly as possible as I am sure Stewart has his own experts to aid you."

"I do indeed General and the sooner the better." Menzies agreed.

[1] *Moslem Northwest Territory became Pakistan after the partition from India. SMkIII*

[2]*Higgins Boats, small flat bottom assault craft that carried the bulk of the soldiers and equipment to the beach. They were manufactured by Higgins Industries of New Orleans. LCMs (Landing Craft Mechanical) and some were specialized as platforms for launching artillery rockets and other special needs. SMkIII*

[3]*LCVPs and LCTs: Landing Craft Vehicles and Personnel, and Landing Craft Tank. Larger flat bottom boats designed to carry personnel, vehicles, tanks and heavier artillery from Allied ports to a beachhead. In addition LSTs (Landing Ship Tanks) were ships some 327 feet long and with a loaded weight of 3800 tons capable of carrying 12- 20 tanks depending on size, 200 soldiers above the ships complement, and 20 or more other vehicles such as trucks and jeeps. LSTs were also converted to carry multiple LCMs, and two LCTs or LCVPs.*

Chapter 45: Upset its homeostasis

M. Larsen, V. Fuller, E. Dietsch,
Excerpts from the meeting minutes

August 22, 1943 08:00
A converted carriage house at Bletchley Park

"VINCENT, YOU THINK that infra-red film will help us find the dragons?" Ernst asked.

"Yes. Actually their carrying case, the *Drachenspringteufel*. If nothing else your Voronstov seems to have a sense of humor still. A dragon jack-in-the-box doesn't sound too awesome, but it sure could be an unpleasant surprise to the fleet."

"How's the IR film going to help?"

"Ernst those boxes contain the dragon and they're big metal shipping crates. Very sturdy and all the same size. By late afternoon they will have absorbed enough heat to be distinct from the cooler trees and ground and their uniform shape should show up pretty clearly through the camouflage netting. We may find all sorts of other things under those nets, but the boxes should stand out."

"Sounds good Vince, we'll wish them good hunting." Max Larsen said. "Our navy is sending over a Captain Michael Pinkerton, who is supposed to be an expert on anti-aircraft systems. Everything from guns to barrage balloons, including a new device that shoots up a small rocket that deploys a long steel cable with parachutes on each end. Apparently it's supposed to tangle up around a wing and then yank it off."

"Max, I don't see how that will help much against the dragons. By the time it deploys it's already well above the dragon's path." Vince replied. "Hopefully he'll have some other tricks. I still think our best bet is to spoof them out to sea somehow. Any attempt to shoot them down will just decimate our own people. They don't have all that much range. Get them out far enough and they just fall into the Channel."

Ernst spoke up, "I dislike the idea of trying to lure it out to sea. Do we even have an aircraft fast enough to weave it between all the ships and keep it in play long enough to burn out? A suicide mission may be called for in the balance of saving more lives, but let's hold it as the last option."

"What about the UV projectors of the Germans, anyway to knock them out of commission. If not, how bright would our light sources have to be to attract the missiles?' Larsen asked.

"In order, no, I agree, and yes it would have to be very bright. We don't have an aircraft fast enough to lure them far enough. Suicide is a lousy option and we don't have a safe way to bail out of an aircraft at speed. And to add to the problem, while a Spitfire or a Lightning or the new Mustangs in a dive might be able to target and safely hit a dragon, they will have to ignore both the German flak, artillery, and our own ships shells heading toward the landing. Being hit by a fourteen inch shell or any of the smaller stuff is not a good situation.'

"The UV projector is almost as ingenious as the dragon. It has a d/c motor spinning a very small hi-voltage a/c generator feeding a transformer that excites the bulb to the point where it's emitting in the UV range so their filtration is minimal. The optics use a front surface mirror in a tube that I can only describe as an inverted tubular Fresnel lens. It is the most cohesive beam of light from a projector all of two feet long that I have ever heard of. All this is surrounded by a mineral oil filled jacket that transfers heat to an ammonia tube that percolates like a heat pump to pull the excess heat out. I will definitely steal this idea for something sometime. The battery takes up the rest of the box and the thing only has to work long enough guide the missile to its target. Five to seven minutes max. Then you replace the battery, let the projector cool down for a few minutes and you're good to go. Put several of the lights deep in the artillery revetments on the shore and unless you are the target, have the proper filter, and looking straight back along the beam you would never know for sure where it is coming from. As it will be beamed on the hull there won't be anyone on the ship who can see it. Other ships observers with filtered glasses will be able to see what ships are targeted, but all they can do is warn them and you can't do high speed evasion without running into other ships. Besides any ship's high speed maneuver is still too slow. We're screwed so far."

Gloom was the first thing to greet Capt. Pinkerton as he was shown into the room. "This looks bad. Either I am not at all welcome or the three of you have some very serious problems."

The three men rose to greet the captain. "Excuse us Captain; we do have a bad problem and we keep making it worse. Hopefully you'll see something we missed." Larsen said. He went on to make introductions and then explain the weapon and what they had considered as countermeasures.

Pinkerton stood looking at blueprints and pictures while rubbing his chin. "I'm afraid I'll need to start working on my scowl. I can't shoot it, I can't catch it, we can't evade it, and it runs faster than we can. You've taken me out of my competency zone, that's for sure."

Ernst looked up from the table covered in data, "competency zone, Mike your zone is not the answer, but the missiles zone may be the key." Dietsch stood up and started pacing back and forth. "Design parameters. How can we force it out of its zone? Max for your edification and benefit I want to upset its homeostasis."

While providing a digital salute to Ernst, Max turned to Fuller, "It flies in ground affect. What happens if its target goes up?"

"It would try to follow it, but it can't carry that load out of ground affect. It needs the air compression under the wings. It would slow, maybe stall, fall off. If you had a series of UV sources going up it would reacquire and try again, probably start porpoising beyond its ability to correct. Either stall or dive into the water. It has a combination proximity and contact fuse so it might not even blow up. Could depend on the entry angle."

"This sounds like the best so far. An actual real possibility and we couldn't have done it without you Captain Pinkerton. You're just as brilliant as the admiral claimed. Didn't take you ten minutes after we explained the problem." Ernst said while vigorously shaking the captain's hand.

"Glad to be of help, however if you don't quit pulling my leg I'm going to end up with a limp. Let's see how we might pull this off." Pinkerton said as he loosened his tie and unbuttoned his jacket.

Max threw out the first question, "Do star shells emit UV light? How about parachute flares? Tow one from the back of a fast launch like an air rescue boat and let it rise up like a kite on the end of a cable. Reel it in or let it out as needed."

"Possible, I need to look at the autopilot a bit more and try to figure out how quick it could react." Fuller said. "

Pinkerton added, "I have no idea how much UV light any of our flares, star shells or searchlights can put out. Hasn't ever been a factor the Navy needed to know. I'll send out a request and see if there is anything in the archives."

"Mike, I'm sure they told you how important this is. You can't send out a blanket request or the Germans may hear of it. Keep it a very discreet search." Larsen advised. "I have a couple of other venues to explore. I'll use the shipping company's system to send a radiogram in our company cipher, we use one time pads, to have Hiram's firm start researching any patents that might be out there on UV propagation. And possibly quickest I'll use it to ask Tom."

"May I ask who Tom is and doesn't this get into the same problem as a blanket request?" the captain asked.

"Dr. Thomas George Fixx is the owner and lead researcher for Columbia Pharmaceuticals in Chicago. He is also a genius with a photographic memory. If he has ever read or heard of anything to do with UV emitting flares or other sources he can lead us to the references in an instant." *'That he was once Hugo DeValle the teenage mastermind of the Devall criminal family is probably something the good captain does not need to know.'*

"Of course I've heard of Columbia, and Dr. Fixx. Doesn't he have some kind of educational foundation that provides grants? I'd never heard of his photographic memory. How I could have used one when I was going through the academy." Pinkerton said.

"You really don't want an eidetic memory Mike. Yes it's a big help for a scientist or a student. It's also a curse to anyone who has ever lived. Every memory for him is fresh and instantly available. Good memories and bad. Every time he thinks of his first wife he can remember every detail of her dying due to eclampsia, losing their unborn daughter as well. Every moment spent in the trenches of World War One, every friend and how they died or were maimed. You would be unable to forget anything. All as fresh as the day it happened. You probably have a very good memory, one doesn't become an acknowledged expert or graduate from the Naval Academy without an excellent memory, but you don't want what Dr. Fixx has. He is one of my closest friends, but I pity him every day."

It became very quiet in the room as Larsen and his two friends thought about the doctor and some of their own shared memories, good and bad.

Finally the captain broke the silence, "Thank you Max. I'd never considered the downside of a perfect memory. I think I'll be happy now to look up standards and tables and count my blessings."

"Mike I didn't intend to bring down the party just when we might have a solution to one of our problems. Let's go get a late breakfast or an early lunch. Being gloomy makes me hungry. Gentlemen, my treat. Let's check the canteen."

Chapter 46: Mr. Morton-Smyth

August 22, 1943, 16:00 GMT
Col. Osgood's Office

"COLONEL MENZIES SENDS HIS regards. By no means is this operation his only one and he has to get back to those currently running." Hiram Snowden told the crew helping him locate the Fire Drakes. Col. Osgood, George Lee, and Mr. Gadson Wilson Morton-Smyth, the personification of a milquetoast minion of Lloyd's. Blessed with minimal physical dimensions and who, according to Col. Menzies, had the testicular fortitude of a platoon of Royal Marines; Morton-Smyth had just returned from surreptitiously touring the Channel ports of the French Coast.

"Brigadier, I believe I may be of some help. I have witnessed some of these boxes being transported from Canal de Calais a Saint-Omer to Dunkerque. The dimensions are exact and the rigging used by the cranes to place them onto the German [1]MFPs, their landing craft, as well as the change in draft marks would suggest an equivalent weight." The little man mentioned while his eyes, behind old pince-nez, never left the plans and specifications.

"Have you seen them anywhere else Mister Morton-Smyth?" Col. Osgood asked.

"Colonel please call me Will. Gadson resulted in numberless futile bouts of pugilism when I was in school. One of the incentives helping me forge a persona of inconsequence that has served me well as I cowered from Dunkirk to Portugal. Yes I have seen them. The sites correspond with the material presented by Mister Lee. I didn't range too far from the waterways, but I did see them being lightered along the coast and trucked up into the hills behind the ports. Whoever designed the cargo box did a beautiful job. Eyes at all eight corners let them be quickly hooked to a crane or boomed to a truck or flatcar with a minimum of fuss. They were offloading one every three to four minutes. A large forklift would also be able to move them."

Col. Osgood spoke up, "We should have photos later tonight or early tomorrow morning. The recon F-4s will be going out shortly and taking pictures of as much of the areas covered in camo netting as possible. I hope the film's fresh. The storage requirements for infrared film are pretty stringent. The lab boys test each batch before they load it."

"Kodak not keeping up with demand?" George asked.

"No, that's not a problem, the film is sensitive to heat even in the canister. Much easier to shield from visible light than it is from heat."

"Ok, that makes sense. Do they refrigerate it?"

"George I really don't know. It sounds likely, but I don't know the details, just that it's difficult. Ask Hiram if you want a technical answer." Osgood said.

Snowden held up his hands in protest, "I'm just an old lawyer. Don't expect me to...."

Osgood interrupted, "George, don't listen to his I'm just an old country lawyer shtick. His first degree was in math and after he became a criminal defense lawyer he switched to patent law because of his fascination with machines and they were easier to understand than people and much more lucrative. Believe me when I tell you that the Brigadier can hold his own with most engineers and scientists."

"Not supposed to interrupt superior officers Albert. George the film has to be stored in certain temperatures. Not a problem in the North Atlantic as long as you keep it away from the engine room. In warmer climes they do use refrigeration."

"Thank you Hiram." Lee replied. "Will, just how well do you know the French Coast?"

"George I was a young naval rating in the Great War and I ended the war supervising offloading in a few of the French ports. I stayed in France after the war as a civilian expediter of certain cargoes, especially of Bollinger."

"A man after Max's heart if I've read between the lines correctly." George said to a questioning frown from the two American officers.

Morton-Smyth had the grace to allow a slight blush of his features, "Youthful indiscretions George. To put not too fine a point on it General, Colonel, I smuggled champagne for quite a few years. I parlayed my expertise by investing in the Lloyds' market where I did quite well. I was later encouraged somewhat forcefully to join the ranks of Special Enquirers for the consortium. The Admiralty was also quite happy to make use of my knowledge and contacts. I have been keeping an eye on the French coast for King and Country since 1932."

"I believe we have our expert General." George said. "Will, what locations come to mind when I say 'cutting out party?'"

[1]MFP Marinefahrpram: German landing craft originally designed for Operation Sea Lion, the invasion of England that never happened. 160' long, 21' beam, draft of 4.5'. Capacity 85 to 140 tons, and constructed of riveted steel plate. Powered by 3 Deutz diesels providing a top speed of 10.5kn and a range of 1340nm at 7kn. Most were usually armed with 2-20mm AA guns, 1-37mm, and 1-75mm gun. Some were converted to other duties, the artillery model (AFP) was armed with 2-88mm or 2-105mm cannon, 1-37 mm AA, and 8-20mm AA. All MFPs had .8" of armor with the AFPs adding 4" of concrete to the inside for additional protection from splintering. SMkIII

Chapter 47: A Cutting Out Party

OSS Logs, H. Snowden, A. Osgood

August 22, 1943, 17:00 GMT
Col. Osgood's Office

"Damn'it George, Max and Vince have been planning this insanity all along. Admit it, those two are going to try and steal a Fire Drake!" Brigadier Snowden yelled and then added some choice cursing.

"Of course they're going to steal some. The bastard things are too damn good to ignore. If they are going to design a defense then they want better information than just what the plans show. They want to fire up an unarmed and unfueled unit and see how well the tracking system works, how fast it reacts, and how well it tracks UV. They don't want to trust defense to theory and neither should you." George riposted.

The brigadier was still fuming, "What, they plan on waltzing into the French coast with a German flagged *LaDonna*? Rowboats with muffled oars and his men with cutlasses clenched in their teeth. Max has called his crews pirates for so long that it's gone to his head."

"No General, that isn't the plan. At least not yet. Would you like to hear the proposal or do you want to go throw a few paratroopers around in a so called [1]training session until you calm down?"

"I'll hear you out and then I'll go teach some of those young kids how to survive. God, they teach'em a few throws and a choke hold and the guys all of a sudden think they're the Shadow or [2]Doc Savage. And don't start looking all smug you big lug or I'll show you a few things your papa never taught you."

Looking remarkably unperturbed by Snowden's threat, George continued, "Yes sir. Now as to your questions: First, *LaDonna* will be headed for the South Atlantic. The consensus amongst the naval types is that she will be more effective by herself. We know the Germans have at least two Q-ships running around down there now. Also any German subs she lures in will most likely be working alone and she can hunt them down with all her weapons free including active sonar. Lieutenant Commander Archer is getting a well-deserved bump to full commander and it will be a Navy crew along with a few of Max's older chiefs who will be carried as warrant officers with all pay and privileges. Plus Max will keep paying his chiefs their regular salary in hopes of not getting his ship bent. He's worked out a lease agreement with the Navy against what they owe him and he retains the *LaDonna* when the war is over."

"Ok George; that takes care of Max's Q-ship and makes surprising sense for Max and the Navy. So what is the plan for the Fire Drakes?"

"With Will's help and knowledge now available to us and the *Manta's* ability to loiter and observe we intend to capture a German landing craft. They are moving some of the jack-in-a-box units along the coast at night to evade British planes and MTBs. By using the remora to put some of Major McDougal's men along with Ardison and Max on board they should be able to capture or kill the crew. The Nazis can't afford the manpower to fully crew the *marinefahrprams*. Max and Ardison should be able to take out the crew without causing an alarm and the major's men will be in reserve for insurance. Any E-boats acting as escort will be either evaded or engaged by British MTBs which will be vectored by the *Manta*. Once they secure the German MFP it will head west and drive right into the *Caroline Maverick* which will then head under cover of the MTBs, the *Repulse*, and Max's sub for Southend-on-Sea and the Thames as quickly as possible. Both the *Manta* or the remora are capable of towing the Nazi MFP if for some reason it loses power."

Col. Osgood could no longer contain himself, "Their plan is centered on two people quietly taking out the entire German crew. That's ludicrous! Yeah, Max is a human juggernaut and Ardison is big and strong, but this would be laughable if it weren't so absurd."

Hiram turned to his friend and fellow officer, "Al, I have to say that the part of Max and Ardison clearing the ship of crew is the least risky part of the operation. Yes Max can be a juggernaut, he can plow through a football team and not break a sweat. I've been with him in the wild though. I've witnessed him stalk a mature black bear to touching distance and the number of sentries that Max has killed or caught is staggering. There is much more science to his ability as a fighter than you would think, he rarely needs it, but he has learned it in the grimmest of schools. Ardison is nearly his match in the wild and his martial skills put mine to shame. I learned them and practiced out of interest and practical considerations. Ardison learned his from necessity, pride, and a commitment to freedom the equal of Max's. Don't let his easy humor and singing fool you, he and Max are probably the two most deadly men you will ever meet."

"That's true Albert. Listen to Hiram, if anything he's understating their ability." George added.

Osgood answered, "Understating I'll take on advisement. You two really think they can take over a *marinfahrpram* without alerting her escorts? I guess if the major's men are along it might work."

Snowden replied, "Yes Al, we do. There's possibly other reservations I have, but Max and Ardison clearing the ship isn't one of them. Frankly I believe the major and his men are there just to make Colonel Menzies happy. Max's pirates are even better trained and more experienced than the SOE contingent. The difference is small enough though to make little difference to Max. If he didn't think the Brits could handle their task, he never would have included them."

Osgood capitulated, "All right you two. I've heard some of what Max and his crews have previously accomplished. How they did it without half a dozen countries screaming for his hide I haven't a clue. Go ahead and ask your other questions so George and Will can answer them. Considering how you were defending Max it sounds like the agreement has already been struck."

"I'm still going to hand out a few lessons on general principles." Hiram grumbled. "And Albert, several countries have tried to put an end to Max and his crew: they eventually decided that the price was too high."

[1]*In 1905 in Atlanta, Georgia and while still practicing criminal law Hiram witnessed a slight Asian man subdue two large men who were attempting to rob the man's wife. Hiram stepped in to keep Sung Lei from seriously harming the two bumpkins. Hiram brought assault charges against the two men, winning his case with the statement: "the assault is predicated on their intent, not their miserable ability." Hiram gained lasting friends and employees in Sung Lei and his wife Sung Jing. Hiram learned kung fu, karate, and Mandarin while developing a lifelong interest in martial arts. As his work and riches took him further afield he learned a Berber form of savate, different types of African and Indian stick fighting, as well as Hungarian and Indian swordplay. Hiram and Ardison Mitchell will later supplement the Ranch training provided by Captain Quartermain and Leboo Larsen. During WWII, Hiram occasionally gave "finishing lessons" to paratroopers and OSS agents undergoing training. SMkIII*

²*Doc Savage, Clark Savage Jr. was another popular pulp fiction hero published from the 1930s until after WWII by Street and Smith Publishers. A protean scientific genius of immense physical abilities aided by five associates who were all masters of different professions and adventurers par excellence. Lester Dent, who wrote most of the adventures under the house name Kenneth Robeson, was nearly as talented and adventurous as his creation. SMkIII*

Chapter 48: Quiet Death
Log of the *Manta,* Reports from M. Larsen, A. Mitchell, Maj. Ian McDougal

August 26, 1943, 01:00
Off the French Coast between Calais and Dunkerque

"DEFINITELY JACK-IN-THE-BOXES; Will was absolutely right about the shipment. Looks like maybe four units. He has to be the bravest man I've ever known. How he gets in and out of France whenever he wants is truly amazing. Any idea how he does it?" Max Larsen asked Major McDougal while continuing to observe the German landing craft through the *Manta's* periscope.

"I have some ideas, but I don't pretend to know for sure. Colonel Menzies is satisfied and as far as I know he and Will are the only two who know. My favorite theory is he's portraying a French smuggler assisting some officer in the German marine patrols to do his own bit of smuggling." the major answered.

"That's how I'd do it. As long as your leverage is good and the officer and his crew know that a double cross will cost them more than it would Morton-Smyth; he should be good." Larsen agreed.
Larsen lowered the periscope and turned to his crew, "The E-boats are even farther ahead and aft of the MFP than we'd hoped; better yet they are both seaward so the remora can come up on the starboard side without their observing. The craft is doing about eight knots, and I couldn't see any crew amongst the cargo. Two men on the twenty millimeters, two at the helm and probably a radioman just inside the companionway, a lookout in the crosstree behind the helm, figure a cook, and ten to fourteen deck hands, gunners, and two engineers. Once Ardison and I control the helm and the gunners Ian, you and your men take over the helm and the radio while the two of us finish the capture or kill of the crew. Most will probably be in their bunks or the ready room. Once we control the radio and helm the hard part will be done."

"No Max, the hard part will be if the rest of the crew discovers us and decides to die rather than surrender." Ardison said.

Max's reply was a simple grunt of agreement. "Major, time to go. Fau, don't hesitate to turn the British MTBs loose on the S-boats if either does anything suspicious or breaks radio silence. We need to take them out at some point anyway. I'd rather the Germans think all three vessels were sunk rather than one was stolen. Preferably we'll already be in control of the MFP, but if not we'll cross that bridge in a much noisier fashion."

"Don't worry about the *Schnellbootes,* they won't interfere. Be careful Max, don't bend any of the Fire Dragons or we'll have to do this again." *Manta's* second officer replied.

01:15

The remora was very crowded, Lars Anderson was at the helm; Max and Ardison, a crowd by themselves were at the hatch, all but the helm seat had been removed and Major McDougal and six of his men were standing hunched over in the space between. Max and Ardison were dressed in dark clothes, broken by occasional gray lines zigzagging across. Their tunics had fringe and odd shapes built in to destroy recognizable outlines. They were also festooned with numerous knives, garrotes, and suppressed .380 ACP model 1908 Colt pistols as well as regular model 1911 .45s. All the weapons were dull and darkened and vigorous shaking had not elicited a sound from them.

The British commandos were attired all in black and had their standard weapons of Sten guns and pistols. Three days before they had been the recipients of a very instructional and frightening lesson in a dimly lit warehouse. All had been subjected to quiet taps on the shoulder as Max and Ardison had moved through their ranks while they guarded a keg of beer held in an office. Most sobering was that the beer had been spirited away before they had received the shoulder taps of implied death. They were now convinced that only divine intervention would save the German crew.

A Perspex dome had been made to cover the remora's hatch to allow Max to coax Anderson alongside the Nazi ship. The dimmest of red lights illuminated the interior of the sub. Sufficient only to allow the commandos to egress. As the underwater tug matched speed alongside the landing craft and slowly rose up, Max and Ardison moved silently forward and aft, quietly attaching rubber coated grapnels to the German gunwales. A heavy rope stretched between the two and a few feet of boarding net hung from the rope. The *Drachenspringteufels* actually hung over the side of the little ship by a couple of feet, raised on racks and with just room to crawl beneath them to access the deck. Max quickly tightened the line and then he and Ardison slithered over the ships side. Major McDougal and his men quickly moved to the cargo net, clinging to the side. One man stayed behind, closing the Perspex dome and then acted as lookout.

The remora silently peeled away to wait for the rear S-boat to pass and then follow in trail of the three ships.

Ian McDougal was watching the helm station while his top sergeant was keeping the two 20mm guns under observation. Ian thought he saw a shadow obscure the lookout above the helm and then the shadow went away and the lookout had taken an unnaturally stiff position against the mast behind him. McDougal's sergeant suddenly realized that one of the gunners was no longer to be seen and as he looked toward the other an indistinct shape enveloped the second gunner and then both disappeared. The sergeant shivered slightly as the hair on the back of his neck rose up. The silent and sudden nonexistence of the gunners was unnerving and a silent prayer ran unbidden through his thoughts.

At the helm a small penlight flashed twice toward the commandos and as one they gained the ships deck and advanced as quietly as possible. At the helm they found Larsen on the wheel, two Germans dead and placed against the aft bulkhead. McDougal looked up at the lookout to see a young sailor tied to the mast and his unseeing eyes staring down in surprise, the slow drip of blood was the only sign of his fatal injury. The sergeant looked into the small compartment for the radio operator and saw a mass huddled over the desk and the radio turned off and dark. Larsen directed the commando who had been a fisherman before the war to the helm and then melted below. Several of the soldiers said a silent prayer and one who was Catholic crossed himself. Proximity to a veritable angel of death can have that affect.

Down below Max moved towards the wardroom while Ardison moved into the engine space. The noise in the engine room allowed Ardison to use the suppressed .380 Colt to quick effect and then proceed toward the berthing space. Max dispatched the cook dozing in the small galley before finding three sailors engrossed in a card game in the wardroom. Two died before the third realized they were under attack and he died as a dagger pierced his throat and penetrated the brain stem. The two men continued their inexorable passage through the truncated bowels of the little ship. Meeting in a small passageway they stopped for a moment, "For the Reverend Jepson and his family." Ardison intoned in a voice so low it couldn't have been heard five feet away.

"He wouldn't have approved, but yes, for the Reverend and all the others." Max said, then the two returned to the helm, sending the fisherman to the engine room with Ardison accompanying him.

"Major if you will alert *Manta* we will see what we can do with these E-boats before we head west. The rest of the commandos manned the various guns onboard the German ship. Once the men reported that all were manned and ready the major took an American SCR-536 handie-talkie from a pack, extended the antennae to turn it on and blipped the transmit button three times. He had started a lethal chain of events for the two S-boats. Max increased throttle slightly, bringing the German vessel closer to the lead S-boat.

Two British MTBs, one keeping pace forward and inshore and the second trailing the three ships were alerted to attack once the *Manta* started the action. Silently the giant sub surfaced, its unique design keeping the water flowing smoothly over its surface and precluding a visible wake or bow wave. The quad-40 was directed at the helm of the trailing S-boat. The *Manta fired,* instantly destroying the helm and radio station of the German torpedo boat. With the first crack of the subs' gun the 75mm cannon on the landing craft fired at the lead boats helm, but instead hitting a rack of depth charges on the stern. The resultant explosion destroyed the rear half of the vessel. The lead British MTB's 20mm guns and 2-pounder cannon made quick work of the forward half of the defenseless ship. Meanwhile the *Manta's* cannon continued to decimate its target. Joined by the trailing MTB the Nazi vessels were soon sinking, some burning fuel on the water the only marker of the German vessels' demise.

As soon as the 75mm cannon fired on board the MFP. Larsen spun the wheel to head west and soon had the sturdy little ship at its top speed of a little over ten knots. The *Manta* left the final destruction of the German escorts to the British torpedo boats and followed the pirated landing craft. The big sub slowed for a moment to recover the remora and then again closely followed the prize. Once the two MTBs confirmed the destruction of the German patrol vessels and the absence of survivors, they too sped up and formed a protective screen in front of the escaping vessel.

At 02:40 the MFP slid into the darkened confines of the *Caroline Maverick* which as soon as the landing craft was secured, started pumping ballast water out of her twin hulls and was soon doing over twenty knots towards England. Escorted by the two MTBs and *HMS Repulse* the huge ship headed for the Thames estuary and the protection of England's shield.

The *Manta* quietly continued north toward its shelter in the Orkneys.

Chapter 49: Shell Game

Log of the *Caroline Maverick,* V. Fuller, B. Crabtree, M. Larsen

August 26, 1943, 02:45
The *Caroline Maverick* in the English Channel,
15 nautical miles west of *Dunkerque*

VINCENT FULLER WATCHED as the German MFP floated into the cavernous central bay of Larsen Shipping's best ship transporter. The dimmest of red lights illuminated only the landing crafts helm as a gangway was adroitly placed alongside by an overhead gantry crane. "Everything ready for our guests Ben?"

Ben Crabtree smiled grimly as he observed the precision operation performed by his crew. "Oh yes. All's ready. A keg of beer, steaks, baked potatoes, and all the trimmings are waiting for Major McDougal and his men. We've also added a bit of two hundred proof ethanol to the beer and one of the cooks was almost in the bag before they determined that the beer tasted innocent of the addition. I don't envy their heads later today or tomorrow."

"You think they'll have gotten a good count of all the Fire Drakes?" Fuller asked.

"They had no flashlights, the ship ran without any lights and they concentrated on the helm and the guns. The only seaman among them was either at the helm or in the engine room. And don't forget what being around Max and Ardison when they're hunting is like. First time I saw their handy work I didn't sleep for two nights, spent all my time looking over my shoulder and spooking at any little sound. And I'd bet this ship that I was older and had witnessed more mayhem than any of those lads down there."

Vincent nodded in agreement, "Yeah, I've been there. I didn't want to be alone with either of them the first time I witnessed their act. Max and Ardison will be as quiet and grim as a graveyard for the next few days. Their gifts are burdens few men could bear."

"Amen to that. They won't shirk what they can do, but neither of 'em takes any pride in their abilities. Everything else is ready. Five containers down there. I'd never pack that many on an MFP. They have the first four overhanging the sides of the ship. You think we can get away with hiding two of them and then spacing the rest out? We also have a kubelwagen that we can tarp and put in one space."

"Two should do it, we'll learn how to use them with the ones we use for testing. You're sure Janelle can alter the shipping manifests?"

Crabtree just smiled, "Remember that Winchester 50/110 that Max gave you ten or so years ago. Janelle did the engraving on the receiver. We have several German typewriters so as to get a close match, German paper and carbons. Not a problem; who do you think makes all the passports and other papers Max uses. When he can't steal or safely buy the documentation he needs, Janelle provides."

"Damn, I had no idea. That rifle is my favorite. I don't know how many times I've pulled out a magnifying glass to show people that tiny Pearl Beer bottle next to the campfire. Amazing work."

"My darling wife usually only engraves our own guns or for good friends. She knew that Max set store by your friendship and she was happy to do it. All right the boats secure, time to go and Ardison's leading those Brits to a celebratory dinner they'll all regret later. As soon as they're out of sight we'll start hiding the pea."

Max Larsen joined Ardison and the British commandos at the wardroom table where a truly impressive and aromatic display of food had the commandos salivating. "I hope you don't mind Ian, but I think you and your men deserve a small celebration. The work all of you have performed in the last few months has been outstanding. It's not much, sirloin steaks and all the fixings, potatoes, fresh green beans, even apple pie a la mode for dessert and of course the keg of beer that was the prize a few days ago."

"Mind, my word I don't mind! Your ships serve the best food I've had since the war started. Do you feed all your crews this well?"

"The difference in cost between bad food and good is a pittance. A good cook and good quarters are small enough reward for what my sailors do. Besides a well-paid and happy crew makes more money for the company. Less downtime, better maintenance, and less turnover of properly trained people. I won't hire someone I don't like, why not treat them like the friends they are." Max answered. "If you will excuse me, I need to meet with Captain Crabtree."

"Of course Max. Thank you for this. Frankly what my men have witnessed tonight may lead them to empty that keg."

"Don't worry about that. We'll tell Colonel Menzies that we need you on board for the rest of the day. You can return to your barracks the next day and I can supply stevedores if we need to carry you in."

The major laughed and turned to his men who were impatiently waiting to be turned loose on the feast before them. With a nod of his head they took their seats and began passing plates around.

Max went to Ardison and in a low voice only his first officer could hear said, "Thanks Ardison, keep them entertained and in here. I know that a party is the last place you want to be now, but they can't see us shuffling the containers about. As soon as we have the containers hidden I'll send Anderson to relieve you."

"Don't worry Max, the way they're knocking back those schooners they won't be sober long. I'll be sure that the gallyhands empty the keg into the scuppers if the Brits don't kill it. Max we did what was necessary. You didn't start this war. Unfortunately the politicians who allowed it to happen will never have to pay appropriately. I hope Hell has a special place for them."

Max just nodded, turned and left the room, none of the revelers able to see the pain and sadness in his face.

Larsen crossed the foredeck to the opposite hull and was in time to see a section of deck complete with track for the gantry crane swing back into place over an unmarked storage hold in the port hull. He found Vincent Fuller watching the operation. "We took two of them Max and the men are spreading out the other three and putting a kubelwagen under a tarp to help take up space."

Max looked down at the German landing craft for a moment noting the activity, "Thanks Vince, did you find the manifests?"

"Yeah, we did. Demetrius opened the safe. The kid is good, just held a glass up to it to listen; didn't take him two minutes. Janelle has the paperwork and once she finishes the new manifest we'll put it back into the safe and let the Brits open it up. Why don't you look in on her and then get some rest."

"I doubt I'll sleep tonight, if you need me I'll be on the starboard bridge wing. Thanks Vince and goodnight."

"Night Max."

Max paused for a moment before the door to the captain's suite and then knocked.

"Come in." Janelle Crabtree was a regal woman, tall as her husband, her hair still dark and her tanned face marked with laugh lines deeply etched. She looked up as Max entered, a jeweler's loupe in one eye as she examined a sheet of paper. "Max dear come here." She said as she removed the loupe and stood up. As Max walked up she raised her arms and caught him in a gentle hug that lasted for several minutes.

"Go up to your perch dear, I'll come get you if you're needed. We'll talk later." Reaching up she brushed his long hair back off his forehead.

"Yes ma'am. I'll join you for lunch." Max left the cabin and went to the starboard bridge wing where a chair had been secured near the rail. The crew knew not to bother him as he sat a quiet vigil staring out to sea until the ship took a mooring as the sun rose.

End of Book One

AAR#0002-11231943 will be concluded in the imaginatively titled:

The Fire Drake
Book Two

Read the first two chapters now.

Book Two
Chapter 1: Letters from Home
                    Log of the *Manta,* Letters delivered to M. Larsen
January 3, 1944, 03:20
Aboard the *Manta* off the French Coast.

CHEN FAU WAS mildly amused to see his captain wander into the control room of the *Manta.* When off watch Max always seemed to appear whenever anything even remotely out of the ordinary occurred. The aroma rising from a large mug of coffee barely visible in Max's hand heralded his approach. The sub was currently at snorkel depth running two of her four diesel engines, charging batteries and adding some warmth to the sub. Radiators, using heat exchanged from the engine cooling system, were in most compartments. The English Channel in January was not the most hospitable location, though on reflection certainly not the worst Fau mused. The second officer was sure that Max had come in because the remora was due to arrive shortly. In fact sonar had reported its approach a few short minutes before Larsen's arrival.

Max contented himself with a quick survey of the instruments and a brief exchange with the helmsman who chided the captain for not bringing coffee for everyone. Smiling, Max handed his cup to the helmsman and continued towards Fau, one eyebrow raised in query.

"Ah Captain, what a surprise that you showed up now. I'm sure it's coincidental, but Ardison will be docking in a few minutes." Chen Fau said somewhat irreverently.

Max just nodded in reply, "I had to use the head anyway so I thought I'd check to see if you were about to run us aground or found a new route to Crimea."

"At least Crimea would be a change. How much longer are we to be enthralled by the OSS or the good Colonel Menzies? Running errands grows old regardless of the importance."

Max nodded in agreement, "Morton-Smyth and Gerard should be returning tomorrow. Hopefully they will have pinpointed the last of the Fire Drake sites. Once we get Snowden and Menzies that information we should be free for more interesting jobs."

"Bridge, Sonar: The remora is on final approach. Docking.....now."

Both Max and Fau looked toward the annunciator board in time to see the telltale light up designating that the clamps were in position. A second light came on showing that the hatch connection was secure. Minutes later Ardison appeared, two mailbags in hand. The smaller of the two had a simple lock and seal in red. That one was handed to Max as the larger bag was placed under the map table for the yeoman to distribute at breakfast.

"Not anything new that we haven't already heard on the BBC." Ardison said by way of greeting. "Boys are unloading the remora now. Max, Hiram met me at the supply ship and handed me that small mail bag and said to warn you that it has an incendiary device that he said only you would know how to render safe."

"How long did it take you?" Max asked.

"Almost two minutes, tricky little bugger. Took much longer to resew the bit of bottom seam I went through for access." Ardison said smugly.

"Pirates." Max muttered while breaking the seal and using a small key to open the lock. Without any hesitation he opened the pouch. "Letters from home!" He took a quick sniff in the bag and shuffled through the letters to come up with one. "Verna! Fau, don't call unless we run hard aground or do end up in Crimea. Thanks, Ardison." Max said over his shoulder as he headed for his cabin.

"Perfume?" asked Fau looking to Ardison.
The big man shook his head and grinned, "Disinfectant."
"Ah, romance." Fau intoned as the control room succumbed to laughter.

Manta's Captain's Cabin:

After stopping for a fresh cup of coffee Max settled in front of his small fold down desk, letters spread out in front of him. He quickly prioritized the letters: Verna's first, Hiram, then Ernst, and last one from Herman Wolf.
Sipping his coffee he opened Verna's letter:

December 18, 1943
Darling, First thing I miss you terribly. You must stay safe, or as safe as you can, Dr.'s orders.
Hiram has assured me that I can write about anything in a letter that he forwards to you. I'm quite sure he'll cut out anything untoward if I tell tales out of school.

Nancy Cuny and I went up to Bletchley last week. We have become the de-facto visiting medical staff for OSS and MI6. We saw Robin and Susan. They are good and Robin's leg is quite recovered. The two of them and the twins are instructing recruits and preparing to return to France before the inevitable invasion. They are to contact members of the Resistance and help coordinate their actions to aid in the invasion.

Robin, or rather Leftenant Jarvis was once again passed over for promotion. Some pencil necked British major took it upon himself to tell her that due to her "un-natural proclivities" she should never expect a promotion and would find herself cashiered the day after victory is declared over Germany and whatever is left of the Axis powers. Adding insult to injury he left the door to his office open so as to make sure everyone could hear the little insufferable prig dressing Robin down. I had to restrain Nancy who was determined to see how far the "the bastard's knee would go up his ass". Robin was just as cool as could be. She laughed and simply asked if that was all, then turned and marched out. She grabbed Nan's other arm and we went out to gather Susan and the twins for lunch. Robin confided that she was sure that the British military would never accept her regardless of her contributions. She said that Col. Menzies has already told her that he would be happy to find a place for her as a civilian, especially if she wants to continue living in France after the war.

Susan encouraged her to forget the service and that years of her ill-gotten gains were converted to gold and banked in Switzerland before the war. One tends to overlook Susan, I'm sure that's a blessing in her profession, but that little body encases the brain of a Moriarity minus the murder and blackmail. I'm going to talk to Hiram and see if there is anything he can do for both those brave ladies.

Speaking of brave ladies; Nancy and Lysette are becoming an item. Marie has mentioned that she, Lea, Frankie, and of course Hiram have wondered when Lysette was going to be willing to admit to herself what they all suspected. While neither of the twins would ever be considered a shrinking violet, Lysette has just blossomed lately. She may be an ultra-competent spy and warrior, but her newfound social ease is a revelation. I can't wait for you to see her joy. The girls are discreet, they do know where they live at the moment. However the twins are competent spies and between their abilities and Robin and Susan's advice and assistance the affair is going smoothly and under cover.

Nancy too is radiant. I found out that her "trouble" at medical school was that she had turned down the attentions of an instructing doctor. Apparently he comes from a wealthy family and a new wing for the teaching hospital preceded his appointment. According to Nan he was a short, rude, "all hat and no cattle" type of smarmy bastard. He assumed that anyone who turned him down was simply playing hard to get and when he decided on making a physical attempt found himself being thrown out a window sans culottes. He was probably lucky not to be sans cojones. Shortening a long story he wanted to press assault charges against Nancy. The Dean assured him that he would happily help press charges and would call for a news conference with the prosecuting attorney to get the entire story out about how a nursing student had thrown him pant-less out a window (unfortunately it was only the first floor). He would also call the doctor's father and mother to assure them that no stone would be left unturned in the prosecution and that all of Texas would soon be reviling the female nursing student who had so viciously thrown him out a window thereby exposing the doctor's shortcomings for all the campus to see. Of course the doctor decided that possibly he had made a mistake, he simply fell out of the window while dressing after surgery. Also it was time to inflict himself on the unsuspecting public and go into private practice. Almost the end of the story; the Dean was happy to rid himself of a subpar instructor, but after interviewing Nancy and realizing her "un-natural proclivities" was reluctant to have her continue, despite being one of his top students. I'm assuming that being an Amazon style lesbian in Texas is either illegal or at a minimum a sin against the pantheon of Texas' rather inflated self-opinion.

I'm sure that you or your Texas connections can smooth over this little bump in the road. I know you consider the twins kin. Well it looks like you will have a new kin-in-law after the war and a nicer smarter one Lysette will probably never find. I've come to love the twins as my future nieces/sisters and I'm just as determined as you to see to their happiness. I know that Nan and Lysette have a long hard road ahead. Society does not reward being outside the norm and no lesbian woman nor homosexual man ever chose to be their way, especially not because of the world's universal admiration. Just one more cause to add to your others.

Love you so much and I hope to be in your arms soon, Verna

Max folded the letter and added it to Verna's other correspondence in his safe. *"Well that's a good bit to think about. Sounds like the Dean isn't all that anxious to get rid of Nancy. With the letters and better yet certificates of appreciation from the Brits and OSS I'm betting we can get her reinstated for a lot less than a new wing. Maybe a Victory class freighter to the marine engineering school and a bit of quid pro quo."* Max decided that the rest of the letters could wait until after breakfast as he heard the off-watch heading for the galley.

Book Two
Chapter 2: Waiting Game
                    Log of the *Manta*, Letters delivered to M. Larsen
January 3, 1944, 04:00
Aboard the *Manta* off the French Coast.

AFTER FINISHING BREAKFAST and a turn through the ship Max went
to the control room. Anderson had the watch with Ardison dozing in
the ready room, a small alcove with a bunk just aft of the control room.
Max had always appreciated the small private captain's space many
merchant ships had adjacent to their bridge and replicated it on the
Manta. With a smaller crew than a military sub he had to optimize the
crew's ability to rest while still keeping officers handy to the control
room. The snorkel had been stowed and the ship was one hundred feet
below the surface and station keeping by heading into and matching
the current. They would listen for other ships, but the Channel in
daytime was relatively free of German traffic other than an occasional
German sub traveling to or from the sub-pens in Brest.

        Max conferred with Anderson for a few minutes and then
returned to his cabin to start on Hiram's letter. As usual Hiram's letter
had been typed on the portable machine that was always part of
Snowden's luggage. The lawyer's handwriting, never good, had
devolved into a scrawl that Hiram alone could decipher.

12/26/43

Dear Max, I hope all is well with you and your boat. I was corrected
by Capt. Pinkerton the other day who assured me that submarines
in American service are called boats rather than ships. I take it that
the Navy as an institution has been breathing salt air for far too long
and must therefore come up with all these misbegotten rules of
nomenclature simply to confuse people of rational and logical mind.
Also Merry Christmas, afraid that was an afterthought.

        I spoke with Verna and of course read her letter to you
before adding it to the pouch so I know that she has informed you
about Lysette and Nancy. My Episcopalian upbringing faded long
before I started college, but I'm willing to say a prayer or two for
their success and happiness. I haven't seen my daughter so happy
in years.

Also Marie has been seeing quite a bit of a certain Patrick Henry Donovan, Captain USMC seconded to the OSS. He is apparently a third or fourth cousin to Wild Bill, but has never met him. He broke a leg parachuting into Denmark early last year. Even so he stayed for 4 months coordinating supply drops and assisting the Danish resistance. When he returned his leg had healed so badly that the surgeons re-broke it and did quite a bit of work straightening it out. Like the twins he is acting as an instructor while convalescing and waiting for a new assignment. Interesting fellow, political science major with a second in Scandinavian languages. Marie and Patrick seem to be hitting it off and I may end the war with both a son-in-law and a daughter-out-law.

I have also given some thought about Lt. Jarvis and Mouse. As you know my firm has an interest in Sullivan & Scardino, Enquiry Agents. They have offices in England and had offices in France, Germany and Poland. It is an old and very able company of private investigators. Their ranks though have been decimated by the war. Most of the British staff was co-opted. Mostly MI5 and 6 and most of the staff in France are members of the resistance. The firm has suffered the death of several good agents including Mr. Scardino. I proposed to Ernst that we should acquire the remainder of the company for the trust. It will be invaluable after we win the war, especially for researching companies we might want to buy and finding engineers and scientists we will want to hire. Anyway I propositioned Robin and Susan about taking charge of the Paris office after the war. The thought of working for people they have come to know and trust and who don't give a fig about unnatural proclivities has a fair allure. We'll see what comes of this venture and I hope they take my offer.

Vincent has been working with Mike Pinkerton and they have come up with some possibilities. Tom Fixx came through with a reference to a material that burns in the ultraviolet spectrum when mixed into a flare. Some god awful long chemical; something-something-tetra-flouroethylene I think. However, it works and Vince thinks he can get the FD porpoising bad enough to crash. Pulling a large and sturdy kite, similar to the delta winged glider Vince designed, with a flare attached. They winch it out behind an Air-Rescue craft, similar to your suggestion.

Pinkerton has come up with something like a cross between a Hedgehog spigot mortar and a depth charge Y-gun that fires two shells that pull a wire mesh net between them and spread out in front of a Fire Drake. They're still debugging it and I'm fairly sure it would take a combination of luck and skill for it to tangle a missile in ground effect; very short range. The small craft would have to try to intercept a missile from dead on and then risk a large explosion, not something conducive to making sailors happy.

I hope their efforts work as I must believe that no captain of a ship would refrain from firing everything he has at an incoming missile, especially one with the destructive power of a Fire Drake. The collateral damage in the invasion fleet from a capitol ships efforts is not something I want to contemplate.

Ernst has been working with Barnes Wallis, but I'll let him explain what he's doing in his letter to you.

Stay safe and your bird dog duties should be over soon.
Hiram

04:30

Max was thinking about a reply to Snowden's letter when the intercom called for him. "Captain to the radio room please." Max checked the depth gauge and compass over his desk, he had felt the sub rising earlier and the slight reaction to surface swell as Anderson surfaced for a radio check before sunrise. They were already returning to depth, so whatever the radio shack had received probably did not require an immediate response.

Max activated his intercom, "On my way." He then closed his desk to prevent any sudden maneuver from scattering his letters and headed aft.

When Max stuck his head into the compartment he found his operator finishing the decoding of a short message, "'bout done Artie?" Arthur Dietel held up a hand in brief acknowledgement as he finished transferring letters from the one time pad to a form in front of him.

"Here you go Max. Looks like it's time to be picking up Gerard and that little fella tonight." Dietel said as he passed the message to Larsen.

"Gadson Wilson Morton-Smyth." Max said reflexively as he read.

"Yeah, him." Art responded.

Max looked up to see Dietel grinning at him. "Yeah, him. Ready to do something, be somewhere else?"

"Yes Sir."

"I'll probably have some traffic for you before sunrise. Give me a few minutes while I check the charts." Max said as he headed for the control room. There he found Lars Anderson and Mitchell looking at the chart and drinking coffee. Ardison handed Max a fresh cup as he came up to the nav-station. "Expected you a bit sooner." Ardison said.

"We may make pick up tonight. Between 23:00 and 03:00 tomorrow morning. There's the coordinates." Max said as he placed the message form on the table.

"Sooner the better. I'm starting to name the fish swimming by. By now they think we're one of them." Mitchell said while plotting the location on the chart. "No problem, plenty of water under us there. And a bank not too far away if we need to rub a Nazi ship off our track."

"Usual procedure Ardison, I'll have you and Rajko make the meet with the remora. I think we'll wait on the southwest side of that bank. That way we can hear anyone coming. Go ahead and come to periscope depth long enough for Art to send off my confirmation."

On his way to the galley Max handed Dietel a short message confirming the pickup. Next he refreshed his coffee. "*Verna thinks I drink too much coffee. I'll have to look into the science on caffeine. It can wait until after the war. No sense doing anything rash. I need to do more research on excuses not to do the research.*" With that last happy thought Max opened Dietsch's letter;

12-19-43

Max, I'd ask if your head's still above water, but since you're in the Manta I know it's probably not.

I'm working a lot with Barnes Wallis, man's a damn genius. He developed the spherical bombs that took out all those hydro-electric dams in the Ruhr Valley. Vince should be here. Too bad he's stuck working on the spoofing system. Even in a letter that Hiram assures me will stay secure I'm going to refrain from saying anything substantive about the current [1]project other than I'm doing some of the structures and

221

materials calculations and helping turn the idea into something factories can actually construct.

Saw Hiram the other day and he brought me up to speed on the twins. I'm glad that shoe has finally dropped. Met Nancy Cuny a couple of weeks ago, she was with Verna and seems mighty nice. Only fault is I got a crick in my neck talking to her. That and Nancy's thick West Texas drawl has me a bit homesick. Not sure why as I heard as much German and Spanish growing up in the hill country as I ever did Texian. Must be getting old, probably time for another nip of Doc Tom's elixir.

I had Col Menzies office do a little research and they found Petro Romaniuk. He is fighting with the Free Polish Air Force and is a Major now. I was sure he'd not be part of Stalin's Red Army. We're going to meet in two weeks and I'm betting he can shed a bit more light on Voronstov's life after Russia.

That's about all happening with me. Got a letter from Big Herman, but Hiram says you have one too so I'll let that suffice for now.

Stay out of trouble until I can join you. Ernst

[1]Dietsch was making reference to the "Earthquake Bombs" that Barnes Wallis designed. Recommend the Wikipedia articles and if the member desires more information contact the Trust Archives. SMkIII

Afterword:

Writing a book about World War II is a humbling experience. It is easy for the author to ignore some realities and to fudge facts and timelines to better allow his heroes to triumph. I've attempted to fudge as little as possible aside from the obviously imagined constructs such as Fire Drakes, the *Manta*, early hang-gliders, and a purpose built Q-ship. I have endeavored to make these possible if improbable.

Compared to the reality of millions of brave men and women engaged in the war on both the battle ground and the home front my small cohort of fictitious characters enjoy the privilege of fiction to keep them alive, well, and successful.

Timelines have not been overly altered and many footnotes are true, though not all of them. There was a bombing raid on Peenemunde that occurred at the time and date used in the book. MI6 disguising Griffin as a Polish scientist to protect him was invented by me. To the many warriors and spies whose names I used in a strictly "coincidental" manner I did it in respect and hope I have not offended you or your relatives.

Glenn W. Cunningham